The

Keeper

Ghosts of Texas

Dedication

To the people we meet along the way.

Table of Contents

Texas: 1867

The storm lurked in the overcast sky most of the day. When it broke, the rain came suddenly and poured heavily. Lightning split the sky and thunder cut deep into the heart of the solitary figure walking a carriage trail through the oak dotted landscape. His gray coat, worn and stained, hung from his thin frame like sackcloth. Pulling up the collar, he held it shut with his left hand, tucking his right across his body. It wasn't the cool breeze, but the thunder that brought him shivers as he fought the instinct to crawl into a hole or a ditch and hide. He could now, and no one would call him a coward or a deserter. Though fear ran often and thick in his blood, he decided long ago it was easier to cut it off from his mind and move forward, ever forward until someone called a retreat. Lately, it seemed that was all he did.

Now, he advanced into the storm, hoping for a dry place to sleep. So many nights he spent in the rain, the last few years with no blanket and no fire, he refused to spend another if he had a choice. Ahead lay the hacienda. That much he learned in town before the shopkeeper expelled him from the store with a well-aimed boom handle. The knot in his scalp still throbbed as he trudged through the darkness, silently praying the thunder would quit.

As the hour passed, the storm faded into the east, and the rain eased into a drizzle. When the dark shadows of the hacienda rose into view from the muddy grassland, the drizzle too, ceased falling. Tired, hungry, and now shivering from a chill, the wanderer pushed on.

Nothing moved around the place. He paused outside the gate anyway, still cautious of buildings and places where riflemen might hide. Fighting down the fear of ambush, he stepped through the gate and crossed the open distance to the front door, knocked and waited. Minutes passed while he nervously watched the yard.

The door opened, and a girl peered out at him through the narrow opening.

"*Si?*"

"Is Señor Alvarado home?"

"*Si.*" The girl nodded once. With a measuring glance, she took in his appearance and all it said of him. "What is your business with him?" she asked guardedly.

He hesitated, knowing that for all her youth, this girl could slam the door in his face. He felt awkward and light-headed with anxiety.

"I have some questions," he said. "Private questions."

Her eyes narrowed. Then a male voice spoke in Spanish from the fire lit room beyond the door. The girl replied over her shoulder and frowned at the reply. Then she stepped back, opening the door to admit him with only a sharp wave of her hand.

Removing his hat, he crossed the threshold into the warm foyer. The man, a Spaniard from the cut of his coat and trousers, stood in the arched doorway to the right, silhouetted by firelight. The Spaniard spoke with what sounded like a command. The words teased at a long-buried memory, but understanding eluded the wanderer. The Spaniard spoke again, gesturing him closer. Once tall, his shoulders now hunched beneath the black coat, resembling a perched vulture. As the wanderer moved closer, he could make out the Spaniard's face, weather-scarred like the mountains of Virginia.

The Spaniard regarded him with the same suspicion as the girl had. After long scrutiny, he asked a question that the wanderer did not understand. When he failed to reply, the obsidian black eyes narrowed.

"Your name?" the Spaniard said with a thin vein of impatience.

"Martin," the wanderer replied.

The old man's frown deepened. "And your family name?"

To this, Martin could only lower his gaze having nothing to answer.

The old man blinked and spoke in clear, stern English. "Did your mother not teach you it is rude to not answer when an elder asks a question?"

Martin nodded and responded politely. "She also told me it is better to remain silent than tell a lie."

The old man's expression remained stern a moment longer before giving way to a mirthless smile. He turned away and moved toward the firelight. Two strides away he stopped and turned back.

"Come, *Martín*," he said, giving the name the Spanish inflection and gesturing toward the sitting room beyond. "No guest is denied here."

"Sir, I don't wish to impose on your hospitality," Martin said. "I only wish to ask questions."

"What kind of questions?"

Martin swallowed and reached inside himself to open up a part of him that had lain locked away for nearly ten years.

"About my mother, sir. I understand she may have grown up here."

If there had been any friendliness in the Spaniard's face, it vanished. "And, your mother's name?"

"Maitea. I don't remember her last name."

The Spaniard's mouth hardened and he turned away quickly. "Come sit by the fire. My bones ache with cold."

With little other choices, Martin followed the Spaniard deeper into the room where firelight played over thick adobe walls. A faded rug covered the floor beneath red satin furniture. The old Spaniard settled into a high-backed chair near the fire. Martin sank to the hearth facing him, thankful for the abundant warmth.

"Lolita," Alvarado called. When the girl appeared in the doorway, he told her to bring food and warm wine.

Martin felt a spark of excitement when the words formed meaning in his mind. He extended his hands to the fire but drew back as the heat seemed to sear his flesh.

"Warm yourself. These spring rains chill to the bones, and you've come far from the look of those shoes."

They could hardly be called shoes anymore. The soles were worn through in places as were the knees of his trousers and elbows of his shirt. Only the old gray coat seemed fit for service any longer.

The Spaniard took up a long-stemmed pipe from the table beside him. He bent forward, lit a long splinter, and held it to the bowl. He sat back and puffed quietly for a long while.

"Tell me about your mother," the Spaniard said at length. "What did she look like?"

Martin closed his eyes, summoning the memory. Though his mother's features remained vivid in his mind, kept alive by the picture he carried with him, her live image had faded with time.

"She was delicate in form, golden-brown hair, and green eyes."

"And her character?"

"Gentle and kind, always willing to sacrifice for those in need."

The Spaniard frowned in thought. "Did she tell you anything else about your family?"

"She talked about my grandfather and her brother a little."

"And your father? What of him?"

Martin glanced into the firelight. "She did only…"

"Only what?"

Martin swallowed a twist of sadness in his throat. "He was killed by Indians up in Kansas."

Alvarado's head cocked in curiosity. "And so your grandfather and uncle are your last hope of finding a family?"

"Yes, sir."

Alvarado gave a slow nod. "I see. What do you know of them?"

Martin looked down at his hands as the memory of his mother's dying words came to him. "My mother only referred to them by their first names, but she mentioned this ranch, warning me never to come here."

"What makes you think they live here?" Alvarado took a deep draught of his pipe and Martin watched his face through the smoke.

"I don't know," he said with a shrug. "I figured there were ties here."

"Their names? Your grandfather and uncle?"

"She called them just *Abuelo* and *Tío*. She never told me their names."

Again, the Spaniard descended into thought. Martin waited anxiously, hoping the old man would remember something. He searched the old man's face but saw no signs of recognition.

Hopelessness nagged at the back of his mind until he turned toward the fire and extended his hands again. This time the chilled flesh did not scream in protest.

"How long ago did your mother leave?" the Spaniard asked suddenly.

"Almost twenty years ago." Martin paused. "I was too young to remember it clearly, but I remember some."

"What do you remember?"

Martin glanced over the room again, taking in the heavy Spanish influence in the decoration. He hesitated to explain for fear his heritage might cause the old man to expel him into the cold night. Drawing a deep breath, he resigned himself to the fate of another cold night.

"My father was an American. I believe my grandmother did not approve of their marriage. After my father was killed, I believe my mother left to avoid a forced marriage. That's all I know."

The Spaniard stared down into the bowl of his pipe and shook his head. "I apologize, but your story is unfamiliar to me. I do not recall such a thing happening to any of the families on my *hacienda*."

Martin swallowed his disappointment as once again he was set adrift. He gazed into the fire, trying to think what to do next.

"However, if you require work, that I can give you."

Again, Martin studied the man through the smoke. He was not unpleasant, but something still seemed strange about him. Regardless of his sense of this man, Martin needed a job. For the last three months, he had walked with only the clothes on his back and what food kind souls willingly gave. With this dead-end in front of him, there was no use in pushing on any longer.

"How are you with horses?" Alvarado asked.

"I've only ridden a couple of times, and those were sway-backed nags."

"Well, when Armand's done with you, you'll know them well enough." Alvarado rose and gestured Martin toward the door. "Lolita can show you to the men's bunk room. You'll find her in the kitchen just down the hall from the front door." His attention turned inward then, and Martin sensed the conversation was over.

Martin straightened. "Thank you, sir."

The Spaniard waved his hand dismissively, and Martin retreated to the foyer. Away from the fire's warmth, he shivered, but the old man had dismissed him all the same. He walked down the hall, hoping the kitchen had a fire.

The girl, Lolita, nearly collided with him as he stepped through the door. He caught the decanter before she dropped it and her arm before she fell from the step. She jerked free.

"I thought you'd be in Señor Luis's company a little longer," she said going to the table and setting the plate down.

"It seems he's given me a job." Martin moved to the open fireplace and sat beside it. "Have you a water bucket?"

She scoffed. "Why don't you wring it out of your clothes if you want water?"

Her words hurt. Like the stones they'd cast at him in Port Arthur and Houston, they told him he was unwelcome. He turned his back to her and reached his hands toward the flames in defiance of her anger.

She was silent for a long moment. When she spoke again, her tone was gentler.

"We have water here." She filled a glass and brought it to him. As he drank she reached out and felt his coat, then without pretense she slipped her hand inside the open collar to feel his shirt. "You are soaked through." She spun around, flipping her long black hair as she did. She was younger than him but carried herself with the authority of womanhood. "Stay here, I will get you dry clothes."

Taking the plate and the water, he sat on the hearth and ate. The first few bites knotted his stomach and so he ate little, knowing that it would make him sick.

When Lolita returned, she had a cotton shirt and trousers which she handed over to him. She nodded toward the pantry. "In there, you can change. Leave that cloak by the fire."

He obeyed. The clothes fit loosely and were short in the sleeves and pant legs. The wide belt required a new hole which he cut with a pocket knife, a tricky thing to do in the thick darkness of the pantry. When he stepped out of the pantry, Lolita looked him over and pursed her lips.

"They'll do it."

"Whose are they?"

"None of your business." She took his bundle of wet clothes. "I'll wash these. They smell."

"No wonder. I've been wearing them for the last five years and then some." He returned to his place by the stove aware that she studied him.

"At least you're still alive to talk about it."

He ignored her and continued eating. "Señor Luis said you can show me where to bed for the night."

"Go to hell."

Martin turned a frown on her. "I didn't mean it that way, ma'am. I meant could you show me where the bunkhouse is?"

Her expression softened. "Straight across the yard out that door. Be quiet. The men will be asleep by now." She disappeared through a side door and did not return.

Martin pondered over her while he finished his food. Then his thoughts turned to his own situation and forgot her tantrums while he waited for the fire to drive away the last of the chill.

The bunkhouse overflowed with the scent of unwashed men sweating in the heat of an over-built fire. Even with the thin glow from the stove, finding an empty bed proved dangerous. As Martin crept between the bunks he brushed a blanket draped over an outstretched arm. Suddenly, the blanket flew back, slapping him in the face and a solid force struck him in the chest, knocking him against the wall and forcing the air from his lungs. A knife pressed against his throat.

"Last words?" The man's breath was foul and his voice grating. Martin nearly gagged.

"Just looking for a bed," he said, "Didn't mean to wake you, mister."

In the dim light from the dying fire, the man's sparkling eyes narrowed. The shadows deepened the lines of his face. With a jerk and a shove he threw Martin to the ground and stood over him.

"The top on the end is open." He hauled back and kicked Martin in the gut, causing Martin's gut to twist around the supper he had eaten. "Just don't sleep too deep." He returned to his bed amid the chuckles of the other men who roused enough to watch the brief conflict.

Taking shallow breaths, Martin carefully rolled to his knees and used the wall to stand. Men rolled over or settled deeper into their blankets and paid him no mind. Even the man on the bed beneath the empty one turned his back to Martin and pulled his blankets over his head.

The bunk had no blankets. He glanced at the fireplace and decided to sleep warm. Even the old gray coat would keep him warm by a fire.

The coals danced with thin threads of light as he added a couple more lengths of wood and slid down against the wall, folding like a pocket knife into a ball. He wrapped the coat about his legs and buttoned it, remembering the man who gave it to him so many years before. That man had been the closest thing to a brother Martin knew and died saving his life in the last days of the war, leaving Martin with only memories both comforting and saddening. His death had been the impetus for Martin's journey here, the spark lighting hope that he could find his family.

Tonight that hope died with Señor Luis's certainty that no one like his mother, uncle, or grandfather lived here. Still, Martin could not believe his mother created the stories to quiet his anxious search for identity as a boy. In those days, he never could have understood her reasoning, or her stories and the people in them, but now that he could, the truth was nowhere to be found. This puzzled, frightened and agitated him until his mind, exhausted by emotion and thought, surrendered to sleep.

He dozed until sunlight grayed the windows and a rooster crowed. Martin woke at the first sound of movement. A man rolled out of his bunk, pulled on his boots and coat, and walked out into the morning twilight in a groggy half-stagger. He seemed unaware of Martin's presence.

Martin debated staying beside the dying coals or getting more wood. The night had been long and unsettled, and the last thing he wanted was more trouble.

Taking the poker he stirred the coals and added a few more logs before going outside.

The air was fresh, clear, and cool. As he stood on the narrow porch watching the chickens, the door opened.

"Sleep good?"

He recognized the voice and refused to turn or respond as the man closed the door and came to stand close beside him.

"Grayback, eh?" The man chuckled showing rotted teeth. "Well don't that beat all."

Martin shifted his gaze from the chickens to the corral where a handful of horses stood dozing.

"I heard you boys tucked tail and run after Richmond. Figure that's why we lost the war." He stuck his face to within inches of Martin's. "That true, soldier boy?"

Martin glanced down, watching the man's hands out of the corner of his eye, but said nothing. His heartbeat slowed. In a surly morning mood like this, he almost welcomed a fight.

"Maybe I should put my knife to your throat again. Maybe then you'll talk."

Taking a slow breath, Martin looked up into the man's eyes and waited. The man's grin faltered, his left eye twitching uneasily. He backed off a step and stood there, his right hand resting against the holster and gun strapped over his long underwear. Unarmed, Martin stood no chance against the man and did not care. Martin turned his back and stepped off the porch wandering toward the corral. He heard the door open again followed by quiet conversation.

Putting the indiscernible whispers from his mind, he leaned against the fence and watched the horses as they woke and went about their own morning routine. Lost in consideration, the jingle of spurs startled him. He looked up to see a man in a broad Mexican hat and tall boots approach.

"You Martin?"

He nodded.

"I'm Armand. I run this ranch for Señor Luis. I understand he hired you last night."

"Yes, sir."

Armand looked him over. "You've seen more hard times than hard work." Martin held the man's gaze as Armand studied him. "Can you use a gun?"

"I can."

Armand's eyes narrowed. He smiled. "You must be good to answer like that. No emotion. The ones that cannot make it sound more important."

"Señor Luis said I'd be working with horses." Martin felt the hair on his neck stand up.

"For now." Armand considered him a moment longer before he turned away toward the kitchen. "You'll miss breakfast if you stand there much longer."

Martin's stomach rumbled and he followed at a quick walk.

The kitchen was crowded with nearly twenty men lining the long table in the center of the room. All devoured the food in the ravenous manner of hogs. It reminded him of a time a few months after Gettysburg, when his company devoured all the food they found at a homestead. His hand went to the scar, hidden above his temple, a reminder of that day.

"Dig in," Armand ordered as he took the only chair at the head of the table.

Martin skirted the table searching for a break in the wall of men. Across the table, Lolita cast him a glance that showed both worry and anger. He found a gap between two men and squeezed in, gathering what he could onto his plate. The pickings were already lean, but he got enough to satiate his hunger. As he reached out for the last biscuit, he barely avoided the blade of the toothless man a second time. The point of the knife split the plate and bit deep into the tabletop. Stillness descended on the room. Martin ignored it. He split the biscuit and sandwiched bacon between the halves.

"Pretty fast hands," the man purred. "Bet you're pretty good with a gun or fancy yourself that way, eh, gray boy?"

"Lay off him, Kell," Armand said without much force.

The toothless man, Kell, glanced over at the boss.

"He ain't nothing but a skinny little rat, hardly even worth carving."

"Then get that knife out the table and finish your meal," Armand ordered.

Kell's upper lip twitched in a sneer. He jerked the knife free and, with a facial shrug, went back to shoveling eggs into his mouth.

Martin went on eating. He was the last to leave the table. Armand waited for him on the porch.

"You'll start out in the stables, cleaning." He fixed Martin with a knowing look. "You ever shovel shit before?"

"I've done my share."

"Well, you're going to do more." Armand waved a hand for Martin to follow and led him to the barn where he pointed out a rake, shovel, and wheelbarrow. "When you're done cleaning out stalls, clean the tack room. It hasn't been done all winter." He left it at that with Martin staring at his back as he crossed the yard. As he passed the kitchen, Lolita threw a dishpan full of water from the door, nearly hitting him. Both froze, staring at each other. Then Armand started for her and she retreated inside, bolting the door.

Martin bit his lip. It was none of his business.

Shedding the coat, he hung it on a peg in the tack room and went to work in the stalls. It took most of the morning, but he finished before lunch and had the tack room started.

The weeks that followed he found contentment with the work, for while he worked around the hacienda, the other hands left him alone. Even Kell had nothing to do with him. The nights however left him restless. Having no blankets, he slept in his coat, but good food kept him warm. Then one evening, he found an old quilt on his bunk. It was threadbare, but it was something. As he fingered the tattered edge of a patch cut from the same cloth as the borrowed shirt, he smiled, knowing where the gift came from. But even Lolita's kindness could not ease his mind when it came to the subtle and not-so-subtle threats of the other men.

A month passed and payday came. Martin was grooming one of Señor Luis's favorite mares when Armand brought him his time.

"Will you be moving on now?" Armand asked.

Martin shook his head. "I'd like to work off a horse and saddle. First, I need boots and a few other things."

Armand nodded glancing over the shirt and trousers Martin was gradually filling out.

"Lolita needs supplies. She's leaving tomorrow morning. You can drive the wagon."

"Thanks." Martin pocketed the coins and turned back to his work.

"Just don't get any ideas about her," Armand said suddenly. "Lolita's my woman."

Martin looked at him, wondering if the man could be serious. Armand looked away first and walked out of the barn.

The next morning, in the gray dawn, Martin hitched the team and pulled the wagon around to the kitchen as Lolita walked out. She frowned and started climbing to the seat before Martin had a chance to offer help. When he extended his hand she ignored it and sat on the edge, putting as much distance between them as she could. He stared at her in a silent question. She glared at him.

"Drive, *puta*!"

He understood her insult, but not her motive. He clucked to the team and they started down the road in enduring silence. An hour passed before Martin worked up the courage to speak.

"I want to thank you for the blanket," he said.

Lolita scoffed. "It was the dog's before she died."

A smile, quiet and brief flashed across Martin's face. "Reckon that's fitting the way folks been treating me." He glanced over at her and she looked away. Martin let the silence hang for a while, but gradually, the burning agitation in her wore on him.

"What you got against me, señorita?"

Her hard expression faltered.

"I know you don't have much cause to be partial to me, and I ain't asking you to love me. I'd just like to say 'hello' to you in the morning and you say 'hello' back like you do the other men."

Her eyes were wide and soft as she stared at him. Then she stared at the horses for a long while before answering.

"You're decent. That's what I have against you." She crossed her arms. "No one's called me 'ma'am' the way you do. It's always Lolita or *puta* or *perra*." Her lips pressed hard together as she met his gaze. "You don't belong with them. Yes, men can be rough, but these..." She shook her head. "Have you heard of the Nueces Strip?"

Martin shook his head. "Can't say I have."

"It's a hideout. Miles upon miles of country infested with Comanches and outlaws. Most of the men who work for Señor

Luis lived there, survived there. They're men you have no business working with. Especially here."

"Why is it Señor Luis has outlaws working for him?"

"Because of the trouble with the Terraza family west of here. Their land shares a border and they've been feuding since the time the old men courted Señorita Carmelita de Barcelona y Lopez. Señor Luis and Santiago fought to win her affections. In the end, she chose Santiago, and it was a curse on him. She was beautiful but crazy. Santiago was left fighting her at home and Señor Luis on the land. Señor Luis has sworn to kill everyone bearing the Terraza name and ordered his men to kill any rider who works for them on sight. Once they let you out of the barn, they'll expect you to kill men, no matter the circumstance."

Martin scoffed. "I doubt they'll ever let me away from the hacienda. Seems if I work there much longer I'll turn into another pile of manure. Surprised I haven't already."

Lolita shook her head as a laugh threatened to break free of her throat. Martin glanced over at her with his eyebrows raised with mock seriousness, and the laughter burst forth. She was not given to mirth, and it took her a while to recover. At last, gasping for breath, she sobered, and then her expression became grim as she regarded him. "You have no place here. It will end all that is good in you."

"If there is any good left."

"What makes you say that?" She fixed him with that hard stare of hers that challenged him to defy her. He found it entertaining, even comical that she thought so much about him after what she had called him but answering her question sobered him. He stared straight ahead.

"I don't much care to talk about it."

"Is it really that bad or do you only think it that bad?" she challenged.

It came back to him clear, the two men he killed in the act of surrender. The woman he shot, mistaking her for a Yankee sharpshooter. The four sentries he killed for their weapons and ammunition. Part of him regretted these though his rational mind knew what he had done had been for survival.

Unable to find the words to explain, Martin looked up into Lolita's face. Her eyes widened in fear, and he realized his expression betrayed him. She looked away, shaking her head.

"I will not ask again," she promised.

He silently thanked her.

A new, friendlier silence filled the air between them until they reached the town. As Martin stopped the team in front of the dry goods store, Lolita pointed out the clothing shop.

"That's where you go. Be back in two hours." With that, she turned on her heel and disappeared into the store with a flick of her braided hair.

With a pocket full of money and the Alvarado hands miles away, Martin felt drawn to relax. Ten dollars was more than he ever had at one time before in his life. He crossed the street to the shop and bought an outfit, not fancy, but nice. A dark-gray shirt and tan trousers, a vest and boots. The hat he bought on credit and saved seventy-five cents for a drink or two. The new clothes felt odd, and he worried they would attract attention, but he had earned a drink, and so, he walked down the street to a saloon that looked a little more vacant than the others.

He walked to the bar and leaned on it, waiting patiently for the bartender. He ordered a beer, and when it came it was luxuriously cold. As he took the first sip he noticed a handful of men studying him from the corner table. He lowered his head and tried to think of where he had seen them before.

They spoke softly then were silent, and Martin went on drinking. When they pushed back their chairs and crossed the room to his end of the bar cornering Martin in the back of the saloon.

"Didn't you ride in with that cook from Alvarado's rancho?" the first asked. He was a Texan, tall and broad with forearms of corded muscle. If Martin stood straight, his forehead would come to the man's nose. The other two were a little smaller. The second was a Mexican that fiddled with a quirt. The third had a nose kinked by too many fights. Martin studied them openly then took another swallow from his mug.

"What of it?" he asked neutrally.

"We don't like your kind in here."

"Now, Bucho," the bartender said, his voice trembling faintly. "I don't want any trouble in here."

"I'm not making trouble." The big Texan looked down his nose at Martin. "I'm just kicking some out."

The other two took the queue to close in. Martin straightened and nearly laughed at his reflex. He managed a smile, hoping to hide his nervousness, and slowly raised his hands, palms out.

"Gentlemen, please," he said. "I just wanted to enjoy a quiet drink. Now, if you'll let me finish, I'll leave and I won't come back."

The Texan grabbed his glass and guzzled what remained. Then he smashed the glass on the edge of the bar top.

"You're done," he said. "Now try to leave."

Martin glanced at the other two and shrugged. "I reckon you boys make better fences than gates."

"Are you insulting us?" the Texan challenged.

Martin sighed and felt anger rise in him. After a month of dodging the Alvarado hands and their violent pranks, the last thing he wanted was a fight, but frustration brought an itch to his knuckles and an urge to inflict a little pain.

"Mister, trouble followed me from Pennsylvania to Louisiana. Blue coated trouble you three ain't nothin' compared to."

The Texan's eyes narrowed. He started forward, putting more menace into his action than he had to back it.

Martin ducked under the first swing, slugged the Texan just below the rib cage, and brought his elbow back into the crooked nosed man's face. The Mexican charged, and Martin dodged him, snatched the gun from the Mexican's holster, shoved him into the Texan, and ducked back before either man had a chance to grab him. The Mexican and Texan froze as Martin cocked the gun. The crooked nosed man staggered backward and sat down hard, blinded by blood and pain.

Suddenly, the Texan grinned though he straightened slowly.

"Now what, whelp? You walk out we'll just come after you."

"Put your guns on the counter, belts and all," Martin ordered, hoping disarming the two men would take a little starch out of their backs.

The man with the broken nose growled and looked to the Texan who glared at Martin.

"I ain't got all day, boys," he said. He glanced beyond the broken nosed man, making sure no one sat against the wall. Then he snapped a shot off at the empty shot glass sitting on the table beside the man's shoulder. Shards exploded from it, and the broken nosed man, hands bloody, fumbled with the buckle of his gun belt. He threw it at Martin's feet.

"You too, big man."

The Texan held his ground, lifting his chin defiantly. Martin raised the revolver to eye level and sighted over it straight into the Texan's right eye. That was enough to break the Texan's nerve. Reaching down with his left hand, he unbuckled his gun belt and tossed it beside the other.

"Now, I would like you to pay for that half beer you took."

"I ain't got the money."

"Well ain't that a shame," Martin drawled. "Maybe I should take it out on your knees." He lowered the gun as though to aim, but stepped in and kicked the man instead just below the kneecap. It gave out and dropped the Texan to the floor. Grimacing, the Texan stared cross-eyed into the barrel of the revolver nearly touching his nose.

"You like to bully people, mister?" Martin asked.

The Texan glanced up at him but made no answer.

"From the way you act, I bet you do. Maybe I ought to teach you a lesson about that."

"Bucho!"

The Texan's eyes widened. "Not now, boss," he called.

"Yes now."

Martin stepped back and risked a glance at the man standing in the doorway. He was slender and clean-cut, as tall as Martin with angular features. His dark eyes met Martin's with authority, and from the cut of his suit, Martin doubted he was only a foreman.

"What is this?" the man demanded.

"Nothing, Mister Terraza," the bartender said.

Martin looked at the bartender with a deep frown. Then he understood. If the bartender got these three in trouble with their employer, they would charge him a heavy price.

"This gentleman owes me thirty cents," Martin said. "It wouldn't matter so much to me if he hadn't also disturbed my peace of mind."

"He's one of Alvarado's men," the Texan countered loudly. "Bold as brass he comes in here like it don't mean nothing."

The man stared down at the Texan, still on his knees. "We don't own this place, Bucho. He's entitled to a drink here, no matter who employs him. Understand?"

The Texan's mouth hardened.

"Now get out of here. I'll deal with the three of you later."

The Texan rose, cast a final warning glance at Martin then retreated outside with his companions in tow. The broken nosed man muttered a curse as he passed, but Martin ignored it and watched them disappear beyond the swinging doors before letting down the hammer on the revolver. He reversed it and extended it to the man in the fine suit.

"This belongs to the Mexican. I only meant to borrow it."

The man took the gun and smiled.

"Three against one is not fair odds. Even one against Bucho is bad, especially for one so light."

"I do what I have to."

The man tucked the revolver under his arm and reached into his pocket.

"Please accept my apology, and another drink on me." He laid coins on the counter. Martin considered them then shook his head.

"I appreciate the gesture, sir, but it's neither your apology nor your money I require."

"Ah." The man nodded. "An honorable settlement is what you desire."

Martin's jaw tightened. He spoke wrong. Now he chose to keep his mouth shut rather than make himself out to be more the fool.

At his silence, the man only offered his hand. "I am Fernando Lopez Terraza."

Martin remembered Lolita's warning and hesitated, but this man offered his hand in friendship, and he grasped it firmly. "Martin. I've heard about your family."

"Obviously nothing good if you're working for Luis Alvarado."

"Not exactly, only rumors."

Fernando studied him for a moment. "May I buy you a drink? No bribe, no pretense. I'm curious to know where you come from, Mister Martin."

"Just Martin. It's easier for people to remember."

"And quicker to say when you're in trouble." Fernando smiled. "I had a sister who said much the same thing."

Martin's skin tingled at the distant memory of his mother saying those words. "It's a good saying."

"Well, about that drink?"

"Thank you, but I better be on my way. Lolita ought to be ready to load up by now."

Fernando nodded. "Good day to you."

"And to you." Martin left without a hurry, checking the street before he stepped out. He was aware of Fernando Terraza watching him from the door as he crossed the street and walked back to the wagon.

Lolita stood on the boardwalk, arms crossed, tapping her foot.

"So you got a drink, I see."

"Only half."

"Did that man have anything to do with it?"

He followed her nod to Terraza standing outside the saloon, the gun belts draped over his shoulder. Martin shook his head.

"No." He gripped a crate and loaded it into the wagon.

"Stay away from him," Lolita hissed in his ear. "Do you know who that man is?"

"I know his name and that he saved me from killing a man. Besides that, what's some feud you don't even know how old it is got to do with me?" She recoiled from his reply, but he felt no shame. "You can never tell what a person is like until you get to know them, señorita."

She stared at him, mouth softened, while he loaded the supplies. "I'll not say a word about it, but if word reaches Señor Luis, you better run."

"Thanks for the warning." He helped her onto the seat and climbed up beside her. They drove back to the hacienda in silence.

Answers

Winter passed and yielded to the warm, mild days of spring. Martin passed the time working various tasks around the hacienda and in the stable caring for the horses. He wanted to learn how to ride and train the animals, but that required working with the wranglers, including Kell, and that thought sickened him.

One day, after turning a handful of special saddle and coach horses into the back pasture, he watched as Kell climbed onto the back of a speckled red horse, blindfolded and pinned against the tall breaking pen fence. He gripped the hackamore and settled heavily into the saddle.

"Let 'er go, boys!"

The men jumped back pulling the blindfold. The horse shrieked and leaped into a hard tirade. Kell kicked her flanks with large spurs. The mare screamed in pain and kicked her hind legs against the snubbing post.

Martin watched and felt his heart sink. True to her mustang heritage, the mare had spirit, enough to give her a proud look in her eye and a strong stride, but as time passed with Kell in the saddle raking his spurs across her hide and hauling back against her mouth she seemed to tire. He heard about this horse from the men around the table in the evenings, how she kept fighting, and Kell, ever confident, bragging about how he was going to break her. Over the last few days they deprived her of food and water and kept her standing with front and hind legs hobbled, yet she fought on, and while the men cheered Kell, Martin silently cheered the horse. Not long into this fight, however, Martin sensed it was near the end.

How long it went on, he did not know, but the horse, weak and exhausted, slowed her bucking to Kell's rising anger. Finally, she ran headlong into the fence, turning her body at the last moment throwing her weight into it, causing the posts and planks to pop and crack with the strain. Kell, unseated by the force, tilted sideways and as the mare jerked back to the left, he dropped to the hard ground. She kicked at him, and Kell scrambled under the rails to safety. Finding the object of her torture out of reach, the mare limped to the other side of the corral.

Reaching through the slats, Martin tried to offer her some grain from the small stash he kept in his pocket and nearly lost his hand when she snapped her teeth at him.

"Leave her be, gray boy!"

Martin met Kell's red-faced glare. He was no longer startled by the man, but anger, primed by fear, still struck through him.

Kell marched around the breaking pen toward him. Martin straightened teeth and fists clenched, ready to fight. Kell stood before him for a moment, fists balled, ready. Then the hardness in his face eased and he glanced at the horse. Reaching out, he gripped a rail and scaled the fence. The mare shied away, but Kell caught the long hackamore and brought her up short. He jerked the mare toward the center of the pen. The mare, her spirit still in the fight barred her teeth and charged Kell, nipping him in the forearm. Martin nodded once in approval.

Swearing then cursing the horse, Kell drew his knife and plunged it into the horse's neck.

Blood spurted from the wound, and the mare reared nearly knocking Kell in the head, but any fight she might have given then was destined to fail. She could not know it, and so charged Kell and drove him from the pen again.

Martin knew nothing could be done for the horse, and that feeling tore through him more violently than any pain Kell could have inflicted upon him with his fists.

The mare, blood pouring down her neck staggered away from the fence, turned once as though looking for a way to escape. Then, raising her head to the sky, she bellowed a mournful whinny as her legs gave out. Her proud body wilted as her spirit faded, set free on her final breath, her cry carrying and echoing off the buildings. All around the ranch, the other horses responded in a chaotic chorus that sounded angry, sorrowful, and afraid.

Throat tight, stomach-turning, and chest burning, Martin glared openly at Kell who gazed in apparent satisfaction at the dead horse.

"You deserved that," he growled and spat tobacco juice through the slats into the horse's glazed eye. "Good for nothin' bitch."

Martin's hands, numbed by shock, curled into fists. His legs and arms quivered with rage. Kell gave him a single glance, a sneer, and turned his back.

Before Martin knew what he was doing, he leaped onto Kell's broad shoulders sending both into the dirt. He came up first and kicked Kell across the face sending him back to land hard on the packed earth. At that moment, he forgot the rules. He wanted to kill Kell, and he jumped on the big man, pinned him to the ground, and beat Kell in the face before four men hauled him off.

"You gone loco?" a short Mexican called Chico shrieked.

"Settle down you wildcat!" another voice ordered. "It's just an old scrub pony."

"He had no right!" Martin screamed struggling to shake loose, but they lifted him clear off the ground and pinned him to the corral fence. All four struggled to hold him there.

Armand knelt beside Kell as the big man sat up slowly and rolled to his feet. He tested his jaw and spat in the dust running his tongue over the stubs of his rotten teeth. Then, he leveled a glare at Martin and took a step toward him. Armand stopped him.

"Don't!"

Kell glared at the foreman. "He ain't got no right to jump me like that."

"I wish he'd jumped you sooner." Armand closed the distance between them, and though he was a head shorter than the Texan, his carriage conveyed all the force of a hurricane about to make landfall. "You've killed three of this herd already with the way you ride. You had no right to just kill this mare like that."

Running a hand over his mouth, Kell spat again. "Alvarado doesn't keep me for my way with horses," he said. "He keeps me around for killing."

Armand's jaw hardened, with rage or fear, Martin could not tell. He watched the two men glare at each other. Kell looked away first.

"Saddle up," Armand ordered him. "You'll ride to the south border and haze strays."

Kell blinked. "That's two days ride one way."

Armand grinned mockingly. "So you'll have plenty of time to think about how you'll repay Señor Alvarado for another horse."

Growling in anger, Kell swept up his hat and marched away toward the barn. Armand watched him go then turned to Martin.

"Let him loose," he ordered.

Chico chuckled as he stepped back. "You're one crazy son-of-a-bitch!"

Martin shook his arms. Already he could feel bruises forming where they had grabbed him. His gaze held Armand's. The foreman shook his head.

"Don't keep angering him," Armand warned. "He will kill you one day."

Martin glanced down at his bloodied knuckles, and then back up at Armand. "I don't care much for men like him."

"Neither do I," Armand said. "But, Señor Alvarado hired him for a purpose as he said."

Martin clenched his teeth and turned to the trough outside the pen to wash the blood from his hands.

"Señor Alvarado wishes for you to join him for supper tonight," Armand added.

Martin frowned in puzzlement. "What for?"

Armand shook his head as he stood, gripping the buckle of his cartridge belt with his left hand, his right rested on the coiled whip he carried.

"I don't know, and I don't suggest you ask." Armand turned away toward the cookhouse, head down in apparent contemplation as was his way.

Splashing water over his face and head, Martin looked to the main house and wondered. Suddenly, Kell burst from the barn, astride his horse at a full run. He turned the big animal straight for Martin.

With an instant to react, Martin leaped over the tough and dove for cover, expecting Kell to renew the fight, but the big man rode on up the rise, laughing and whooping as he went.

Straightening, Martin dusted himself off, caking his wet hands with mud, and watched Kell escape into the distance. Then from the far end of the yard, the rattle of a carriage drew his attention as it rolled up to the main house. It was a fine black coach pulled by a pair of proud Andalusian horses, a rig for a person of means.

Señor Alvarado himself greeted it. As Martin watched, a woman dressed in a dark green traveling gown stepped out and took his arm. Together, they strolled inside, leaving Lolita to handle the baggage.

Deciding the rest of his work could wait, Martin hurried to help her.

"What are you doing?" she demanded as he lifted a trunk onto his back and silently hoped he would not regret it later.

"The horses can wait a few minutes, ma'am, if you'll just hand me one of those cases." Before she could protest, he took the bigger of the two from her.

She gaped at him, then hissed. "This is not your concern. Armand will kill you."

"If you are his woman as he claims, he would be doing this himself." He gestured toward the door. "If we hurry, he'll never know."

With a growl of banked fury, she gathered what she could of the luggage and led him inside.

From the parlor, he heard Luis and the woman speaking in hushed tones as he passed. No clear words reached him.

Lolita led him to one of the many extra rooms at the front of the house.

"Put it in the corner there." She nodded toward the window beside the bureau.

Martin set the case on the bed and lowered the trunk to the floor.

"No, not like that." Lolita skirted the bed and gripped the trunk handle. Her hand touched his and she stopped. Her usually blazing spirit ebbed into gentle warmth. She gazed up at him.

"Thank you," she said.

It was a new thing from her. In the months since coming here, she had insulted and berated him, but never once did he feel she spoke with true anger. Now, he knew for sure.

She drew a deep breath and held it as her lower lip curled inward in uncertainty, the first he had ever seen in her. She looked down, blushing.

Knowing the effort it took her to express gratitude, Martin's heart warmed. He cupped her chin and gently guided her eyes back to his.

"You're welcome," he said sincerely, hoping she would understand how much he meant it. He knew what it would cost both of them if he showed how he truly felt at that moment. Drawing back, he flashed a smile and left her alone in the room, staring down at her hands.

At the front door, he met Chico, burdened with the second trunk. The little Mexican grinned at him.

"Next time you tangle with Kell," he said softly, "warn me so I can sell tickets, eh?"

Martin smiled grimly. "Alright, Chico, *if* it happens again."

"*Bueno.* I make a lot of money off that."

Martin shook his head as the Mexican stepped past him headed for the guest room. He glanced toward the sitting room, where Señor Luis and the lady visitor still spoke. Alvarado glanced up, and their eyes met briefly, but Martin could read nothing in the old face though a chill seeped into his blood. Alvarado turned his attention back to his guest with a deceptively warm smile, and Martin stepped outside and pulled the door shut. He wondered if the guest had anything to do with his invitation to join Señor Luis for supper. Soon enough, he would know, but in the time he worked here, he learned there was a side to Señor Luis Alvarado that worried Martin.

The coach rolled away toward the barn breaking Martin's train of thought. He followed it and returned to work, helping the driver unhitch the team.

Despite being used to the confines of the bunkhouse, the spacious dining hall with its dark walls felt close to Martin, as though an unseen entity wrapped its arms around him and squeezed. Luis Alvarado sat at the head of the long table when Martin followed Lolita in. At his right sat the woman who arrived that afternoon. Years of wisdom showed in her pale face, made more so in contrast with the black veil she wore. From her neck hung a sparkling array of diamonds framed against her skin by the low slung collar of her dark blue gown. She glanced up at him with the air of a queen measuring something of interest to her.

Alvarado stood and extended his hand in a formal introduction.

"Martin, I wish to introduce Señorita Eva Maria Garcia de San Marco."

The woman offered her hand. From the recesses of his mind, the lessons his mother taught him returned. He took her hand and bowed over it.

"Señorita."

She smiled, pleased. She turned to Alvarado and, in Spanish, expressed her surprise that he had manners.

Alvarado dismissed it as something Martin had probably learned in a book. Then he gestured to the chair at his left. "Sit."

Martin obeyed and placed the napkin on his lap. He felt awkward in his effort to not seem out of place, but the woman's attention made him blush.

"I apologize if my manners are poor," he said. "My lessons were long ago."

"Don't apologize," Eva said. "I'm really quite impressed and curious to know how you learned."

"My mother was very adamant that I learn proper etiquette. She taught me herself."

"Oh? Who was your mother?"

"Maitea."

The woman frowned and sat back as Lolita served her. "I'm not familiar with that name. Where does she live?"

"She's dead, ma'am," Martin said, managing to hide the pang of loss he felt. After all the years that had passed, he still missed her. "We lived in Baton Rouge."

The woman nodded. "I've heard of the place, but I've always departed from Port Arthur when leaving for Spain."

"Yes, ma'am." Martin offered Lolita a sheepish thank you as she served him, but her face was unreadable, and further unnerved him.

"Tell Señorita Eva about your mother," Luis ordered. "You told me she once lived here. How is it she left this country?"

Martin shrugged. "She only ever told me that she had differences with my grandmother. I don't remember much being too young at the time."

"And your father?" Eva pressed. "What of him?"

"He was an American. He worked at the ranch where my mother grew up. They fell in love and were married. A year after I was born, he went north and was killed by Kiowa."

"A shame." Eva picked up her wine glass and seemed to think for a moment. "What did your mother look like?"

Martin reached into his pocket for the daguerreotype he had carried every day since his mother's death. It was small and housed in a protective brass case which he opened before extending it to the woman.

"This is my father and mother on their wedding day."

She took the portrait in her long fingers and blinked at the image, then leaned over and shared it with Luis. Martin searched their expressions as they conferred in whispered Spanish. Alvarado's face was unreadable; the woman was excited.

Closing the case with a solid *snap,* the woman returned it to him with a smile. "I may know where to find your family."

Martin blinked in surprise and glanced at Alvarado. "Are you sure?"

The woman nodded and cast a knowing smile at Alvarado.

Suddenly excited, Martin fought back the urge to press the woman for more information. A sense that she was holding back something nagged him. He managed to ask the first question without rushing his words.

"Where do you think my family is?"

She set down her spoon and folded her hands, studying him for a long moment.

"How old are you, Martin?"

Her question confused him. "Twenty, I think. I was born in the fall."

"And you said your mother's name was Maitea. Did she have other names?"

Martin fought to remember the name. His mother had spoken it only twice, and the memory returned to him with painful effort.

"Maitea Carmelita Helena Mercer." The name came haltingly from his American tongue, the pronunciation clear and correct because it had been the way his mother said it.

"Was it?"

Martin nodded. Alvarado frowned, and the back of his neck prickled as Martin studied him. The old man was fishing for something, what he was unsure.

"Mister Alvarado…"

"*Señor* Alvarado, if you please."

Martin nodded that he accepted the correction.

"Sir, I'm not asking anything except for answers. I just want to know what happened to my family."

Alvarado frowned as his fingers tapped the table beside his untouched bowl of soup. Silence lingered long over the table before the old man spoke again.

"It's old Spanish custom for children to carry the names of both parents, and sometimes even the grandparents. It's a way of tracing our lineage." He paused and watched Martin's reaction. "Your mother would have kept her maiden name and added your father's to it. Since Mercer is a gringo name, I assume she left out her maiden name." He leaned forward, his expression friendly for the first time. "Or she never had one. There is more I will tell you later," he whispered as he patted Martin's wrist and took up his spoon for the first time.

Martin's appetite was gone, and for this, he received many threatening stares from Lolita. No matter how hard he tried, though, he could not make himself eat.

He was thankful when Eva excused herself. Alvarado stood and took her hand.

Eva apologized for retiring early and expressed her desire to leave for home early in the morning.

Alvarado kissed her hand and thanked her for her company. Eva glanced back at Martin and smiled.

"I hope you find your family, Martin," she said. "I feel strongly that you will."

"Thank you, señorita." He bowed as she sank into a curtsy that spoke of nobility despite her age. How she retained the unmarried title puzzled him.

Alvarado turned to the hall and gestured him to follow with a firm but kind command. "Come."

Martin followed him through a side door into the parlor where the two of them sat the night Martin came to the hacienda.

"Do you enjoy tobacco?" Alvarado asked, opening a dark wooden box on the sideboard and surveying the contents.

"I tried a pipe once, but I don't reckon it was tobacco."

"Oh, how did you know?" He selected a cigar, smelling it before clipping the end.

"It smelled sweeter than tobacco." Martin stood near the door, feeling hunger creep back to him. He surveyed the room, and his attention came to rest on a painting above the mantel.

"Me in my youth," Alvarado said, noticing Martin's interest. "Long ago."

The image was unmistakable, but in youth, Luis Alvarado bore a vague resemblance to Fernando Terraza. The features and build were much the same though Alvarado was longer of limb.

Martin stared as his mind struggled to fully comprehend what his eyes were seeing, and his ears hearing and reconciling the two.

Alvarado filled two glasses of wine and brought one to Martin.

"I didn't want to speak of it in the presence of the señorita, but as a man, I think you'll understand."

Martin took the glass and met Alvarado's gaze with a silent question.

Alvarado smiled and paced toward the row of windows held in iron frames.

"I'm sure you understand a man's need for a woman," Alvarado said slowly.

The memory of brightly painted women enticing men to the upper floors of the rooming house where he and his mother had lived remained vivid because of the mystery it held in his childhood. During the war, he learned of prostitution and came to dislike it in principle. Though he felt the need, he craved more the companionship. "Yes, I believe I do," he responded.

"And, you also have heard the story about my courtship with Carmelita de La Rosa y Lopez?"

"Yes."

Alvarado scoffed and sipped from his glass. "Well, she was the only woman I really loved. After her, all others simply served to satisfy my animal needs. I had no desire to take a wife." He shrugged and turned away from the windows, pacing. "I've had many women in my bed through the years and have fathered several children, including, I suspect, your mother."

Martin met his gaze, unsure if he liked the story. He never knew what he would find when he came here. If this was the truth, he had no choice but to accept it.

"You, yourself, can see the resemblance," Alvarado said, gesturing to his portrait as he paced past the dead fireplace.

Martin glanced up at the portrait again but saw the resemblance as a bare suggestion.

Alvarado sank into a chair beside the hearth, the same he had sat in the night Martin had come in from the rain.

"I'm growing old," he said with a sigh. "Someday, I will leave this world, and I wish this land to go to someone. I would prefer it to be one who shares my heritage."

"What of the others?" Martin asked. When Alvarado silently questioned him, he continued. "You said you fathered many children. Certainly, there are some whose heritage you're more certain of than mine. You said yourself; you only suspect I'm your grandson."

A dish clattered loudly in the dining room. Martin glanced toward the open door and briefly met Lolita's unreadable gaze as she turned and hurried into the kitchen.

Alvarado chuckled. "Many of them, I doubt I'm their father. Others already have an inheritance from the fathers who raised them, but you!" He sprang from his chair with impressive agility and stood within inches of Martin. "You have no one!"

Martin searched the man's face. Something seemed strange. Perhaps it was the light, or perhaps it was because he had searched for so long, never expecting to learn the truth that knowing felt strange. He looked down, trying to make sense of it all.

"Of course," Alvarado went on with a wave of his hand. "I'm not promising you anything. If you stay here, work hard and prove you can carry the Alvarado name with pride, you will stand to inherit one of the biggest *ranchos* in Texas."

Staring into the fireplace's charred walls, Martin thought about this. As much as he knew the proposal would entice most, the prospect of owning a ranch like this held little appeal to him. What he wanted more was to know who he was and know his family's story. He looked into Alvarado's eyes and found himself aching to believe this man.

"If what you say proves true, that I am your grandson, I hope I won't disappoint you."

Alvarado smiled broadly and patted his shoulder. "I doubt you will." Apparently satisfied that the matter was closed, he turned back to his chair, his back no longer as bent as before.

Martin swallowed his wine in a single toss of his glass.

"If you'll excuse me, señor, I have chores I must finish."

Alvarado frowned at him. "Would you rather not leave them to someone else?"

Martin shook his head. "It's my responsibility."

With a shrug of his features, Alvarado dismissed him with a wave of his hand. Martin thanked him and left through the kitchen door. Lolita did not look up from her work when he passed, and he did not wait for her too. His thoughts were too scattered to add her windblown mood swings to them.

He went to the barn, and halfway through filling a bucket with grain, his hands slowed as what Alvarado had said seemed to settle. Still, he struggled to believe his mother was illegitimate, raised by *peons*. How could she have been so refined and been raised by servants?

But she also had raised her son in a brothel, making fine dresses for the parlor girls who plied their trade in the brightly painted rooms below their attic home. Would a well-bred lady reduce herself to such a state over an argument with her mother?

Martin shook his head. His mother had no other choice, and a seamstress was the best she could do. He could accept being a bastard for himself, but he refused to think of his mother as such.

Deciding to let the matter settle before considering it further, he shoved the scoop deep into the grain. By the time he filled the bucket, his thoughts remained a gentle roar inside his skull.

Wildcat

The border ran north and south along the wash, where the last trickle of spring runoff cut a narrow swath through the sand. Martin drew rein on the edge and stared across onto Terraza land. He saw no cattle, but Chico nodded toward the rock outcropping less than a mile across the wash.

"Bet you ten dollars; there are cattle in those rocks."

"Do we dare go over there?" Martin asked, uneasy at the idea of trespassing on Terraza range.

"Who's going to know? There ain't a Terraza rider in miles." He kicked his little pinto down the slope. "Come on. You can always run back here if you get scared."

Martin bit his lip. He disliked the idea, but at the same time, he hated going back to the roundup empty-handed. It had been at Alvarado's insistence that he participate in this operation, miles away from anywhere at the mercy of Kell and the others. Though their treatment had improved since Luis Alvarado announced that Martin would be his heir, a subtle threat remained in Kell's every look. If it had not been for Chico, Martin would not have slept the last week.

With a kick to his mount's flanks, he followed, hoping the Mexican was right. Continuously scanning the open country around them, they approached the rocks and found the outcrop a mile wide and two miles long.

"This isn't going to be a quick task, Chico."

"Ah, so what?" Chico turned his horse up a narrow trail. "Terrazas never come this far south."

"Then, what are those fresh tracks from? A ghost?"

Chico turned in the saddle and looked to where Martin pointed.

"Ah, those are mine," he responded with a grin. He kicked his horse again. "Come on. I don't want to spend more time here than I have to."

Martin knew little about cattle, but he knew tracks, and the fresh, shod hoof prints did not belong to Chico's mustang. He glanced back in the direction of the wash. He could leave Chico on his own, but if trouble came, he doubted he could live with having left Chico to harm. Martin chose to go on. His bay horse balked at the idea, and Martin had to kick the gelding hard to get him up the slope.

They reached the top and looked out on the green late-spring land.

"See." Chico grinned. "I told you we'd find cattle up here."

"Yeah, and they're not ours."

Down below, a herd of twenty head milled in a small canyon flanked by two riders on horses Martin did not recognize.

Chico watched, and his tanned face lost a little color. Then he smiled.

"They won't be there long. A lion stalks the one."

Martin watched a long, lanky form move down along the canyon wall. From their position in the canyon, neither man saw the cat, nor would their horses alert to its presence with it approaching from downwind. Martin turned the bay along the canyon edge, searching for a way down.

"Martin!" Chico's voice was shrill as he realized what Martin was doing. Martin ignored him.

He found a chimney, rocky and sloped gently enough he could descend on foot, but too steep for the bay. He pulled his rifle from the scabbard and started down.

The herd and riders were out of sight beyond the rock that lined the chimney. Martin scrambled down, half sliding as he went. Then he heard the growl and the screams of horse and man. Shots broke out, and as Martin came into view, he saw the second rider charge the cat as it stood over the first man. The cat leaped, knocking the second rider from his horse three hundred yards away.

Martin knew he could not cover the distance in time. He dropped beside a rock and levered a round into the rifle's chamber. He sighed and held his breath as the rider tried to rise. When he fired, the cat staggered and looked up. Martin worked the leaver and fired a second round into the cat's face. The cat wailed in pain, and Martin shot the third bullet through the animal's vitals. The cat fled toward the rock slope a few yards away. It tried to ascend to safety but fell, too weak to continue.

Moving cautiously, Martin approached the cat. It hissed and growled at him then took a swipe at his leg. Raising the rifle to his shoulder, he put a bullet through its eye. The head dropped limply to the hot stone. Though blood still pulsed from the wound, every muscle relaxed as the life drained away from the cougar.

He turned to the two riders. The first one Martin recognized as the Mexican from the saloon. He was dead, slashed through the jugular. A strange sadness passed over Martin and was gone as he moved to the second man who still breathed. Martin knelt beside him, shading his face from the sun. His dark eyes opened, and Martin saw fear and pain in them.

Behind him, Chico let out a string of curses in Spanish as he dropped the reins of Martin's bay and dismounted.

"You know who he is, gray boy?" Chico asked in English. "That's Filipe Terraza. Fernando Terraza's son. Grandson of Santiago Terraza. You bring him back to Terraza *rancho*, and you'll not ride away."

"I'm not leaving him here." Martin shrugged his vest and unbuttoned his shirt.

"Mister, he isn't wrong," Filipe said weakly.

Martin's heart sank. He did not know if the Terrazas knew him as an Alvarado, but even as one of Alvarado's hired hands, the Terrazas likely wanted him dead for trespassing on their land. He knew for certain if he took Filipe to Alvarado's ranch, Alvarado would kill him or leave him to die slowly for lack of care. Martin had no other choice.

"You got a mama?" Martin asked as he tore his shirt into bandages.

"Yes."

"Think of her and how she'd feel not knowing what happened to you. Women can be funny about things like that. Especially mothers." He cut the sleeve away from Filipe's left arm, which had taken the worst of the cat's attack, and wrapped most of the bandage around the wounded limb.

"Let's go. We'll only complicate things by staying here." Chico grabbed his arm. Martin jerked free and glared up at his companion.

"Go on back if you're so inclined. I'm not leaving him to die."

Chico blinked, and Martin went back to bandaging the wounds.

"You can't take him to Alvarado. They'll kill him, and town is too far."

"I'll take him to Terraza. What they do with me is my concern."

Chico looked grim. "If they don't kill you for being an Alvarado, Señor Luis will when you come back to the rancho. He certainly will disown you as his grandson."

Jaw flexing, Martin realized he was burning a bridge, but a closed-door meant less than a man's life, even if the man was the son of someone who would kill him for no other reason than the fate of his birth. Martin went on, committing his mind to the idea of never fully belonging.

"Go on, Chico," he said, staring into the eyes of Filipe Terraza, confident he was doing the right thing.

Chico sighed heavily. "I hope you know what you're doing, amigo. *Adios.*" He climbed onto his paint and galloped back toward the wash and Alvarado land.

"I thank you, stranger," Filipe said a moment later when the pain eased.

"Don't thank me yet," Martin said, leaving him to bring the bay close to offer shade while he rounded up the other horses. "It's still a long ride ahead." He gave Filipe no chance to reply. He caught the horses, then loaded the dead man on one, and brought the palomino for Filipe, who now sat up braced against his good arm.

"I'll be able to ride alone," he said.

"Are you sure?" Martin brought him a canteen. Filipe nodded.

"If I fall off, you can tie me on." He took a swallow and handed back the canteen with a weak smile.

"Right now, you falling off is the least of my worries." Martin took his arm and pulled him to his feet. He helped the wounded man into the saddle then climbed on his own horse. "You'll have to direct me some. I don't know the way to Terraza ranch."

Filipe nodded south. "Follow this wash 'til you come to a trail. Then head west along it. It will take you there."

Already, Filipe swayed in the saddle, but Martin hesitated to tie him on his horse. He knew what damage ropes could do and, with the chance his existing wounds would fester, the last thing Filipe needed was more injuries. After a mile, Martin took to riding alongside, holding Filipe in the saddle. It was over ten miles to Terraza ranch. By the time night fell, he gave up and rode double with the wounded man leading his own horse and the horse with its dead burden.

Filipe was out of his head by the time the main gate of Terraza Rancho emerged into view among the shadows. Brightened by the moonlight, it became a beacon on the open, barren land. Martin paused at the end of the trail leading to the door, his eyes tracing the top of the fortress. He expected to see guards pacing the fire step, but nothing moved. A sound, a motion, no matter how slight, would have eased his mind.

Filipe stirred and raised his head, staring at the gates, delirious. Martin felt him tense and groan softly.

"*Lo siento*," he said quietly.

Filipe shook his head. "You've already done more than…" He tensed as another wave of pain passed over him.

"Easy, now." Martin shifted his grip on the reins. "I'll take you up there."

He nudged the horse forward at the same slow walk that had carried them over many miles. All the while, he watched, waited, knowing the strong likelihood of a bullet ending his life.

They stopped less than ten feet from the heavy, iron banded doors built to hold off attacks by Comanches.

"Hello!" Martin called. Silence answered.

"Why don't the guards answer?" Filipe asked.

"I doubt they're sleeping." Martin listened a moment longer and then called again in Spanish for Fernando. This time the response was a pair of rifles extending from above the gate. Martin released the reins, raised his left hand, and called out in Spanish to see Fernando.

"He sleeps, *gringo*," one snarled. "Be on your way."

"I have his son, Filipe, here. He needs care, and I won't leave him on the doorstep."

The speaker scoffed. "Señor Filipe is in the hills far from here."

"He was attacked by a puma. I've brought him here for help." Despite the rise of anger, Martin kept his tone calm. His words affected a sober silence from the man.

"Be on your way," the voice said again, and when Martin remained, someone fired a shot into the dirt between the horse's legs. The palomino jumped and bucked. Martin gripped the horn and held on to keep them both in the saddle, but Filipe, weak and disoriented by pain, went limp. When he fell, Martin did his best to ease the fall, but they hit hard, and he felt the shock in his left shoulder as the joint popped out of socket. Fortunately, the horse turned and bolted down the trail with the others in tow, sparing Martin and Filipe a trampling.

"The next will find your heart, *gringo*."

Martin ignored the guard and turned to Filipe. His wounds bled again, and Martin did what he could to stop it.

"Didn't you hear me, *gringo*!"

"Paco." Filipe's voice was weak. Martin doubted it carried to the guard, but the young man had spirit. He filled his lungs and called out again. "Paco!"

In the faint moonlight, Martin saw the guard's mouth soften.

"Señor Filipe?"

With great effort, Filipe raised his head so the man could see his face.

"Let us in."

The guard hesitated, but he and the other lowered their weapons. Beyond the wall, voices shouted, and the gate opened.

Martin felt relief at the sight of Fernando, shirt un-tucked, coming toward them with a lantern.

"Your father's coming, Filipe."

Filipe's eyes closed. As the lantern light fell across them, Martin looked up, and Fernando stopped dead in his tracks.

"What is this Alvarado scum doing on my land?" he said a moment later.

"I mean no harm," Martin said. He rose and faced Fernando raising his right hand. "I freely admit to trespassing, but your son and his companion were attacked by a puma. The other was killed, and I brought Filipe here to be cared for."

Fernando frowned. He gave orders in Spanish, and two men carried Filipe inside.

"What do you hope to gain by this?"

Martin shook his head. "Nothing. Only, I understand a mother's grief and how that grief can be made worse by not knowing what happened to her child."

Fernando's expression softened. "Where's the other man?"

"Down the road on one of the horses, I led in."

"Paco!"

The guard stepped forward, and Fernando ordered him to track down the horses since it was his shot that spooked them. Paco grudgingly obeyed and disappeared into the night.

"Ordinarily, I would turn you away," Fernando said. "Considering the circumstances, I will give you what I can, but cannot let you inside the gate."

Martin nodded that he understood.

Fernando looked him over. "Come to the gate. I'll have someone look at that shoulder."

He could not refuse what Fernando Terraza offered. His arm hung useless, and the pain nearly took his breath away.

"Bucho!"

He nearly groaned when he looked up into the face of the big Texan from town. He held up his good hand.

"No trouble."

Though Bucho's face was grim, he put down his rifle against the wall.

"He can fix your shoulder," Fernando explained, casting a warning look at the Texan.

Reluctantly, Martin let the Texan take his arm. With one hand against Martin's ribs, he pulled almost gently. The pain eased, and as Bucho relaxed his grip, the numbness left his fingers.

"You'll want to put that in a sling for a few days," Bucho said.

Martin nodded. "Thanks."

Without a word, Bucho took up his rifle and stood beside the gate. Not even Fernando spoke as they waited. Once Paco returned with the horses, Martin climbed onto his bay.

"Don't let the sun rise with you on this land," Fernando commanded. "I give you your life for saving my son, but no more."

Martin nodded that he understood and turned the bay down the road east. With no bedroll and no provisions for the trail, he had little choice but to find his way back to the Alvarado camp and try to get his gear. He was uncertain what to expect. The very least his grandfather could do under the circumstances was let him have what he bought himself. Less than an hour of the night remained when he rode into the camp. The cook, already at work, went to Armand's bed and woke him before Martin dismounted. Within moments the camp came alive in silent motion. Martin went quickly to the gear wagon and collected his bedroll and rifle. Then he turned and found ten men fanning out, surrounding him and cornering him against the wagon.

"Where are you going?" Armand asked.

"Leaving."

Armand chuckled. "So you're just going to tuck tail and run?" A chorus of chuckles, sneers, and overall agreement ran through the men.

Martin glanced around at them, sizing them up. They had waited long for this moment, and a few of them grinned in anticipation. Kell grinned the widest, his mouth a mottled gap in his ugly face.

"I want no part of this," he told Armand. "If I can't help a man I harbor no ill toward, I want nothing to do with you."

The lines of Armand's face deepened in the shadows from the chuck wagon's lantern. He stepped forward into shadow, and his face disappeared, but what Martin had seen was already enough.

"You're not worthy of the Alvarado name. You betrayed us and helped our enemy." Armand stood close, rubbing his knuckles. He seethed theatrically. "You don't walk away from that."

Martin knew it was coming but was slow to react. Armand's left caught him in the middle of his stomach, just below the ribs, and forced the wind from his lungs. He doubled over, fighting to straighten. He didn't see the next blow as it caught him on the left side and knocked him to the ground. He fought back, but they never let him rise as far as his knees before someone knocked him down again. A boot caught him on the side of the head, stunning him. After that, all he knew was pain and darkness. Armand's voice, growling a command in Spanish, penetrated the scraping of gravel.

They stripped him of his boots, belt, and vest. When Kell reached into his hip pocket for the watch, he struck out and landed a solid blow on Kell's mouth. Kell reacted by gripping his throat and squeezing. Martin reached up, trying to dig his fingers into Kell's eyes, but Kell held his face out of reach, and darkness descended, consumed him, and he felt nothing.

When he stopped fighting, Kell took the watch, pocketed it, then dragged Martin to his horse and threw him across the saddle.

Chico saddled his paint and waited for Kell to saddle his horse. Then they led the bay out through the scrub in the morning twilight. They rode the three miles to the range border. There they brought the bay alongside a gully and shoved Martin's limp body into it. Then Kell, thorough in the job, drew his pistol and cocked it.

"He's good as dead already," Chico protested. "Why waste the bullet?"

"Because he's worth making sure." He fired a round into Martin's back. Mercifully, Martin had lost his senses and did not move. "See. Didn't feel that, *if* he's still breathing." He holstered the revolver and leaned down to gather the bay's reins. "Let's go. I got me an appetite."

Chico lingered beside the gully staring down at Martin's remains. If he felt remorse, he only showed it with a brief prayer. He signed himself and kissed his fingers before turning the paint to follow Kell.

The sun rose, bringing with it the heat that drew lizards from hiding. They scurried over rocks and Martin's body with equal caution, wary of the shadows that played over them. Vultures circled, landed, and moved close, but when he moved, they fell back and waited. Martin, with one good arm and no strength, crawled down the gully to an overhang. He knew nothing of what he did, only that he had to flee the vultures and the sun, but as he neared the overhang, he knocked the dirt loose, and the overhang collapsed, burying him. Though the cloud of dust, he stared at the pile of dirt and felt despair descend in a constricting air as close as the building heat of the day. In a mind not quite clear, and a world bleached by the sun, he broke down inside. He thought of the family he long dreamed of meeting and would never know. How close he came to finding out what happened and why his mother had left this place! It all ended here in a dry wash in the middle of a land that killed, surrounded by heartless people. He was alone and had no more strength to fight. So he put his head down and wept silently. Perhaps if he slept, he would not feel the vultures tear into his flesh.

The plume of dust carried high in the windless air. It caught the eye of a rider nearly a mile away.

Paco frowned at it.

"Hey, Jinx," he called to his companion in the day's search for cattle. "See that?"

Jinx squinted. At his age, the glare hurt his eyes.

"Yeah." He shifted the tobacco in his mouth and spat. "Ain't enough wind to stir a devil."

"Maybe we should go see. Could be one of our cows."

Jinx shook his head. "With all the buzzards around, I doubt it's anything we can do much with."

Paco thought for a moment then shook his head. "We've been all day out here and seen nothing. I'm going to look." He turned his little buckskin and kicked it into a lope.

"You're going to make that ride for nothing!" Jinx hollered after him. He spat again and glanced around at the brush, deciding he was bored with the search. "Awe, hell!" he growled and followed Paco, cussing Mexicans as a whole for the simple fact it made him feel better.

Vultures leaped into the air as Paco drew up short of the wash. He frowned when he saw nothing resembling a steer or cow. Then he moved closer and rode along the edge. Then he saw the form of a man, face down, half his body covered in dirt from a collapsed side of the wash. Paco jumped from his horse and slid down the steep side of the wash. He knelt beside the body, searching for signs of life.

"What'd you find?"

Paco shook his head. "Must've been *banditos*. They stripped him." Then he turned the man over and recognized the face. He cursed.

"What?"

"The *gringo* from last night, the one who brought Señor Filipe home."

Jinx spat. "Alvarado must not've liked what he did." He worked the plug and settled it in his cheek again. "You're going to have to do most of the digging. My old bones won't take that kind of work."

Paco removed his hat and bowed his head. "Stubborn *pendejo*. I might've liked him." Then Paco saw the exit wound and realized it bled afresh. He reached out and touched the blood to be sure, and then he put his fingers to the parted lips and felt the stir of the man's breath. "He's still alive," he called to Jinx, who had turned away to find a burial site.

"Well, damnit, stop squawking, and do something!" Jinx dismounted and brought his canteen to Paco. "Clean that wound out and get the bleeding stopped."

While Paco worked, he hoped the gringo would wake and show he still had strength, but he remained senseless. Jinx held out hope as they wrapped the wounds in his chest and back with Paco's shirt.

"Hopefully, your Mex sweat doesn't infect those wounds."

Paco shot Jinx a look. "Any infection he's going to get he already has. You see how far he crawled?"

"All the same, ain't nothing out here going to save him. Let's get him on my horse."

Jinx rode double, holding Martin's limp body in the saddle in front of him. When they rode into the yard at Terraza Ranch, Fernando was first to meet them with his wife, Lucia, close behind.

"What's this?"

"*El gringo*," Paco answered. "The one from last night."

Fernando's lips tightened in anger. "I'll take him."

Jinx handed Martin down to Fernando, who carried him inside.

"The spare room." Lucia cut past him and led the way up the hall past Filipe's room. She turned down the blankets and supported Martin's head as Fernando laid him down. Jaw tightened, he unwrapped the makeshift bandages.

"It looks bad," Fernando said after examining the wounds. He sighed. "Clean him. Make him comfortable. I'll be back." He marched back outside to where Paco and Jinx watered their horses. "Who did that?"

"Wasn't us, señor," Paco replied. "We would have left him out there."

"Nice to know you have a heart, Paco," Fernando snapped. "Did he say anything? Anything about Alvarado?"

Jinx shook his head. "No. He's been like that since we found him. Never would've known he was still living if he hadn't been bleeding."

Fernando grunted in rage. "Had to be Alvarado. Only he would be so hard."

"Anything we can do to help, señor?" Paco asked, removing his hat. "I feel a little responsible."

Fernando's temper cooled. He shook his head.

"No. You men have done what you could." He nodded in the vague direction of the corral. "Go on about your work."

"Thank you, señor." Paco led his horse away, but Jinx remained behind. He sat on the edge of the water tank and removed his hat.

"Mister Fernando?"

"Yes?"

"I got a real good look at that boy," Jinx said quietly. "Kind of reminds me of someone."

"Who?" Fernando asked over his shoulder.

"Your sister."

Fernando's eyes widened. He turned to face Jinx, who raised his hand, patting the air as though to calm Fernando's fresh rise in temper.

"Just hear me out," he said with that same calm tone. "I ain't saying anything in particular, but something in his face reminds me real strong of her. That's all I'm saying."

Fernando squinted at Jinx.

"You've been out in the sun too long," Fernando said finally.

"Maybe I have." Jinx shook his head. "Truth is you don't know what happened to her and her son. Maybe they died. Maybe they just got lost. Maybe that boy is hers, come back looking for some answers."

Frowning, Fernando turned and stared toward the house. "Go back to your work, Jinx."

"Yes, sir." Jinx pulled on his hat and stood with a sigh. "I will." He led his horse away to the corral, leaving Fernando alone with his thoughts.

Santiago Terraza

Cool, quiet stillness surrounded him. In delirium, he believed that he had slipped quietly into hell. Now, he wondered if Heaven claimed him by mistake. He reached for his pocket, for the watch, but a strange force held his arm back. In his half-conscious mind, this puzzled him. Earth would have no give. He could move a little, but not enough, and that restriction came from pain and weariness. His mind cleared, and he could feel soft cloth surrounding his body, like the sheets of the bed where he had lain ill as a child, but that was as far as his mind reached. The sensation faded, and his thoughts grew muddled. He felt as though he floated on the swells of a sea, twisting, bending, and turning on the waves as everything around him grew surreally distant. Then the feeling calmed, and he slowly woke again and heard the sound of men's voices speaking in worried tones.

Martin opened his eyes, but the lids were too heavy, and they closed before his vision focused. He tried again to see the men speaking nearby. Their voices were clearer now, speaking Spanish, and his sluggish mind struggled to grasp understanding. He blinked, and the ceiling above cleared. The voices stopped. One man spoke again, and Martin turned his head toward him.

He sat beside the bed, a white-haired man with sharp features and a close trimmed beard. His eyes sparkled in the lamplight as he smiled a kind, gentle smile. His right hand gripped a cane which he passed to his left and reached out to touch Martin's forehead.

"You live as yet," he said, gently stroking Martin's hair as he tested the warmth of Martin's skin. He turned and spoke again in Spanish to the other man. Martin understood enough to know they talked about him. The other man came near, and Martin recognized Fernando Terraza. Fernando's face was heavily lined with worry and darkened with something that remained when the worry lifted.

"Filipe?" Martin asked with an effort. His throat was dry, and he nearly choked as a cough tore through his windpipe. The old man calmly took a glass of water from the bedside table and helped him drink. The coughing left his throat raw and his chest with a sharp pain running through it.

"He will live too," the old man said. "The infection was severe, but he survived. Without you, he would not have lived."

"I don't remember coming back here," Martin said, fighting grogginess. He looked at Fernando. "What happened?"

"Paco and Jinx found you in a wash near the border of our land. You've been beaten and shot. It seems they left you for dead. Jinx said the vultures were about to take their first bite." Fernando's mouth remained tight. Martin knew his presence displeased the man.

"I'm sorry," Martin said softly.

Fernando waved his hand. "You've nothing to be sorry for. Filipe told me what happened, how the puma jumped him and Alonso, and how you saved him." Martin felt the heat rise in his cheeks. He looked away as Fernando went on. "He also told me there was another man with you who warned you not to go back to the Alvarado herd. It appears you didn't heed his warning."

Martin closed his eyes, searching his memory.

"I needed my gear," he explained when his thoughts finally organized. "Didn't care about my pay, but my gear..." Then he remembered the watch and the picture, and his heart sank into his stomach. He looked from one man to the other. "Did they find anything with me?"

Both men looked grim, and for a moment, Martin feared he had lost the two most valuable things in this world. Then, the old man sat forward, leaning on the cane whose scarred wood matched the gnarled skin of his hands.

"They found only this." The man's expression was gentle as he reached over and picked the daguerreotype off the table and slipped it into Martin's palm. "We had to pry it from your hand to clean the blood away."

Relief washed away the pain. Though the watch too had value, the picture was the only proof he had of his heritage. Without it, he was as lost as any maverick. He closed his eyes and felt thanks in every fiber of his being.

The old man told Fernando he would stay if the younger man had other things to attend. Fernando nodded, calling the old man father and telling him not to excite Martin, but even through their Spanish, what Martin understood confused him. His mind was still weak, and he quickly gave up puzzling over their conversation.

"That picture," the old man said, gesturing to Martin's hand. "Is of your mother and father?"

Martin nodded. "Their wedding day."

"Are they dead?"

Again Martin nodded. "I came here hoping to find what remained of my mother's family. Now..." He shook his head, staring at the brass case. "Not anymore."

The old man nodded. "Alvarado has long hated us. If only he knew the truth, but he would never listen."

"Señor Fernando called you '*Padre.*' Are you Santiago? The winner of Carmelita's hand?"

The old man chuckled. "Ah, yes. I am Santiago, but a winner..." He shook his head. "That is the story Alvarado never knew, but I like how you put it. It shows openness. If you were truly devoted to Alvarado, you would have called me a thief." He smiled, and Martin felt a sense of familiarity. "They call me Grandfather here, even our hired hands. I'm too old and broken to work anymore. I can only tell stories." He regarded Martin for a moment. "I tell the stories of how my grandfather came to this land from Spain so that my grandchildren will know their heritage. Everyone should know their family's story as well as their own. Don't you agree?"

As Santiago gazed into his eyes, Martin felt sadness. He looked away, feeling lost and lonely as his throat tightened.

"I think you agree," Santiago said. "That's why you look away. You don't yet know your story, but you will in time, and even if you never know the story of your family, yours will be the beginning of a new line of stories that will be treasured by your children for generations to come."

As Santiago spoke, the life in his eyes spread, animating his whole lean body. His gnarled hands gestured, artfully emphasizing his words. When he paused, his eyes grew contemplative. He nodded as though coming to a decision.

"I will share the story with you," he said. "Because of what you did for my grandson, and because..." He shook his head in a subtle theatric gesture. "When you're old, sleeping holds no interest."

Martin smiled at this. He understood and felt honored to have the kind old man's attention.

"I don't know if I can remember it," he said in a quiet apology.

Santiago saw how tired he was. He placed a hand over Martin's.

"It cannot be told all in one night," he said. "What I tell you tonight will only be the beginning."

Martin listened as his eyes grew heavy and finally closed. He felt like a boy again, and in the deep recesses of his memory came the image of his mother telling him a story like this one so long ago time blurred the names and details. He did not know when his mind completely separated from Santiago's lively voice, but he remembered the image of ships tossed in a storm and harboring off the Texas shore.

In the days that followed, Martin regained enough strength to listen without falling asleep, but it was several days longer before he regained enough strength to walk more than the few feet between the bed and the high-backed chair by the window with Santiago's patient assistance.

Martin was not used to the fussing Filipe's mother and sister bestowed on him. He knew it was because they were grateful to him, and he did his best to accept their care graciously, but he felt smothered. Four days after awaking from fever, Santiago convinced Lucia to let the two young men sit on the veranda outside Martin's room. The day was hot, and this side of the house was in the shade, cool and comfortable.

Filipe sat in a broad, high-backed chair. He smiled when Martin stepped onto the porch with Lucia steadying him and muttering in Spanish about young blood being too anxious to heal right. She commanded him to sit while she gathered a blanket for him.

"Ma'am, please..."

"A boy as thin as you with much blood to make you'll catch a chill," Lucia countered.

"Calm down, Daughter," Santiago said with an upraised hand as though to fend off her feisty temper. "Martin has been alone for a long time. I'm sure he knows what's best for him."

"He's hardly older than Filipe there," Lucia countered.

"And I'm sure he appreciates your concern." Santiago poured wine into small, stemmed glasses. "But he needs room to heal as he must. Like any wild thing, he's not used to so much attention."

Martin was unsure if he should be flattered by the comparison, but knowing Santiago, he chose to feel flattered.

Santiago straightened and, without his cane, carefully brought two glasses to Martin and Filipe.

"Don't fret," he told Lucia. "If he becomes chilled, I'll get a blanket for him."

Lucia looked down at Martin, her eyes blazing. He had faced his share of danger in his life, but women carried their own category of danger against which he had no defense. He looked away.

She relented by folding the blanket from the bed inside and placing it on the chair beside him. When her cool fingers touched his cheek, it startled him. He looked up into her eyes now tender with motherly love. She kissed his forehead, then turned to her son and did the same, commanding them to behave. Once she departed, Santiago raised his glass.

"Let us drink," he said. "To consequences."

"Isn't that a little odd, Grandfather," Filipe asked. "It's not as though consequences are ever very good."

"Ah, but that is where your youth puts you at a disadvantage, grandson." Santiago raised his glass. "To consequences, whatever they may be."

The old man's toast puzzled Martin, but out of courtesy, he raised his glass and drank.

"I still don't understand," Filipe protested after drinking.

"You will in time." He moved the blanket and sat beside Martin.

"Filipe knows this story well, but he could do to hear it again."

Martin saw Filipe's jaw flex. Santiago saw it too and ignored it.

"Do you remember, Martin, where I left off?"

Thinking for a moment, Martin remembered. "Diego and his move to this country was the last I remember."

Santiago smiled, satisfied. "He was my grandfather, a man of light hair and green, gold-flecked eyes, a tall man of lean strength, wise for his youth. He fought for Spanish conquest in the south and earned his land here, whatever land he chose. When he came, he saw the people of this land, Los Indios, live as they had for thousands of years and was fascinated by it. He helped the brothers of San Francisco build their church in the nearby town and taught those that came how to ranch. Their descendants still live on this land today. Maria Luis is the great-granddaughter of the first Indian to bring his family to this rancho. The name Juan was given him. He also brought with him his sister, whom Grandfather Diego fell in love with. It wasn't a quick love, but one that grew with time. When faced with the choice of marrying the daughter of a Spanish don and the Indian maiden, he chose the latter, Helena. She died a year after giving birth to my father. My grandfather married again, this time to the Spanish woman. She bore two sons and a daughter. The daughter went back to Spain, and one son went to California. The two sons of Diego that remained here never got along. They fought over the littlest things. Before Grandfather Diego died, he divided his land equally between them, knowing they would never live together as brothers should."

"That's what became Alvarado land," Filipe offered.

"Yes." Santiago nodded sadly. "The son of the Spanish woman, Manuel, fathered only daughters, the oldest of which married a Spanish man of that name who inherited the land through his wife. The son of the Indian woman, named Juan after his uncle, remained here. His sons ran the ranch together, but only I survived to marry."

"How is it, then," Martin asked, "that the rivalry continued? Isn't it usually the father that passes that on?"

Santiago thought a moment. "Perhaps, but in this case, the daughter of Manuel passed it on to her son. While it seemed quiet in those years, her cunning kept the rivalry going. They bought more land and nearly doubled what they began with. While she was only a woman, she ran that ranch before and after her husband died with all the strength and wisdom of a man. Her son, Luis, has never married."

"He and father have never gotten along," Filipe added. "Between his arrogance and Father's temper, it's no wonder."

"He doesn't seem to know why," Martin explained, nearly referring to Luis Alvarado as "grandfather" but caught himself before uttering the first sound. "Señor Alvarado never spoke of his motivations. Only that if we ever met Terraza riders, he didn't care if one was killed."

Santiago nodded slowly. "Four of our men have been found dead in the last six months. It makes it hard to hire new help. Those still here have lived and worked here as their fathers did. Only loyalty keeps them here."

"But they're not fighters," Martin pointed out. "Not with guns and knives. Alvarado has no less than three known gunmen working for him. The rest are simply mean. They know how to cause trouble and enjoy killing; it doesn't matter if it's man or beast."

Filipe and Santiago shared a look that spoke volumes. Likely, this was an old argument between them. Santiago looked down at his empty glass and sighed.

"We know," he said. "But we can't fight on those terms. We haven't the money, and it's not right."

"Not right to defend what's ours? Or ourselves?" Filipe sat forward, his eyes aflame.

Santiago was silent as he continued staring down into the glass. When he looked up, it was into Martin's eyes.

"Filipe doesn't know what war was like," Santiago said slowly. "From the scars you carry, I believe you do. I fought against Santa Ana at San Jacinto, and I don't want this land bloodied by violence."

An expectant silence fell over them as Santiago awaited an answer. Martin saw that in his eyes, but how to say it was hard to find.

"Respectfully, *señor*," Martin said. "I only half agree with you."

Santiago's eyebrows lifted a fraction. "Why is that?"

Martin took a deep breath before continuing. "Well, when two sides have a disagreement, they settle it according to the terms of the side with the most advantage. Sometimes that's by simple talk, but sometimes, there's no alternative but to fight. Alvarado is no longer rational. All he wants is a fight. You've tried for how many generations to settle this peacefully, and it still goes on. Only now it's getting worse. Your men have been killed for no more reason than that they traveled a public road. You can't negotiate with that, not in civil terms anyway."

"You think we should fight him with lassos and pitchforks?" Santiago sat forward, his gaze leveled at Martin. Martin didn't look away.

"I'm saying it's time your men learned to fight with guns and knives."

For a long moment, Santiago said nothing. The conversation completely changed him from an animated storyteller to a brooding philosopher. Martin disliked the prospect of an all-out war between the two ranches as much as Santiago, but knowing Alvarado, he was confident in his words. Still, he felt a pang of shame as Santiago set his glass on the table and rose with his cane.

"I think I'll take a walk," he said. "Supper will be ready soon." He turned away and walked along the veranda and disappeared around the corner of the house, leaving Martin with a sinking feeling.

"Don't worry," Filipe said, reaching out to pat Martin's shoulder. "He just needs time to think. Father's been trying to convince him of the same thing for nearly a year. Grandfather always says that Father's never seen real war and how it destroys land in the minds of the men that see it."

"Sometimes it has to be done," Martin said quietly. He shook his head. "But that's no excuse for charging into it." He fixed Filipe with an intimating stare. Filipe did not hold it for long.

"He's old and tired," Filipe stated in his own defense.

"Don't value him any less for it." Martin smiled at the memory of a parlor girl in Baton Rouge who had lived to be 90. "The best thing an old man can teach a young man is how to be an old man."

Filipe said nothing to this. He sat, staring off into the distance. Only a few years Martin's junior, Filipe seemed a decade younger. If things went the way Martin guessed they would, Filipe would catch up quickly.

The Horse

He stood sixteen hands high, a stallion with a dappled brown coat and long, black mane and tail. His intelligent eye looked out on the world with inquisitive understanding. His black ears swiveled, one always trained on the man in the corral while the other picked up on the quiet conversation of the men on the fence.

Martin watched through the rails as Jinx waved the handle of a long carriage whip with a flag at the end and cued the horse into a trot around the circle. Martin marveled at the ease and grace of the stallion's gait, smooth and strong. Even with his somewhat limited knowledge of horses, he recognized that this was an animal to be admired. From the tones of the gathered vaqueros, he knew this was the consensus.

The horse watched Jinx as he circled, and when the man switched the whip to his other hand, the horse quickly changed direction, light on his feet as though it were all a game. After a few more turns, Jinx lowered the whip, leaning on it almost casually, and the stallion walked to him.

"He certainly knows what he's doing."

Martin looked up at Fernando. His attention had been so focused on the horse he failed to notice Fernando's approach.

"Should you be out of the house?" Fernando asked.

Martin gave a weak smile and shook his head. "I needed to escape. Been inside too much lately."

Fernando chuckled knowingly. "Alright. Just be careful not to overdo it."

Martin nodded and watched as Jinx played an odd game with the stallion. The horse nickered in what seemed like laughter.

"Jinx has trained all our best horses," Fernando said as he leaned against the rail beside Martin. "This one he's trying to train for all uses, but I think he's a fool."

"Why?"

Fernando pointed. "That horse has a fighting streak in him. He doesn't like everybody. Last week he threw Paco quicker than a sneeze just because he could."

"Is that what Paco said?"

Fernando looked at him with a frown of thought. "Yes." He shook his head. "The point is, he's unpredictable. The only man he's not thrown yet has been Jinx, probably because he's spent so much time training him."

As they spoke, Martin watched Jinx untie the halter rope from around the stallion's neck and loop it around to the other side. The tall cowboy had no trouble vaulting onto the bareback. The stallion stood still without even shifting his weight.

"You crazy, cowpoke!" a man yelled from the other side of the corral. "He'll buck you quicker than he bucked Paco!"

"Pay them no attention, boy," Martin heard Jinx say to the horse. "Just do like I taught you."

With the lightest of signals, Jinx turned the horseback into the circle and trotted him around once, then crossed the corral, shifting direction in a tight figure eight, all the while flapping the whip near the horse's head.

The stallion paid no attention to the whip or the hoots of the men as Jinx worked him. He slowed to a walk and stopped at the center. Jinx turned him in a tight circle. The stallion bent his body willingly in a dance that raised dust from the hard-packed earth. Then they went back to the circle, only this time as they crossed the corral, they did it sideways. Martin had seen such maneuvers done by cavalry. The stallion performed them with the precision that excelled the best cavalry horse.

Off to his right, Martin heard Paco chuckle.

"I'll make him buck."

Martin looked over in time to see Paco draw and fire his revolver into the dirt. The crack and whine as the bullet bounced and flew past the horse was enough to make the other men duck, but the horse went on almost casually and only stopped at Jinx's signal. The stallion looked at Paco with an expression akin to puzzlement.

Jinx slid from the stallion's back, walked over to the fence, and stared up at Paco's grinning face. Then in the blink of an eye, he grabbed Paco and hauled him to the dirt, pummeling him in a rolling brawl.

As the other men descended into the corral to break up the fight, the stallion looked over at Martin; ears pointed straight at him. Then with an almost casual gait, he walked over and stretched out his nose for a curious sniff. Martin offered his hand through the rails and felt the stallion's warm breath on his fingers. Then the stallion stepped closer, and Martin stroked his tan muzzle. By the time the fight had run its course, and the two combatants separated, the stallion had turned sideways to the corral fence and remained firmly planted by Martin. As quiet descended, the stallion looked at them with almost lazy comedy. Martin smiled at the incidental humor of it all.

The men shook their heads and walked away, some throwing up their hands as though waving away the animal's insult. Jinx stood alone, looking stunned by what he saw. He picked up his hat and walked over to the horse.

"Just came over here all by his self, did he?"

Martin nodded. "I'm new, and he seems the curious type."

Jinx shook his head. "No. He doesn't do that with new people." He untied the halter lead. "Come in here. I want to see what he does."

Martin walked around to the gate, not trusting his still weak limbs to climb the fence and stepped inside as Jinx again tied the dangling lead loosely around the stallion's neck. Then he picked up the whip and handed it to Martin.

"Can you take that sling off?"

Martin hesitated before reaching behind his neck and undoing the knot. As the sling came loose, he moved his arm with care. His shoulder still hurt from Kell's lazily aimed bullet, but he had seen and guessed what Jinx would have him do, he reckoned it wouldn't do any harm. He tucked the sling in his back pocket and took the whip.

"Run him in a circle."

Knowing the look he gave Jinx was more question than confidence, Martin felt suddenly stupid, but Jinx just nodded toward the horse and said nothing.

Deliberately, Martin moved toward the stallion flicking the flag at the end of the whip and pointing the direction with his weak arm.

The stallion responded readily and moved out, picking up pace with each hard flick of the flag.

"Change his direction."

Martin winced at the pain in his shoulder as he moved the whip from one hand to the other, but the stallion turned without missing a step.

"Call him in."

He lowered the whip, and the stallion slowed, and though he stood next to Jinx, the stallion came to Martin and lowered his head. Martin scratched his forelock of long, coarse, black hair as Jinx had, and the stallion nudged him before tossing his head.

Jinx watched them, stroking his beard in deep contemplation.

"Hope you don't intend for me to ride him," Martin said. "Don't know if my shoulder will take it."

"No." Jinx shook his head. "Not today, but you will ride him." He stepped forward and reached out to stroke the stallion's sleek mottled neck. "I'm a firm believer that for every rider there's a horse, and for every horse, there's a rider. The choosing is as much by the one as the other. You understand?"

Martin nodded.

"Haze, here, has just chosen you. If Mister Fernando agrees, he's yours." He looked past Martin at Fernando, standing forgotten outside the gate.

Fernando's mouth thinned in a satisfied half-smile.

"Since you lost your horse because of my son, I believe it would be a fair trade."

"No." Martin shook his head. "I don't know the worth of horses, but a blind man can tell this one is worth much more than the one I had."

"Consider it a favor to me then," Fernando countered. "Jinx already has three horses of his own, and no one else can ride that one."

Martin gritted his teeth. He could not deny he wanted the stallion, but it was a gift greater than any he had received before in his life. He knew it was not a fair exchange.

Fernando, though, took his silence as acceptance. He pushed off the corral fence.

"See that he gets the loan of a saddle and bridle."

"Sure thing, boss."

Martin watched Fernando walk back to the house, his hand absently stroking the stallion's cheek. He had no words to express his gratitude and so remained silent.

"You know," Jinx said into the silence as he untied the lead rope again. "When that gun went off, I just about jumped out of my skin. The only two that didn't were you and this horse. That says more than enough to me that he rightfully belongs to you." Jinx took the whip and handed Martin the rope. Martin took it, still saying nothing. Jinx chuckled. "Just goes to show sparsely worded folk got no business among people. Let's go put him in the corral."

Martin lingered where he was looking at the stallion in the eye. He could not help the sense that the horse expressed understanding, as though this animal understood him better than any human he knew. For the first time in his memory, Martin felt comfortable, confident, and strong.

"Well, I reckon," he said and led Haze from the corral.

The Coming Storm

At Santiago's request, Martin continued to take his meals with the Terraza family. He felt like an intruder at first despite the efforts of Lucia and Maricruz to make him welcome. His increasing independence drew more and more motherly criticism from Lucia. Upon learning about what happened at the corral, she scolded him for removing his sling and risking injury to his wound.

"What if you bled again?" she demanded. "What if you fainted and that horse stepped on you?"

"Men don't faint, mother," Maricruz defended. "Besides, I think Martin's been on his own long enough to know what he can and cannot do."

Lucia gave a feminine scoff, eying her daughter with exasperation. Then she turned her piercing gaze on Martin, who raised his hand as though to ward off further onslaught.

"I'm fine, ma'am, really."

"Yes, darling," Fernando put in. "Martin risks losing more strength keeping you from spoiling him."

The livid indignation rising in Lucia's face drew smiles from her husband and Santiago and left Martin fighting to not make eye contact lest he further draws her ire. Even Filipe and Maricruz seemed on the verge of laughing. Lucia looked around at them, and their brimming mirth settled her. She shook her head.

"Oh, you!" She waved her delicate hand at them. "All of you! You're enough to drive a woman insane." She giggled, showing her insult was meant in jest.

"Don't worry, dear," Fernando said with perfectly feigned seriousness. "You're not far from it."

Her eyes flashed at him briefly. She gave him a warning look.

"Keep that up," Santiago whispered to Fernando. "And I'll give you one guess where you'll be sleeping tonight."

Lucia blushed but said nothing as the two kitchen maids cleared the table. Then she pushed back her chair, signaling her departure.

"Well, if you'll excuse me," she said with deliberately exaggerated elegance. "I believe I'll take the air before retiring for the night. Maricruz, you will join me?"

Maricruz glanced up at Martin as she rose from the chair beside him.

"Will you walk with us, Martin?" she asked, blinking her soft eyelashes. She was a beautiful girl, and after the roughness of so many working women, Martin craved her company. Before he could accept her offer, Santiago spoke up.

"We have some things to discuss, Mari," he said firmly. "Maybe later."

"Meaning 'no.'" She fixed her grandfather with the look of a young woman frustrated by someone she should respect.

Santiago's eyebrows rose in a facial shrug, and his eyes widened with exaggerated graveness. "Very possibly," he said, nodding.

Her lips thinned. Had she been less disciplined, she would have stomped her foot and stormed out. Instead, she gave a single nod, like a bow first to Santiago, then to Martin.

"Perhaps later," she said, smiling wanly up at Martin.

"Yes, ma'am."

She stepped past him, and her light perfume reached him. Though it was pleasant, it failed to heat his blood.

His attention shifted to Fernando, who was helping Filipe. Santiago led them into the parlor, where he poured brandy into plain glasses. After Filipe was settled in a chair beside the fireplace, Fernando set about packing his pipe. The silence continued well past the time it took them to settle in. When Santiago finally broke it, his tone was reserved, even pained.

"I've thought about what you said yesterday, Martin, and I've come to the conclusion you're right."

Fernando stared at his father through a plume of smoke unmoving. Filipe's eyes widened with excitement.

"Good, now we can do something about Alvarado."

"Take it easy, Filipe," Martin counseled. "Your grandfather struggled with this decision for a good reason." He looked over at the younger man. "It's nothing to celebrate."

Filipe sobered under this gentle scolding. He sat back in his chair and looked from Martin to his grandfather.

"What do you propose we do?" Fernando asked, looking to Santiago.

Santiago thought for a moment while he sipped his brandy.

"Until now," he said at last. "We've tolerated them on our land. No more. We've turned the other cheek each time Alvarado has struck. Now we stand. Our men will have to learn to fight, not just shoot and defend themselves whenever necessary." Santiago looked at Martin. "You fought in the war. Would you teach the men what you know?"

Martin met Santiago's gaze. Something about accepting made him feel dirty. He would be hiring out what he knew about killing for pay, even if it was only room and board. How much different was that from the raiders during the war? Men who killed and raped for profit still wore that mark wherever they went. Would it be any different for him? He would be training men to fight against his grandfather. For that reason alone, his mark should be especially indelible, but as he looked from Fernando to Santiago, he realized it was different for one reason. These men were asking his help to defend their homes and families, not make a profit, or even to exact revenge. In light of that, he believed he could reconcile his conscience to what came.

"I'll help you on one condition," Martin said. "I'll work here as an ordinary hand and earn the same pay."

"That's reasonable," Fernando said with a nod. "I can understand that."

"Your men already know how to shoot. They just need to learn how to move in a fight, but ultimately the question of whether they'll stand and fight won't be answered until the day they must stand and fight." Martin saw Santiago's agreeing nod. He sat forward, leaving his drink untouched on the table. "The best I can do is teach them what I know and try and prepare them for the unexpected. I won't lead them in raids or any other such thing. If it comes to anything like a war, we'll deal with it as such when the time comes."

"And if the time is now?" Filipe asked.

"It's not, I'm sure of that," Martin said. "As you know, Alvarado is the last to carry the name. Once he is gone, the fight may leave those who remain."

"What if it doesn't?" Fernando asked.

"Then, we'll have gained enough of an upper hand that we may be able to negotiate with them." He looked to Santiago, hoping he had gained approval.

Fernando puffed on his pipe. "There is a rumor that Alvarado has found an heir. What do you know of that?"

Martin's heart sank. He forgot that word traveled even between enemies.

"I know that Alvarado will not pass his land to another generation."

"Perhaps." Fernando's gaze lifted from the bowl of his pipe, and he gazed knowingly at Martin.

"What do you mean, Father?" Filipe asked with a frown of deep confusion.

Fernando's gaze didn't waver. "What do you think I mean, Martin?"

Martin's heart raced. He could feel the pulse of it in his wounds. He sank back in his chair and looked to Santiago, but the old man seemed equally as puzzled.

"Martin?"

The words took an effort to say. All strength had gone from him, but he drew a steadying breath and spoke without pride.

"Luis Alvarado claims he's my grandfather."

Filipe's expression hardened. Anger showed through.

"You're the heir to the Alvarado estate?"

"Not anymore." Martin shook his head.

"Not anymore? You don't just stop being an Alvarado! His blood runs in your veins!"

"As it runs in yours, Filipe," Santiago stated calmly.

"But with the promise of that much land, what else could be his motivation other than to trap us? His intentions here cannot be…"

The sharp rap of Santiago's cane against the hearth silenced Filipe.

"Keep your tongue!" The old man stood over Filipe, and at that moment, Martin did not doubt the danger he promised. "You are a Terraza! No Terraza has shown ingratitude as you have just now!"

Silence fell. Martin's chest felt tight as though he dared not breathe. All the while, he felt Fernando watching him. Santiago's attention remained focused on Filipe. He waved his hand at Martin.

"You owe this man your *life*. Such ingratitude has no place here."

Martin dared not look up as Santiago retreated to his chair and sank into it.

"Whatever proof Luis has I say is false," Santiago declared. "Martin is no grandson of his."

"Are you sure, Father?" Fernando asked pointedly. "You know what it will cost us if you're wrong."

Santiago stared at his son for a long time. Then his gaze shifted to Martin. Unlike those times when Luis Alvarado studied him, Martin felt at ease, as though everything was right in the world. Santiago gave a confident nod.

"I am sure."

This seemed to satisfy Fernando. He nodded in return and sat back to smoke his pipe in silence.

For a long while, none of them spoke. Though Martin felt uneasy in the quiet, he feared speaking might break open a new flood of anger.

"I don't like it," Santiago finally said. "But I will accept that the time has come." He leveled his gaze on Martin again. "I hope you will help us with this. I believe what you have told me of your quest to find your family, your home, and I believe you will help us with good intentions."

Again, Martin felt the reassurance of Santiago's trust. "Shall we start tomorrow?"

Santiago shook his head, adamantly. "Not on *Domingo*." He rose. "We'll not taint a holy day with such things." He rose from the velvet armchair. "I am sorry to retire so early, but this discussion has worn my last wit."

"Good night, father," Fernando said as Santiago hobbled past him. Santiago did not reply, a manner, unlike his normal self. Martin felt something sink inside him.

Once Santiago was gone, Fernando went to the hearth and knocked the embers out of his pipe. "We should retire as well. It is a long ride to Mass." He looked at Martin. "You are welcome to join us."

"Thank you."

Fernando put away his pipe. Filipe rose and seemed to hesitate.

"I'm sorry for what I said."

Martin gazed up at him and smiled to show Filipe he forgave him. "I understand. I only hope I will defend my family with the same determination as you."

"Thank you," Filipe said sincerely.

Fernando took Filipe's arm. "Will you sit up a while, Martin?"

Martin nodded, his mind too agitated to sleep. "Until the fire dies."

Fernando nodded. "Good night to you."

Fernando and Filipe disappeared down the hall, leaving Martin alone.

For a long while, he sat staring into the flames, slowly sipping the brandy Santiago had poured for him. He welcomed the calm it brought his body and mind, though he did not savor the sensation. Too many things weighed on him. Chiefly, it was Santiago's insistence that Alvarado was not Martin's grandfather. Did Santiago know more than he was telling in the long stories of his youth? Perhaps his was the same path as so many young men leading from the bed of one woman to the next. Martin shook his head at the thought, believing Santiago too devoted in things, even in years past, to be so fickle. Still, he could be wrong. Likely, Santiago knew of a family whose daughter had fled home with her infant son but bore no relation to them.

Martin drew a deep breath and sighed. He drained the last of the Brandy from his glass. He could sit for hours and wonder, or ask Santiago why he was so confident. However, tonight was not a good night to ask the question. It would have to wait for a better time.

Returning the glass to the sideboard, Martin turned down the lamp and paused for a moment, watching the fingers of flame play over the coals in the hearth. Somehow, it reminded him of the fragility of the world and how easily faith, trust, reputation, and life itself could change direction with a breath of air. How quickly the direction of his own life had changed! Thankful it had changed for the better, he turned away from the hearth and followed the line of windows down the hall to his room.

Heat shimmered against the distant buttes in a phantasmal dance between dry earth and cloudless sky. From the top of a ravine, Martin sat and watched. The brown stallion fidgeted a little, discontent with stillness.

"Settle down, boy," Martin advised. "Won't be here much longer."

The spring was to the south. It promised work, clearing out silt that had fallen in during the spring rains, but for the moment, he was content to simply watch the landscape. Twenty feet away, a rattlesnake stirred.

Aware of the animal, Martin made no move but kept an eye on it. Sensing the presence of something too big to eat, the snake flicked its tongue and crawled toward the edge.

The land was beautiful and dangerous, Martin thought, like the landscape of the human mind with the ability to dream of things that could be and possess the horrors of the past at the same time. Through the months since he left Alvarado's employ, he walked carefully among the Terraza family and their ranch hands. He stayed away from town, intent on avoiding Kell and the others, hoping he could make a new life among the Terrazas. He always rode with someone and wanted to avoid rumors that he remained in contact with Alvarado. He rode alone today only because Fernando sent him out despite Martin's insistence that another man accompanies him. No other men could be spared, and so Martin rode west, away from Alvarado land, and savored his first time without another human in sight in many months. He could have remained on this bluff all day, basking in the sun and the heat, but work waited.

"Alright, boy, let's go."

The horse turned along the edge, and Martin searched for the trail down. As he rode, his mind wandered to Lolita. He had not thought of her in the last two months, and for a moment, he wondered if she was well. A strong urge to ride to Alvarado's ranch to find out came over him. He shook his head and felt a pang of guilt.

Halfway down the slope, he noticed tracks of another horse. He paused and studied them. In the time he spent with Jinx, riding, and learning how to train horses, he also learned to read their tracks. This trail looked familiar. Teasing at the memory, he failed to recall it and continued down toward the spring.

The air turned sour with the smell of rot a quarter-mile from the spring. Haze hesitated, sniffing the wind.

"I smell it too, boy." He patted the sleek neck reassuringly. "Let's find out what it is."

Picking his way through the juniper along a narrow cattle trail, Haze expressed his concern with a soft nicker. Martin felt the same unease and worried they might stumble across a dead man from either side of the boundary. The thought turned his stomach.

As they rounded a bend in the trail and came into view of the waterhole, Martin felt relief at the sight of a dead deer beside the earthen dam, but the feeling evaporated at the question of why it died.

Dismounting several feet from the water source, Martin tied Haze to a stout juniper and approached cautiously, watching the rocks above.

But the deer had no marks, only a swollen tongue, and glazed eyes. Not even buzzards had descended upon the young buck. Looking up at the water, Martin understood why. Another deer, bloated by the heat radiating off the rocks, lay at the water's edge just above the earthen wall. No cat stalked this place. It was the water, likely poisoned by human hand. Like so many others in the area, this water hole was dug out and dammed into troughs by the early Spanish settlers and had provided water for hundreds of generations of cattle and wild game. Before now, the water from this spring had always run sweet.

Going back to his horse, Martin took out the shovel. On the low side of the dam, he started to dislodge the stones and dirt until the pressure of the water broke through and washed down into the gully below. He scrambled to higher ground and watched the leading tide uproot and wash away tufts of grass as it went. In a day or two, he would have to return with others to rebuild the dam. For now, it would have to drain and dry.

"Sorry, boy, no cool water for you." He tied the shovel behind his saddle and took down his canteen, still half-filled from the morning. He gave the stallion a share and took a little for himself. Then he mounted and turned Haze back toward the trail, but the horse shied, refusing to go forward. His ears perked toward the brush, and Martin felt his skin crawl. He was in the open, exposed to anyone hidden in the juniper.

He listened hard, but the heavy silence yielded no clues. Even the songbirds perched silently in the trees.

Then, from far back along the trail, he heard the scrape of a hoof against a stone.

It could have been a cow or a deer, but Haze did not relax, and so Martin reached for his rifle, quietly opened the breech, and chambered a round. Sliding from the saddle, he ground-hitched the stallion and slipped into concealment among the junipers to wait.

The rider made little effort to hide his approach. Martin tracked his progress by sound and let him ride past into the clearing around the waterhole. It was then Martin recognized the white-faced sorrel.

Letting down the hammer, Martin stepped back into the clearing.

"Hello, Paco."

Paco jumped, reaching for the gun on his hip. Reflexively, Martin trained the rifle on him. When Paco saw who he was, a laugh bubbled to his lips.

"Who did you think I was?"

"Not sure." Martin lowered the rifle. "Maybe you were the one who poisoned this water hole."

"Poisoned?"

"*Si.*"

Paco's eyebrows rose. He glanced over and saw the deer. Then he stepped down and bent to study the nearest carcass.

"Cyanide, I think," he said. "And a lot of it. Small amounts take a while to work."

Martin nodded and returned the rifle to its scabbard tucked under the right fender of his saddle. "What are you doing out here, Paco? I thought Señor Fernando sent you north this morning."

"He said for me to start around here and sweep north. Little Lupe is with me, but he didn't want to come down here."

"Why?"

Paco frowned. "Can you keep a secret?"

Martin studied him uncertainly a moment before nodding. Paco glanced around, then leaned in close and spoke in a conspiratorial tone.

"He doesn't like to climb hills. Neither does his horse."

Martin laughed hard and long. Despite his name, Little Lupe was one of the biggest men Martin had ever seen. He nearly passed out fighting laughter the first time he saw Lupe balanced on the back of a cowpony with hardly any room left for anything behind his saddle. The thought of that same cowpony carrying the oversized man down that rock face resurrected the mirth.

"At least he has mercy," Martin said, still chuckling as he wiped tears from his eyes.

"*Si.*" Paco surveyed the water hole again and shrugged. "Well, no point in staying here with no water to drink." He climbed back into the saddle and waited for Martin.

Martin let Paco lead as they climbed back to the lip of the canyon.

Little Lupe waited, reclined against the trunk of a lone scrub pine with his hat pulled down over his face. His snores rumbled through the stillness. As Martin and Paco neared, he woke with a start and rolled to his feet.

Paco called out to him, teasing him for his laziness. Lupe waved a hand at him and hauled his bulk into the saddle. Lupe told him about the waterhole.

"*Bastardos*." Lupe spat into the dirt.

Paco scoffed agreement. He turned his attention back to Martin. "I forgot to tell you, Señor Fernando wanted you back at the ranch. He wants you to go with the wagon for supplies tomorrow."

Martin frowned at this. The last two days, he spent out here, riding from waterhole to waterhole without seeing another soul. He liked it that way. The thought of meeting up with Kell or Armand in town sent chills through him. Protesting to Paco, however, would be pointless.

"Alright," he said. "You two take care. No telling if they didn't poison other water holes."

"*Bastardos*," Lupe cursed again.

"*Bastardos*," Martin agreed before he turned Haze northeast and gave him his head. The long-legged horse reached out in an easy lope that devoured the miles in a few hours. The supper hour neared when he rode through the south gate.

Seated in his usual spot on the porch, Santiago waved and called for him to come over. His expression was sedate and ever warm and inviting. If Martin could wish for a grandfather, Santiago was such a man. Even on days when his worn body hurt from age, Santiago smiled graciously and offered thanks for every bit of kindness showed him, and every little thing he considered a blessing.

Martin tied Haze out of reach of the flower bed, but the stallion tried for the roses anyway and flinched when he stuck his soft muzzle on the thorns.

"That should teach you," Martin scolded. He tugged off his gloves and tucked them in his belt as he stepped through the little iron gate. "What can I do for you, *Abuelo*?" His greeting brightened the old man's expression, and Martin felt a bit of satisfaction in return.

"Yes. Sit. Talk to me." There were two glasses on the table, and Santiago filled the second with cool water before he offered it to Martin.

Sinking into the chair across the table, Martin stretched his legs with a thankful sigh. "The shade feels good." He drank deeply of the water and smiled at its sweetness.

For a while, silence hung in the air. Santiago stared down into his still full glass, his face pale and his hands restless. Something bothered him, and this worried Martin.

"What do you wish to talk about?" Martin finally asked.

Santiago opened his mouth to speak and seemed to lose the words. Several moments passed before he attempted again. His voice was soft and almost fearful. "I do not believe you told me why your mother left her family."

Martin sipped the water, sweet and cool. He told Santiago his brief story several weeks before in a poor return for the rich history of the Terraza family. This last remained unspoken because of Maricruz and her excitement over a new dress. Now, asked to tell it, Martin felt reluctant.

"She said it was because of her mother," Martin said finally. "After my father was killed, my grandmother wanted Mother to remarry to a man she didn't love. When Mother refused, my grandmother disowned her."

Santiago's attention drifted to the garden. He was silent for a long moment then asked. "What of your grandfather?"

"Mother said he was a kind man, and gentle, too gentle for my grandmother. She said she left because she could no longer live with what my grandmother expected." He studied Santiago as he spoke. The old man's gaze was distant, thoughtful, and haunted. Excitement stirred in Martin's breast with a rise in hope, but he kept his tone neutral. "Why do you ask?"

Santiago shook his head and smiled wanly. "No reason." He glanced over at Martin and changed the topic. "I see you're not wearing a gun like the other young men. Even Filipe has one."

Martin let the conversation take its turn. He would await another chance.

"The rifle is good enough," Martin said with conviction.

"But it is wise to keep a weapon close to hand in times like these," Santiago countered.

"It also invites trouble where it would not come otherwise." Martin stared grimly at the little fountain a few feet away, puzzling over how to ask Santiago the question he needed to be answered. When Santiago did not say more, he decided to push forward. "Santiago, what do you know of my parents?"

A look of pain washed over the old man's face, betraying a depth of knowledge Santiago did not wish to dredge.

"Must you ask such a question?" Santiago stared past the fountain with a weary, distant gaze.

"Yes, sir. That's why I came to this country to learn about my family."

Slowly, painfully, the old man nodded. He understood, but even as his lips parted to form words, his voice remained silent. Twice he started to speak. Both times he failed, adding to Martin's frustration. Despite it, Martin forgave the old man who had proven that few things were so hard for him. It was harder for him to reconcile himself with knowing that the truth was there just out of reach and that his love for the old man prohibited him from causing Santiago any more sadness.

"Perhaps another time," Martin said, finishing the glass of water and rising. "Soon?"

Santiago's gaze lifted from the fountain. He blinked as though returning to the present. Whatever memories Martin's question unlocked were strong, and Martin felt a pang of guilt for bringing them to the surface. But, Santiago smiled and bowed his head gratefully.

"Yes," Santiago said. "It will be soon. I promise."

Martin reached out and rested his hand on Santiago's shoulder. Then he retreated down the path through the gate. Haze gave him a confused look as he untied the lead rope. Rose thorns had scratched small tracks of blood over his delicate nose.

"For an animal with so much brains, you're awfully slow sometimes," Martin said and led Haze toward the corral. He glanced back at Santiago, who still stared into the distance. Martin wondered if asking the favor of reaching for the moon would have been an easier task for Santiago.

"Patience is a skill upon which all other skills are built," his mother once told him as a child.

"You never said how hard patience would be in practice, Mother," Martin whispered. But he knew now that such a thing was hard to teach a child. Silencing his own impatience, he unsaddled Haze and found other chores to fill his time until supper.

Cowards

"Damn you, José!" Jinx unfastened the harness on the big black mare. "How many times've I got to tell you not to twist these? It rubs the poor animal raw."

"*Lo siento, señor.*" The boy appeared thoroughly crestfallen. "I can't seem to remember."

Jinx stared at him. "It ain't hard. You just got to remember. Look here."

Martin crossed his arms and leaned against the wagon wheel as he watched Jinx show the boy again how to run the harness, but the damage had already been done. The boy was too dejected to focus on what the old horseman told him. When Jinx dismissed him, José turned to leave and saw Martin's empathetic face.

"I tried, *señor*," he said.

"*Si.*" Martin patted the boy's shoulder and told him he would learn with time, then sent him away to his chores.

"You go too easy on that boy," Jinx said when José had disappeared beyond the barn.

"He's a little slower than most," Martin said. "He doesn't do it out of spite."

"True." Jinx took up the reins and released the break. "But I still wish he'd pay attention when I talk."

The wagon jostled forward. As they pulled onto the road, Martin glanced back and saw Jose standing by the stable door watching them. It reminded Martin of something, but the memory remained out of reach of his recollection.

"How's Haze working for you?"

"Very well. He's a good horse."

"That he is!" Jinx declared proudly. He leaned forward, rested his elbows on his knees, and held the reins loosely in his gnarled hands. "You know I've heard a few things, rumors really," he mused.

"What rumors?"

"Like why Santiago wanted to keep you around."

Martin shook his head. "I don't want to talk about it."

Jinx held up a hand. "Now hear me out. I've worked for the Terrazas for a long time. Over twenty years. I started here when I was no more than fifteen. I'm almost forty now, and my memory's good. My memory for faces is better than the rest of the old-timers."

"What are you getting at?" Martin asked after a long silence. Jinx did not reply immediately, making Martin uneasy. Martin wanted answers, but he doubted he wanted to hear them from Jinx.

Jinx's jaw flexed. "Santiago had a daughter. Fair-haired with the most beautiful green eyes you ever saw. Tried to catch her fancy myself when I was about your age, but she had eyes for another man. He was an American from back east somewhere. A gentleman of sorts looking for a new life." He chuckled and shook his head. "When I first saw him, he was still wearing what had been a fine suit of clothes, worn by travel. He was a big man, tall and strong. He could outwrestle any man who dared try him. He had two sons. Both, I imagine, grew to be like their pa. Identical twins they were. Those two got into a tussle with some of the boys around the ranch. Out-numbered six to two, and dang it, they won! Looked like hell when it was over, but they won."

Martin frowned inwardly and felt worn. The last thing he wanted was another ploy to win his loyalty or another story to pass the time, but Jinx seemed disinclined toward silence. Gritting his teeth, he decided to keep the conversation going for no other reason than to get his mind off the whole thing. "I don't follow you. What's this got to do with Santiago's daughter?"

"I'm getting to that." Jinx waved his hand. "Where was I? Oh, yeah. Well, this feller started playing for Miss Izzy's affections. When he went to ask permission from her father, Santiago refused." He shrugged and played with the reins. "We all guessed it was really the old woman who said no. She hated gringos with a passion. My wife once told me she wished them all dead."

"I still don't see the point of this."

Jinx glared benignly. "If you'd hold y'er tongue and listen, I'll get to the point."

Martin sighed and pretended to listen. Before long, Jinx's rhythmic tone started to wear him down, and he wanted to sleep, but he watched the road, only distantly aware of the man's ramblings. When they reached the outskirts of town, Martin felt the back of his neck tingle.

The Alvarado's supply wagon was hard to miss. Painted red from seat to wheels, it stood out against the white adobe of the grocery. Jinx fell silent, and his keen eyes swept the street. Martin glanced back for any sign of the driver. He guessed Lolita drove the wagon, as was her usual routine. Then he saw Armand step out of the cantina. Kell and Chico stepped out and flanked him, hands hanging loosely at their sides.

"Keep going," Martin advised. Jinx nodded and flicked the reins.

They rolled up to the gunsmith's shop and stopped. Before Martin could think what to do, Jinx climbed down to the boardwalk.

"Stay with the wagon," Jinx ordered as he looped the reins around the brake leaver. "I'll only be a minute."

Martin nodded. "They probably think they're seeing a ghost." He glanced back at the three men. Kell and Chico were talking, but Armand's attention rested solely on Martin. Lines of anger covered his face.

Despite the summer sun, Martin felt a chill, yet he held Armand's gaze until the other man looked away. Armand stepped off the boardwalk and started across the street toward the Alvarado wagon. Casting a deliberate, sideways glance at Martin, Armand strode past the wagon and into the grocer's store.

Climbing down to the boardwalk, Martin watched Kell and Chico lounge in front of the saloon, eyeing him in cold silence. Martin wanted a gun in his hand if, for no other reason than to reassure himself, he was not helpless this time, but the act of reaching for the rifle under the wagon seat could touch off the brewing fight.

A while later, Jinx stepped out of the shop and placed a large, paper-wrapped package under the seat.

"They ain't left yet?" he asked

"No, but they know I'm here. Not sure if it shook them up or just primed them for a fight."

"Either way, I hope two things." Jinx spit tobacco juice between the wagon wheels. "I hope they finish up and leave, or they do something foolish."

Martin swallowed and prayed for the former. He harbored no love for either Armand or Kell, but he remembered Chico's plea to spare him the bullet when he and Kell dumped him in the wash. Though Chico had not been what Martin considered a friend, he was not a true enemy either.

"Wish we could have a drink," Jinx commented as he leaned against the wagon.

Martin had no desire for alcohol or even water. While part of him wanted a fight, another feared it, not death but the implications of a full fight. A fight started today would end as a bloodbath between the two ranches. He took a deep breath and tried to calm his quivering nerves.

"Bastards," Jinx hissed.

Down the street, a woman shrieked in Spanish. She stumbled suddenly from the grocery and fell against the wheel of Alvarado's supply wagon. Martin squinted and recognized Lolita's familiar form.

Heat flooded Martin, and he started for Lolita as Armand grabbed her and shoved her against the wheel. Jinx caught Martin's arm.

"Don't, son! He's trying to goad you into it!"

Martin fought him. Jinx surprised him with a burst of strength as he shoved Martin into the mercantile wall.

"You do this; you'll touch off a full war!" Jinx hissed in Martin's ear.

"No one deserves being treated like that!" Martin lunged, and Jinx slammed him against the wall again.

"Fool! You aren't even wearing a gun. Armand will shoot you like a dog. He's probably looking for an excuse as it is."

Martin stilled, knowing that Jinx was right. Even with that realization, Martin hated the sudden wash of cowardice that overcame him. He watched as Lolita spat at Armand. With a gloved hand, Armand reached up and wiped the spit from his cheek then slapped her across the face. Again, Martin tried to break free.

"Armand won't kill her. She's too valuable to him alive. Think about all the men that will die if you do this!"

Jinx's words had a sobering effect. The images of countless dead scattered over fields and through forests passed before Martin's eyes. It brought back the old sickness and a new, helpless ache.

Martin's body relaxed as Lolita, ever defiant, tossed the hair back from her face, holding her head high. Then she climbed into the wagon with a flip of her skirt. Armand climbed up beside her and took up the reins. Only then did Jinx relax his hold.

Martin picked up his hat and stood staring after the wagon as Armand reined the horses into the street and passed by at a trot. Kell and Chico followed on horseback and drew up where Martin and Jinx stood.

"You saw that, Gray Boy?" Kell demanded. "That's what he'll do again if we see your living ass again." His attention shifted to Jinx, and he leveled a finger at Martin. "Remind your friends back home that if he is brought to Alvarado dead, there's a lot of land in it for them."

Martin felt Jinx stiffen beside him. He knew he should feel fear, sharp and sickening, but instead, he only felt rage. What stayed his hand was the knowledge that the rifle was too far away to give him a decent chance at killing Kell.

Kell grinned with the same enjoyment as he did the day he killed the roan mare after she threw him into the fence. "Yeah, Alvarado says you're his sole heir, and if you won't have his land, the man who kills you can."

A strange calm came over Martin. Now it was plain the door was shut, and he had no regrets for walking away. He filled his lungs and spoke with confidence. "Then tell Alvarado I have no use for him. Once I did, but not anymore. I want no part of a family like his."

Again, that grin, like a Gila monster sunning himself, sent rage through Martin. Kell leaned down and said to Martin alone.

"By the end of this, you will want Alvarado's favor. The only way you get out of this is if you bring the bodies of every last Terraza to him. Your only other choice is a slow, painful death."

The battle fever rose in Martin again, and his face betrayed him. Kell saw it and laughed out loud as he jerked his horse's head around and laid spurs to her flanks. The horse screamed and leaped into a dead run to catch up to the wagon.

Chico held back. His expression betrayed shame.

"Tell the others not to come to town again," Chico told Jinx. "Señor Alvarado has ordered any Terraza rider should be shot on sight unless they have Martin's body with them." When his attention shifted from Jinx, he could not meet Martin's gaze. "I'm very sorry."

Martin studied the Tejano's face. Unlike the others, Chico genuinely hated bloodshed. Perhaps it was the loss of his mother to Comancheros in his childhood, but regret at what lay ahead showed plainly in his eyes. Martin nodded in forgiveness.

The gesture did little to ease Chico's conscience. His expression resembled that of a beaten dog as he turned his horse and rode away at an easy trot.

"Makes you think, don't it?" Jinx asked, stepping to the edge of the walk beside Martin. "All that land, good land too. And all you have to do is kill a few people. Hell, you could slit their throats while they sleep."

Indeed Martin could. He lost count of the men he killed that way during the war, but the Terrazas had been kind to him, something he valued far more highly than land. He asked himself if he could kill them to save his life. Each one he considered, and each one his heart and mind responded with an unwavering "no," leaving him with two choices. Stay and face certain death or flee and be hunted for the rest of his life.

Martin's attention shifted to the saloon across the street. Suddenly, a drink of whiskey sounded good. It was foolish, he knew, but Fate rarely favored him anyway, and he was tired of fighting her. Martin started across the street without a word to Jinx.

Santiago climbed into the carriage and sat back comfortably on the leather seat. Paco latched the door and climbed onto the driver's seat. He flicked the reins, starting the pair of lean bays out into the road. Santiago watched the land roll past and smiled at the memories it recalled. Here he spent his childhood wandering among the brush in search of lizards and rocks of different shapes and colors. Here, he played and learned the value and fragility of life. In the hills and prairies far to the east, he had fought beside the Texans against Santa Ana and learned what killing and death truly meant. He went to war an idealist with only dreams and come home fragile with a new idealism. Here in this land, he had fallen in love and helped create life, his effort too small a token to make up for his sins against life. In his mind, his children had grown into good people despite his deficiencies as a father and husband.

As the carriage pulled into the yard of the old mission, he remembered again his wedding and how that single day changed his life forever and set the course of events that now unfurled.

Carmelita had been a beautiful woman but demanding and proud to a fault. Never could he fully satisfy her desires for prestige and fashion. Only after years did he finally learn of her hatred for the Americans who moved to Texas and drove out the Spanish. To her, Texas belonged to Spain and always should. By the time he learned this, it was too late.

Paco opened the door and offered a steady hand as Santiago climbed from the carriage.

"Water the horses and wait here," Santiago told him. "I'll be an hour at most."

"*Si, señor.*" Paco bowed his head respectfully.

Inside the old mission chapel, the air was cool and carried a faint scent of damp earth, which seeped up through the stone floor. The narrow windows offered little light. In the shadows around the altar, candles flickered and danced like so many souls burning in purgatory, suffering their final penance before entering Heaven.

Santiago knelt at the communion rail, laid down his cane, and prayed as he had prayed for so many years, only now, instead of pleading for his only daughter's health and return, he prayed for her soul and for the soul of her only son.

The old black-robed priest stepped out of the vestibule, genuflected stiffly, and retired to the confessional as he always did upon Santiago's arrival.

Heart pounding with a fear he had not known since he was a young man, Santiago signed himself and took up his cane. He made his way behind the partition, his footsteps echoing against the high ceiling.

"Have you come to confess, Santiago?" the priest asked.

"Yes, father. I apologize that my confession today will be long."

He saw the priest's eyebrow rise through the mesh screen. For years this routine had been familiar to both of them, and while they had often discussed philosophy for hours, never had Santiago's confessions been more than a few minutes. The priest's reaction brought a soft chuckle from Santiago as much to ease his concern as to ease Santiago's unease.

"I never thought an old man could sin so much." Santiago sighed as a wave of emotion hit him. The priest said nothing, only waited with his head bowed.

"Forgive me, father, for I have sinned many times in my life. As a boy, I cared little for others and so caused them hardship and anger. I used others to gain what I wanted. Out of negligence, I caused many animals to pain unnecessarily. Twelve times I took the lives of my enemies in battle, though that fact makes me no less guilty. I lusted after a woman, believing unwisely that her faults could be overlooked and made her my wife. Many times I neglected my husbandly duties and sought refuge in excess drink. I beat my children without just cause at times and believed lies that were told me." He paused as the true weight of guilt settled on his old shoulders. "These are my greatest sins, father, but the greatest of all is I am a coward." Santiago reached for the words to continue as shame and anguish closed his throat. He bowed his head but could not speak.

The priest waited a moment before gently asking, "How are you a coward?"

The question gave his mind direction. Santiago reached into his pocket for his handkerchief and pressed it to his eyes, giving his throat time to open again.

"Many years ago," he said through tears. "My wife tried to force our daughter to remarry after it was believed her husband had died. She wanted Maitea to give her child away and raise a family of 'good Spanish blood.'" He bit out the words angrily and felt suddenly guilty. "Forgive me; I am as guilty as she for my lack of action against it." He paused to let the anger dissipate. "Once, she beat our grandson nearly to death because he was half *Americano*. He had not yet reached his second birthday." He sobbed quietly, and when he continued, his voice sounded brittle with age. "I did nothing to stop it. I did nothing to keep my daughter from taking the child and leaving because I believed it was for the best."

No longer could he hold back the tears that, for so many years, lay ignored deep in his heart. He buried his face in his hands and wept.

The priest waited in silence. When the tears eased, he spoke with compassion and kindness.

"Why do you confess this today? Your daughter left after I arrived twenty years ago, yet I have not heard you speak of this until now."

"Because, father, I believe with all my heart that her son has returned."

The bench creaked as the priest shifted, and understanding flashed on his face. "The young stranger who has joined your family at mass." He nodded. "I remember his eyes when I baptized him."

"Yes, father."

"And you have not told him of this?"

"No."

"Why?"

"Alvarado has already claimed him as his own grandson. My son doubts me, but my memory is not weak." He paused, framing the other part of his explanation. "I fear, if I tell Martin, he will only believe me mad or that I am attempting to use him as a pawn in this absurd feud with Luis."

The priest nodded in understanding. Then another question occurred to him. He considered it for a moment before he spoke.

"You said your daughter 'believed' her husband was dead. Was he?"

Santiago shook his head. "My wife lied to both my daughter and son-in-law. She told each the other was dead. Then, a year before she died, a letter came from Bodie, my son-in-law, inviting us to his ranch in the north. That was when she confessed what she had done. I could not speak to her again after that." He cleared his throat, regaining his composure. "I feared her too much, as I now fear telling my grandson the truth."

"You must tell him," the priest counseled. "He needs and deserves to know. If there is any chance left of finding his father, he should have the choice to take it."

"But how? How can I tell him that he and his mother were driven from our home, and I did nothing to stop it? And what of Luis? What will he do to Martin if Martin accepts the truth?"

"You must tell him. You will only drive him farther away by continuing the lie."

This fact struck through Santiago's heart. He knew it was true and nodded assent. But how would he tell Martin the story without the young man feeling some anger toward him? Then he remembered that Martin possessed his mother's compassion as well as his father's fighting spirit. Martin was blessed that the one tempered the other.

"Since this seems a great task for you, let it be your penance and reparation to God and your kindred."

Santiago smiled wryly. It was a fitting penance. "Thank you, father," he said sincerely.

"Now go in peace, and God bless you, Santiago."

Santiago bowed his head and made the sign of the cross as the priest spoke the words of absolution.

Ghosts of Spain

They rode back to the ranch in silence. Martin, nerves eased by several shots of tequila, stared at the land deep in thought. Jinx respectfully let him. Little could be done about the young man's circumstances, and the old *caballero* knew it. Though Martin knew it consciously, his mind remained restless, searching for a way to change his fate.

The sun crossed the sky in white indifference and hung two hours from setting when they pulled into the yard. Martin climbed down and wordlessly began unloading the wagon. Fernando appeared on the house veranda dressed in his range clothes.

"Where have you two been?" he demanded. His face was livid, and his eyes burned with anger.

"It took us a while to get everything," Jinx replied, eyes tight with concern.

Fernando jerked his head in Martin's direction. "Was he with you the whole time?"

Jinx openly frowned. "Yeah. Why? What's something wrong?"

"Santiago," Fernando said, his expression softening enough to betray worry. "He and Paco should have returned from the mission hours ago. We've heard nothing." He looked to Martin and seemed to debate himself. Then, he appeared to reach a decision he did not like. "Saddle your horse. You'll ride with me."

Despite the lingering burn of liquor, Martin felt Fernando's restrained urgency. He hurried to the corral and saddled Haze. The stallion, usually playful during this process, stood still though his muscles twitched with excitement. Martin dropped the stirrup and swung up into the saddle. Fernando waited for him at the gate, astride his palomino, and they started out along the trail to the old mission ten miles distant.

Fernando was silent, and his manner forbade any word of comfort that might have been offered. For a moment, Martin wondered if it was pure fear for Santiago's safety or the *patrón's* suspicion of him. In his current state, Martin cared nothing for Fernando's opinion of him. His only concern was finding Santiago and bringing him safely home.

They rode opposite sides of the road, each watching the carriage tracks across the hard earth. Six miles from the ranch, Martin spotted where the trail left the road.

"*Señor*!"

He did not have to say more. Fernando's horse reached him in two long strides. His face blanched at the parallel grooves running into the brush.

"Is Paco in the habit of galloping the horses?" Martin asked after a moment.

Fernando looked at him, and Martin pointed to the ground, indicating the tracks of the horse team running side by side between the lines of carriage wheels. The man's expression darkened, and he shook his head. "Where were they going?"

Martin did not know the answer. Rising in the saddle, he traced the trail in a wide circle through the brush and back along the road toward the mission. Santiago was never in a hurry, and so Paco would not gallop the horses without purpose. The way the trail was laid out, Martin guessed something made them retreat to the mission and what safety it may provide. A shock ran through Martin's veins driving away the last of the alcohol and leaving a cold clamminess in his skin.

He turned Haze up the road and heeled him into a lope. Fernando was close on his heels.

It was another mile closer to the mission where the trail left the road again and led down into a steep gully and did not return to the road. There on the edge of the drop, amid broken juniper and sage, they came to a halt and stared down at the wrecked carriage. Both horses lay unmoving in their traces.

Doubt and disappointment cooled Martin's blood. He had hoped the team had made the four miles back to the mission and that he and Fernando faced the simple task of rescue. Seeing the wrecked carriage banished all hope he held. Drawing a deep breath, he started forward, ready to face the inevitable. Fernando caught his arm and held him back. Martin obeyed, knowing it was not his place to charge in and disturb the place of the dead.

It took Fernando another moment to fight back the trepidation of finding his father. When he started his horse down the slope, Martin waited and followed close behind. Once in the bottom of the gully, though, Fernando's surge of bravado dissipated, and he sat his horse staring at the overturned carriage bottom. When he glanced up, his expression pleaded with Martin.

Again there was nothing Martin could say. He glanced at the carriage, then back at Fernando, who nodded his permission for Martin to search it.

Before he dismounted, Martin leaned over to peer inside the carriage. The only sign of Santiago was his cane lying across the far window. Climbing from the saddle onto the side of the carriage, Martin lowered himself inside feeling with his feet lest he land on Santiago's body. Several moments passed while his eyes adjusted to the dim light. As the shapes of the seats formed out of the shadows, Martin scanned the interior. Hope resurged in him when he found no sign of Santiago. The far door rested, open, against the bank. Martin knelt and peered through it.

The coach had fallen against the bank, leaving a narrow space underneath. The crash happened with such force both right wheels were broken off the hubs, and the axles gouged into the ground, but the space was just wide enough a slight man like

Santiago could have crawled through. Martin studied the ground, but the scuffs and scratches were hard to read from his angle. He saw no blood and hoped it was a good sign.

Climbing back into the sunlight, he cast a single glance at Fernando, who searched the ground near the horses. He vaulted off the carriage and walked back to where the disturbed sand showed where Santiago dragged himself from beneath the carriage into a nearby manzanita thicket. The mark of Santiago's stiff right leg was clear. Martin could also see he no longer used his right arm either.

Hurried strides took Martin to the thicket where he dropped to hands and knees and crawled into the tangle of branches.

"Santiago?" he called as the branches grabbed at his head and shoulders, but no reply came. He pushed on, heedless of the scratches the dried manzanita branches inflicted. Then, through the haze of gray boughs, he spotted the maroon of Santiago's jacket. The old man lay curled up against the bank in the shade, his head bloody, his right arm cradled across his body.

"Fernando, over here!" Martin worked his way around to the old man's head. Gently, he turned Santiago on his side.

The old man stirred but made no sound and opened tired eyes. It took a moment for his gaze to focus. Then relief washed over age lined features.

"Oh, Martin." He smiled. "I'm glad to see you."

"Don't talk," Martin counseled. "I don't know how bad you're hurt." He looked the old man over then back the way he came. "Fernando!"

"Martin." There was urgency in his voice, a plea that made Martin's heartache. Santiago reached out and grasped Martin's arm with more strength than Martin believed the old man possessed.

"*Escucha me*," Santiago commanded. "Remember, you asked why I wanted to know about your mother?"

"That can wait, *Abuelo*," Martin said, trying to calm him.

Santiago shook his head, clinging to Martin's sleeve. "You have to know…" His voice faltered, and he forced the words from his lips. "You have to know the truth."

Martin was only distantly aware of branches snapping behind him as Fernando neared them. Santiago's grip was forceful as it drew him closer. Martin tried to calm him. "Shh. Don't waste strength," he said gently.

"*I've no life left.*" He stared up at Martin with a strange, gentle look on his face as he spoke in Spanish, the language of his childhood. Torn between the denial of loss and the need to grant the old man this last request, Martin's mind failed to grasp the meaning of what Santiago told him. He knew Santiago was dying. The pallor in his skin and the coldness of his hands told Martin as much. Distantly aware of Fernando beside him, Martin swallowed his petty grief and held Santiago in the only form of comfort he could offer.

Santiago smiled wistfully as the pain seemed to ease. He reached up and caressed Martin's cheek with a cold, trembling hand. His voice was barely more than a whisper. "*¡Mi nieto! Te quiero tanto, como Como tu madre y padre hizo.*"

Santiago's gaze remained fixed on Martin, the smile unfaltering. Martin caught the fragile hand as it drifted from his face and held it close. He did not know what else to say or do. From somewhere deep inside him, the words came, and he smiled with sad affection as he spoke. "*Sé, Abuelo. Ahora descansas.*"

Even as he spoke, Martin felt the strength leave the slender body as Santiago closed his eyes and rested his cheek against Martin's arm. The long fingers relaxed, and Santiago's last breath rattled from his breast as his soul departed.

Martin felt his throat close. Tears stung his eyes, and though he tried to hold them back, they washed down his scratched and dirt-smudged face.

A hand touched his shoulder. He looked up into Fernando's face. The man was pale with grief as he stared down at the vacant shell that had been his father. Martin remembered holding his mother's hand as she died and how he felt abandoned and broken by her death. Despite the shattered condition of his world, Fernando managed to keep his composure.

"Let us take him home," he said. "That is all we can do for him now." For a moment longer, he stayed there then rose, bending beneath the low branches. "I will bring the horses."

He left Martin, still holding Santiago in his arms. Martin stared down into the death shrouded face and felt something tear part of his heart from his chest. In the first weeks, Martin knew him, Santiago had taken the place of grandfather in Martin's life. That was why Martin called him, *Abuelo*, and why, for the second time in his memory, Martin wept quietly for a loved one lost forever.

A soft breeze rustled through the live oak that cast a pleasant shadow over the open grave. At Fernando's solemn request, Martin joined him, Filipe, and Jinx in carrying the coffin from the parlor to the sprawling oak that shaded the family cemetery. It was a grim honor that Martin accepted numbly.

When they had laid Santiago in his earthen tomb, Martin stepped back behind the crowd out of respect for the family and friends who lived closest to the old man in life. Having known Santiago a short time, he felt no right to mourn as deeply as they did, but the emptiness he felt held on despite his mind's rational thought.

The priest spoke, but Martin barely heard what he said. He stared up into the great sweeping branches of the ancient oak and thought how Santiago must have chosen this place. In his final testament, he refused to be buried in the mission cemetery and, instead, wanted to be buried here among his ancestors in the shade of a tree planted by his great-grandfather. He smiled wistfully at the thought of Santiago, no longer tormented with the pains of a bad leg, stretched out in the grass enjoying the day as he had in life by appreciating the little things like a breath of wind or the warm sun.

Into these thoughts came Santiago's final moments and what he chose for his last words. Santiago would never lie, but Martin could not comprehend the words. He had been too distracted, too determined to calm Santiago to understand. What he remembered confused him, and searching for an answer left him feeling worn and tired. He tried instead to focus on the priest, but his attention drifted over the hills in the distance, noting the faded grass as it cured in the late summer heat. Before long, rains would come, followed by winter. Another season would come and go in a relentless march of time that never heeded the coming and going of life among man or beast. It had been so when his mother died. It would be so now that Santiago was gone. It would remain true when he came to his end. What mattered was the time he had before the world moved on from him, and what he did to make things better for those left behind.

Martin filled his lungs and stared down at his hands, remembering Luis Alvarado's offer. He saw no other way to face the situation, but if he must die here, he would die bringing this feud to an end for the Terrazas. He knew the impossibility of a peaceful ending, and that Santiago would have frowned at the idea of killing his life-long enemy, but maybe he would have accepted knowing it meant the end of bloodshed.

Raising his head, Martin's gaze came to rest on Paco, standing with his head hung in grief and shame. He had told the story of what happened after returning from the mission with what help the padres could offer. Several of Alvarado's riders had caught them on their return from the mission, pulled him off the driver's seat, and spooked the team, sending the animals on a frightened run that ended in the wash. Paco had been beaten and left on the roadside. After waking from unconsciousness, he had walked to the mission for help. His face was bruised, his left eye shut and his jaw puffy with swelling, and his movements stiff from broken ribs. Judging by his injuries, he was lucky to be alive.

Kell must not have been with them; Martin thought wryly, knowing Kell would have shot him for fun. Regardless of who did this, Santiago's death meant the end of waiting.

The priest blessed the grave, and those gathered around it crossed themselves, and all departed in a scattered sea of black.

A fresh wave of melancholy struck him at the sight of the grave, so Martin lingered and watched Bucho and Jinx fill the grave. Each hollow thud of soil against wood sent chills up his back. He knew he could change this no more than he could have stopped his mother from dying. Her heart, her spirit, and her body had been broken, worn down by grief for his lost father and the hardship of striving to provide for her child. His solace was in the hope that she and his father were together now and at peace beyond the torments of this unforgiving world.

"Martin?"

He looked up into Filipe's grim face.

"Papa wants to speak with you when you have a moment."

He nodded, and Filipe turned away toward the house. His stride had lost its youthful strength. It would return in time, Martin knew, but for a while, it would yield to sincere contemplation of mortality.

The men finished their work and left before Martin finally forced his body into motion and crossed the open field to the house. His boots sounded heavy in the still, empty hall. He found Fernando in the parlor standing by the cold fireplace. Martin did not have to announce his presence.

"Come in, Martin," Fernando said without looking up.

Martin moved to the center of the room, hat in hand, and waited. For once, the silence did not wear on his nerves, and patience came easy.

"Have you nothing to say?"

"I'm sorry for your loss, señor," Martin said sincerely and heard the pain in his own voice.

"That's not what I'm talking about." Fernando turned to face him. "I'm referring to my father's dying words."

Martin frowned. "I'm sorry. I didn't understand all what he said."

"Don't lie to me," Fernando snapped. "I know your Spanish is better than you claim. I heard you call him '*Abuelo*'."

The reproach seemed to flow past Martin. He held Fernando's gaze as he spoke with calm conviction.

"I thought it would calm him," he said. "Wasn't 'Grandfather' an endearment for him? Even among those who were not his kin?"

Fernando nodded as anger flared in his eyes. "But he called you 'grandson,' *his* grandson!" The rage seemed to cool. Fernando turned away, running his right hand through his hair as he began pacing between the edge of the rug and the fireplace. Martin wondered if Fernando's anger was spurred by jealousy. Santiago spent his last strength addressing Martin with Fernando there at his side. Not Fernando, but Martin held him as he died because Santiago reached out to him. Martin bowed his head, knowing he had robbed Fernando of the opportunity to spend a final few moments with his father.

"He spoke of it when you first came to us," Fernando continued calmly though he continued pacing. "He *never* deviated from his belief. A dying man does not lie. He knows he will face judgment, and my father feared God more than any mortal."

"I don't doubt Señor Santiago spoke what he thought was true," Martin returned.

Fernando's pacing ceased. He faced Martin with eyebrows raised. "You don't believe you're his grandson?" he said in disbelief.

Martin swallowed and shook his head. He spoke softly. "I don't know what to believe anymore. Your own enemy claims me as his heir. How do I know I've not become a pawn in this generations-old feud?"

It was the first he spoke of it, but the thought had lingered in his mind for weeks, plaguing the darkness before sleep took him at night. He questioned his judgment of Santiago in those sleepless hours, but, remembering Santiago's firm insistence as he died, Martin no longer doubted his belief. Fernando remained questionable.

"I have no doubt some have tried to use you against us," Fernando said. "Just as I have no doubt, my father was not mistaken."

Martin felt his blood heat with frustration. "How?" he challenged. "How do you know? I have no proof. Only my word and a story several years decayed in memory."

Their gazes met, and as they held. Fernando's expression softened.

"When you came here, you had a picture."

Martin became aware of the daguerreotype's stiffness in his left breast pocket, where he always carried it. He suddenly felt cold. Fernando must have seen it in his face for his tone turned patient.

"Come with me."

Obediently, Martin followed as Fernando led him down the hall to Santiago's room at the end. The heavy curtains, drawn across tall windows, admitted thin streams of light that did little to penetrate the darkness.

"Years ago, when I was first married, Papa had a portrait painted of our family as it was then. Even after Mama died, he kept it in here." Fernando crossed the room and drew the curtains aside. Light spilled through, illuminating the room.

Above the mantle of the little fireplace, across from the bed, hung a portrait of a family smiling contentedly, except for one.

It was the old woman in the center, dark-haired with black eyes, who scowled despite the artist's softening of her features. A moment passed before Martin recognized the face of his nightmares and fears as a child. Briefly, the irrational horror returned. He pushed it away and forced his gaze over the other faces.

Then he saw her, the familiar face that the picture in his pocket had kept alive for him. She was younger, happier, with autumnal copper in her hair and wild roses in her cheeks. His memory of her in life had faded to the colorless brown of the image, which he withdrew from his pocket and stared at, unable to force his mind to believe his eyes.

Fernando put an arm around his shoulders.

"I should have known the night you brought Filipe home," he said gently. "There is no mistaking your mother. You have her gentle heart and your father's fiery spirit. He would be proud of you."

Martin's throat was too tight for words, yet he forced the question.

"What kind of man was he?"

"Ambitious...strong. He made things happen and rarely apologized for his mistakes. He came here to learn how to raise cattle. He now has a ranch in the north country."

Untrusted hope drove away Martin's sadness. "'Has?' You mean he's…"

"Alive? Yes, very much."

"But, Mother said he was killed by Kiowas when I was a child."

Fernando nodded. "I know, and that was what your grandmother led her to believe. By the time we learned the truth, you and your mother were lost to us." He seethed. "Mama hated Americans more than anything, and she hated everything. Your father and mother married against her wishes, and she made sure they were separated. She knew the grief her actions would bring about, and her efforts were truly intentional." He fell silent, haunted by his own memory. "When Papa found out what she had done, he threw her out of the house. She went back to Spain and died a few years later. We were all shocked by what she did, but we should have suspected after the way she treated you."

Again, Martin looked at the face of the scowling woman and felt that fear, remembering the pain vividly as the woman beat him. He could not remember what it was for. Now, he knew.

"You have no obligation to us here," Fernando went on. "You are free to go your way. To go to Oregon and find your family."

A thrill filled the emptiness of grief with hope. More than anything, Martin wanted to leave behind this place with its threats of bloodshed and death, but he knew he could not. As much as he now hoped for the safety and prosperity of the family, he believed gone, he wanted the same for the family he had here. He could not leave them with Alvarado's threat of death hanging over them.

"Santiago wanted this war between the Alvarados and Terrazas to end," Martin said when his throat relaxed enough to let him speak. He looked into Fernando's eyes with determination. "I intend to see that happen."

Fernando nodded slowly. "He would be grateful for that." He turned away toward the dresser. There, on the simple linen drape, rested a brown paper package Martin remembered Jinx bringing from the gun shop the day before. He picked up the package and brought it to Martin.

"You know Papa was opposed to fighting, but he believed that when a fight came, a man should be well-prepared. He had these made for you."

Martin pocketed the picture and took the package. Through the wrapping, he could feel the hard contents. He laid the package on the bed, pulled the string, and unfolded the paper.

Inside, nestled together like two cottonmouth snakes in a den, was a pair of revolvers. Slowly, deliberately, he drew one and examined it.

It was a Colt Peacemaker with a slightly shorter barrel and a cylinder adapted for .45 caliber brass cartridges. He pulled back the hammer to half-cock and spun the cylinder. It clicked with a sure *hiss* as unmistakable and unyielding as the sound of a rattlesnake's tail. The hammer moved smooth and firm. As he held it, the dark stained walnut grip felt smooth against his palm and the weapon balanced perfectly, feeling more an extension of his own body than an object apart.

"He knew you had no weapons of your own," Fernando said. "He also ordered this rifle to take matching cartridges."

Fernando extended the Henry to him. Its long, shining black barrel looked unlike those he remembered in the war. Instead of the brass plate, it had black steel. Along with the magazine, a dark forward stock had been fitted to protect his hand from the heat of repeated firing. Together, the three guns looked as though they were forged from the same blue steel and fitted with the same black-stained walnut. The holsters, cartridge belt, and rifle sling, finely tooled with the swirls and puffs of an unfettered wind, were also black. Martin understood the symbolism.

"Instruments of death," he whispered.

"Or life, if used to the right purpose," Fernando prompted.

Martin nodded and hoped that when the time came, he would use these weapons with wisdom and justice and never bring shame upon his heritage. As he thought of this, he felt a new sense of pride, but for so long he had been without a name to honor that he feared his own inadequacy.

"Señor…Uncle, would you promise me something?"

"Certainly."

His knuckles whitened as his grip tightened on the rifle. Once he spoke, Martin could not take back the words. His heart pained the way it had the first time he killed a man.

"Would you please not tell anyone who I am, until this business is over. That way…if I fail to be worthy, no one will be the wiser."

Fernando blinked in surprise. He looked conflicted as he held Martin's gaze.

"Why do you doubt your worthiness?"

Martin shrugged. "I don't know. I just know that in a fight, things happen…things that make you cringe when you think back on them…and that others will judge your actions harshly afterward. I only know how to fight to survive, and that means denying mercy at times."

Fernando remained silent a long while until Martin believed he would not speak. Then he nodded his consent.

"I will keep this secret until you are ready for others to know." Fernando reached out and put his hand on Martin's shoulder. "I have faith you will honor the Terraza name in your own way and time."

A weak smile touched Martin's lips. He hoped Fernando was right.

.

The Breaking

The ranger rode out of San Antonio a week before he arrived at the Terraza ranch. He possessed an easy manner, ever casual, but something lay beneath the surface that warned of his skill as a fighter.

Martin kept his distance from the man. If Fernando had not insisted on his presence when the ranger questioned Paco, he would have remained a stranger. Martin sensed this man was not one to like. A shadow hung over him that held the ranger distant from humanity despite his affable demeanor.

His name was Belden, and he showed no sign of malevolence as he paced the front room of the bunkhouse, but Paco remained nervous. Seated at the bunkhouse table, the light from the windows gave his yellowing bruises deeper shadow and lent him a ghoulish effect as he told the story again. When Martin heard it the first time, Paco told it soberly, like a man disconnected from his thoughts. Now he told it with more emotion and gesticulation. When he finished, his hands settled into his lap, and he sat watching Belden pace around the bunkhouse table, hands behind his back and head bowed in thought.

"Can you describe the men?" the ranger asked after a long silence. "What were they wearing? The horses they rode?"

Paco shrugged. "I don't really remember."

"Yes, you do," the ranger said firmly without threat. "Now, tell me."

Paco seemed to think and again shook his head. "*Lo siento, señor.* I don't remember." He chuckled nervously.

Belden looked at Martin. His jaw worked, flexing in contemplation.

"Yes, you do," he said again in the same tone. "A man doesn't forget stuff like that unless he's witless, and you don't strike me as witless."

Paco stared down at the table in front of him and remained silent. Belden paced steadily toward Paco like a slow-moving rain cloud across the prairie.

"What then, is keeping your tongue-tied?" Belden asked, unclasping his hands and bracing against the table with his left hand. His right rested on the back of Paco's chair, effectively trapping Paco where he sat. "Is it fear?"

There was no change in Paco's expression or attitude. His head remained down, and his hands folded.

"Maybe they paid you to keep silent." Belden lowered his head as though to look into Paco's face.

Still, there was nothing to betray the reason for Paco's hesitation. Yet, Martin saw something in Paco's profile, a twitch of the muscles around his eyes. Three weeks ago, Martin saw Paco play a poker hand in which he won nearly two months' wages. That twitch passed over his face once when Bucho bet a month's wages. Either it had unnerved Paco or excited him. Martin was not sure which. Paco won that pot by a one card difference in a pair of kings and eights to Bucho's queens. Perhaps the tick now manifested because of Belden crowding him. His face twitched a second time as Belden began drumming his fingers.

Suddenly, Belden yanked Paco's chair back, slapped him hard on the chest, gripping his shirt and hauling him to his feet.

"I can make you talk," Belden warned. "You want to find out how?"

His action and his tone startled Martin, but Paco's expression seemed vacant, as though he were only a bystander to the violence. Then he looked into Belden's eyes as though the spirit returned to him.

"I will tell you," he said with a strange calm. He shrugged Belden's grip, straightened his shirt, and sat back down.

Belden stood over him, watching as Paco ran his fingers through his mussed hair.

"There were five of them," Paco said. "Three *Tejanos* and two Americans. One of the Americans was a big man with a round face. He rode a buckskin. The other was lanky, like a fencepost. His face looked like the skin barely covered his skull."

Belden looked at Martin. "Sound familiar?"

Martin nodded. "Sounds like Kell and Rife. Neither was hired for their skill with cattle is my guess."

The ranger nodded and turned back to Paco.

"One of the *Tejanos* was a little man, but broad-shouldered rode a paint. The other two looked like brothers, the same coat and hat."

"Chico and the Morales Brothers," Martin spoke the names then shook his head in unconscious disbelief. "Chico's a good hand with horses and cattle, not with a gun. The other two..." He grimaced. "Let's just say they'd sooner shoot a horse than ride it."

Belden's mouth was hard as he nodded. "I've heard of those two. Came up from Mexico a few years ago. Word has it; they cut their teeth riding with Comancheros."

Martin nodded once in agreement and glanced at Paco, who stared at him hopefully. Paco looked away quickly when their gazes met.

"Can I go?" he said. "I don't know what else I can tell you, and I have work to do."

Belden considered his request and, at length, granted permission with a nod.

Paco pushed up out of the chair and hurried outside without looking at either Martin or Belden. As he took down his hat from the peg beside the door, Martin caught the slightest tremble in the fingers. Doubtlessly he was shaken. Martin did not blame him.

"That's a queer thing to do," Belden commented. He crossed his arms and perched on the edge of the table with his left leg dangling. "That boy has lived on this ranch his whole life. Folks say he loved Santiago Terraza like his own kin, yet he fights to keep the identity of his killers to himself."

"Perhaps he was planning his own revenge," Martin suggested. He said it without thinking and regretted it afterward, fearing he betrayed his own intentions.

"Could be." Belden considered the thought a moment before shaking his head. Then his gaze turned to Martin and swept down to the revolvers.

Still conscientious of their weight, Martin felt suddenly uncomfortable, but he remained still under the lawman's scrutiny.

"You know how to use those?" Belden asked at length.

Martin shrugged. "I handle them well enough."

Belden studied him, his gaze steady on Martin's face as he seemed to measure the truth of Martin's words. Knowing this, Martin studied the ranger in return. He was lean and raw-boned, tall as Martin with hard blue eyes and brown hair bleaching to white. Belden's age remained a mystery, but Martin guessed his years had been hard ones, and as Martin traced the lines of the man's face, a chill ran through him as though he caught a glimpse of his own reflection.

After several heartbeats, Belden gave a single nod.

"Maybe I'll find out for sure," he said. "I want you to ride with me tomorrow. You know the Alvarado boys better than anyone here."

A shock ran through Martin at the suggestion. He lowered his head to hide what might have shown in his face.

"Alvarado has put a price on my head," Martin said grimly. "If I ride with you, it may make things worse. Might even get you killed."

Belden listened in respectful silence, but his expression appeared unyielding.

"It's alright to be scared, kid," Belden smirked with a shake of his head. "God knows I scare easy enough. The truth, though, is that if you don't see this through, you'll be running from it the rest of your life. 'Course, a lot of folks say that who don't know the truth of it." His expression sobered. "So here's the real truth. I don't trust that Paco to be on our side. From what I've heard about that band Alvarado has working for him, I'd rather not turn my back on any of them. Mister Terraza tells me you were in the war and that you're trustworthy. Add to that your knowledge of Alvarado makes you the best candidate for the job."

"You do know why Alvarado wants me dead?"

"Yeah. And I also know that if you really intended to take him up on that offer, you wouldn't have let the Terrazas live this long."

Martin flexed his jaw, mildly irritated at the prospect of going back to Alvarado's place even for this purpose.

"Of course, you could go the other way."

Martin frowned and looked up at Belden in a silent question.

Sliding off the table, Belden paced toward him.

"This feud's been going on a long time. Hell! It's older than Texas. But things now are such that if one key person dies, this thing will end between these families."

The thought had not occurred to Martin. Now that Belden suggested it, Martin found himself wishing he were back in Virginia. At least in the war, things seemed simpler and far clearer.

"Killing Alvarado would be murder," Belden continued. "But some would say that murder might be worth it. Might even save the lives of many on both sides."

Martin shook his head. "No. Santiago would not approve." He looked straight into Belden's eyes. "For that reason alone, I wouldn't do it."

Belden's eyes narrowed. "Perhaps, but things change. People change."

He held Martin's gaze a moment longer as the meaning of his words sank in then turned toward the door.

"We'll ride out at dawn tomorrow. Be ready."

"Yes, sir."

Taking his hat down from the peg, Belden stepped out the door and closed it behind him. The silence that fell over the bunkhouse left Martin uneasy as Belden's suggestion wandered around the back of his mind. He could almost hear Santiago telling him that choice of life and death resided solely in God's power, that he should not assume such power for himself.

In his heart, Martin agreed, but his mind threatened to argue. He pushed the thought away.

"There are times I wish I had your faith, Grandfather," he whispered to himself. "Now is one of them." He took his hat from the peg beside the door and went out to the corral. Trying to focus on what the next day promised, he found work to do tasks by methodical task until the sunset.

A roadrunner called from the brush as they rode through the dawn east toward Alvarado's ranch. Martin rode behind Paco and Belden. Like so many nights before a battle, he had neither slept nor eaten more than a few bites for supper or breakfast. As a result, he was in no mood for conversation. The fact that Paco and Belden had exchanged the few words since leaving the ranch satisfied him. He wanted to be invisible, but he did not wish to be anywhere else. If they could find Santiago's killers, Martin wanted to make sure they made it to their hanging.

With each step his horse took, Martin felt the weight of the revolvers on his hips and with it a resurgence of strength. There was something about a fight that never failed to make him feel alive. It was not that death no longer mattered to him. It was the movement of his body, the reading and countering of an enemy, the defense of an innocent, and the conditions that demanded flawless action, judgment, and a little luck to survive.

The walls of Alvarado Rancho loomed into view over the lip of a high bluff. Belden drew up and sat surveying the place. Martin stopped beside him to watch the compound. He snatched a glance at Paco and felt a chilling uneasiness. Fernando had wanted to come too, but Martin had talked him out of it, fearing if this ride ended in a fight, Fernando, in his inexperience, would be killed, and his family would suffer another unnecessary loss.

The fact of his lineage still felt strange to him. He let his mind wander over the idea. He hoped thinking about it would make the idea settle and become real to him. Again he wondered if he had been wise in asking Fernando to keep silent. He wanted so badly to call Fernando, Filipe, Maricruz, and Lucia his kin, but he wanted with almost equal fervor to feel he deserved their love, trust, and respect. He would earn that today.

"Not very busy this morning," Belden commented.

"Half the crew barely does anything before noon," Martin replied.

"Probably includes the ones we're looking for." Belden quirked his mouth in a wry smile. "Well, we've a job to do. Remember, let me do the talking. Just watch my back and don't start anything."

Martin nodded that he understood. "I'll do my best."

"Good." Belden heeled his horse forward at a casual walk. Martin glanced over at Paco, whose face looked pale and sick.

"The sooner we get this done, the sooner we can go home," Martin told him.

"I want no part of this," Paco grumbled.

Angered by Paco's persistent reluctance, Martin reached out and slapped a hand against the Tejano's chest, grasping his shirt and nearly pulling him out of the saddle.

"And I want no more of your whining. Santiago was like a grandfather to you, and you seem to fight us at every step to find his killers. Why?"

Haze fidgeted under him, reflecting Martin's own agitation as he stared into Paco's face. His dark brown eyes narrowed into slits and his mouth hardened as he stared at Martin. Then he slapped Martin's hand away, flashing his teeth in a snarl.

"I'll do my part," he snapped. "Just make sure you don't get me confused with the others and shoot me for the fun of it."

Martin scoffed humorlessly. "If only I were such a liar."

Paco's nostrils flared, and he kicked his bay hard, driving the gelding after Belden at a run.

Martin cursed silently. Something inside him screamed for Paco's blood for no clear reason, leaving Martin to dismiss his own anger out of hand.

At his cue, Haze leaped into a run, and he soon caught up with the ranger and Paco. When they rode into the yard, Belden held the lead at a sedate walk. Martin and Paco flanked him loosely.

From all around the yard, the Tejanos looked up from their work in curiosity. A few frowned, but none stood ready to fight. The kitchen door opened, and Martin saw Lolita freeze in the middle of throwing out a basin of water. Her beautiful face was marred by bruises. Her lower lip showed a barely healed split. Martin's blood boiled.

Their gazes met and held only a moment before she turned her face away and darted back inside, shutting the door. For the moment, Martin wondered if she would warn Kell and the others.

Belden seemed calm and cool as the stream running just behind the south wall as he led them up to the front porch of the main house. Before the ranger stepped down, Luis Alvarado appeared at the door. His expression darkened when he saw Martin.

"What is the meaning of this?" he demanded of Belden as he cast his glare between the three of them.

Belden held up a hand in a gesture of peace. "Señor Alvarado, please, let me explain. I'm John Belden of the Texas Rangers. I'm investigating Santiago Terraza's murder."

Martin glanced back toward the chuck house at the sound of the door opening. If Belden heard it, he ignored it as Paco did. The Tejano did not move as the line of Alvarado hands filed from the door. Kell was in the lead, swaggering as he always did, conveying malevolent confidence. He squinted proudly up at Martin then reached into his pocket. Casually, he drew out the watch on its braided leather chain and twirled it. Martin's eye caught the flash of the familiar snowflake engraved in the lid, and he tried to swallow the rising anger. He moved Haze to the side and back, keeping Kell and the others in his line of sight.

Paco glanced at Kell and quickly looked away. Seeing this, Kell turned his attention to Belden and wandered toward him.

Martin felt his skin begin to crawl. Kell was the kind to intimidate a person to the point of breaking, and he was good at it. Armand was the one to shoot first and talk later.

Glancing over his shoulder, Martin spotted Chico, holding back by the chuck house with Lolita tucked behind his shoulder. When their eyes met, Chico pushed the girl back inside. Several feet away and behind him, Martin spotted Armand, face bruised and lips split, and realized what had happened the other day. He felt suddenly sick.

Pivoting Haze with his right heel, he faced Armand. Belden would have to deal with Kell alone.

Belden eyed Kell and recognized him by Paco's description.

"My men had nothing to do with that *ijo de perra*," Alvarado was saying. "Now, if you would kindly leave my hacienda..."

"Señor, I have no argument with you, but I'm here as a lawman. Nothing more."

Martin eyed Armand, who stood with his left hand on his hip. His right hung beside his revolver. Absently, Martin wondered how Belden had planned to get out the gate alive even with him and Paco covering his back. As it was, the rest of the ranch hands stood between them and escape. Rife and the Morales brothers were nowhere in sight. This worried Martin more than Armand and Kell combined.

"Maybe we should just kill the three of you and leave it at that," Kell commented. "I know those two won't be missed." He gestured toward Martin and Paco with the watch clenched in his gnarled fist.

For the first time, Belden acknowledged the gunfighter. He turned and glanced at Martin, who nodded.

"Shuck that gun," Belden told Kell so casually Martin wasn't sure of what he had heard.

Armand's hand started to come up. Martin drew his right-hand revolver, so suddenly Armand jumped and brought his gun up.

"Don't!"

But Armand ignored him. Martin shot him, aiming for the center of his chest. The gun dropped to the dirt, and Armand staggered backward, gripping his shoulder. Martin quickly turned to cover the others.

They all stood gaping, frozen. The stable boy they had harassed, threatened, and beaten now had teeth and knew how to use them with skill and speed. Even Chico, with whom he had no quarrel until now, who had been the only one to show Martin kindness, raised his hands to waist height, holding them wide. Martin's heart sank with what he did next.

"Shuck the gun belt, Chico. You're coming too."

Pale with resignation, Chico obeyed. Lolita threw the door open and ran to him. They whispered in Spanish as Chico tried to calm her. Martin risked a glance at Belden and Kell.

The gunfighter looked genuinely shocked. The ranger held him at gunpoint. Likely, Belden had drawn the revolver while Kell was distracted by Martin's shot.

Chico kissed Lolita. She was crying softly. He said something, and she nodded. Then he pulled away and stepped off the porch.

"I'll go without trouble," Chico told him, and Martin could hear a note of regret in his voice.

"I'm sorry," Martin said.

"So am I." He turned toward the others and spoke in Spanish. Two boys ran for the barn to saddle horses. Chico smiled wryly up at Martin. "I'd rather not walk to my death."

Martin grimly nodded his assent. He called over his shoulder to Belden.

"I'm good here." He shoved Kell toward Chico and surveyed the others. "Where are their horses?"

"Coming." Martin nodded toward the barn. He kept his attention moving as though trying to see everything at once. His gaze momentarily fixed on Paco. The man had not moved the whole time. Not even his horse seemed agitated, but the fearful pallor had turned to a deep flush. Martin wanted to say something but thought better of it.

"You've come up in the world, whelp." Kell twirled the watch, wrapping the chain deftly around his fingers, so it slapped hard into his palm each time. His grin broadened when Martin met his gaze. Then he nodded at Haze. "Do all Terraza men ride horses like that, or are you just lucky?"

Belden glanced up at him, and Martin knew he, as well as Kell, waited for Martin to break, but Martin gritted his teeth and continued to stare into Kell's cold, blue eyes. As he did, he noticed for the first time the evil stirring there as the man's mind worked to find the hole in Martin's armor. He took a step forward, and Martin swung Haze's head, cutting the man off.

"No closer, Kell."

A chuckle bubbled up from within him, as though issuing from the devil deep within. Kell shook his head.

"You're afraid," he said softly. "Not of me anymore, no. You're afraid of yourself, 'cause you know you ain't that much different from me."

His words nearly crumbled Martin's guard, which was Kell's entire purpose for saying it. Tenaciously, he held Kell's gaze, determined to hold it until eternity swallowed both of them into hell, but the boys returned with the horses, and Martin was relieved when Kell looked away. Kell grinned as he pocketed the watch, Martin's watch, and climbed into the saddle.

Martin glanced down at Belden. "Get your horse. I have them covered."

Wordlessly, Belden gathered his reins and climbed aboard his dun. He nodded to Alvarado in a farewell gesture.

"*Gracias*, Señor Alvarado," he said. "Sorry to trouble you like this."

"This is nothing compared to the trouble you will face." Alvarado's attention focused on Martin. "Tell Fernando Terraza nothing changes. It is the same between us as it was between his father and I."

For a long moment, Martin held Alvarado's gaze. The old man's sapphire blue eyes sent a chill through him despite the hot summer sun. He nodded once to acknowledge he would deliver the message.

Belden turned his horse and gestured for Paco to lead. Then Kell and Chico followed with Belden beside them. Martin brought up the rear, side-stepping the stallion to cover the remaining men standing on the chuck house porch. Armand looked barely conscious as one of the women worked over him. Lolita stared pleadingly at Martin, but he could no longer offer her comfort, even in gesture. Once they were clear of the gate, Martin waited for a good distance before turning Haze and letting him into an easy lope to catch up with the others. As he neared, Kell glanced back then leaned over and whispered something to Chico.

"Cut that," Belden ordered.

Kell ignored him, and Belden whacked him on the side of the head with his gun barrel. Kell yelped.

"What you do that for?" he yelled.

"You know why," Belden snapped. "Now, keep quiet, or I'll belt you again."

Kell's eyes narrowed. "Keep talking tough, lawman. Your time will come."

Belden stared at him. He cocked the revolver and leveled it with Kell's head. Kell's eyes widened. He brought up his arm as though to ward off the impending bullet and hunched in the saddle like a frightened boy.

"Thought so." Belden stowed the revolver and fell back a step.

Martin stayed at the rear and watched the brush and hills beyond the trail. He thought of Rife and the Morales brothers and tried to figure out where they might be. They could have been sent out to the range and not been privy to the arrest. Or they could have slipped out the back door of the chuck house. That was the difference between them and Kell. The big American's way was showy. If he could make a fight, it would be direct and loud. Chico either thought himself innocent or, as he had at the ranch, admitted to doing wrong and would honorably face the consequences. Rife and the Morales brothers were a different matter. Their way was quiet, deliberate, and rarely predictable.

Belden drew up and fell into step beside Martin.

"Think they'll ambush us?" he asked softly.

"There's a chance," Martin admitted. "Given we're both thinking about it."

Belden scoffed. "Yeah."

"Got any plans if they do?" Martin asked.

"If I were you," Belden said after a moment, "I'd shoot those two. Then do my best to shoot the other three. I'm as much for justice as the next man, but you and I both know what will happen if any of them escapes here. Or what could happen? They'll kill the three of us and wait to pick off the Terraza family one by one. Unless someone kills them first."

Martin admitted to himself he liked the idea of shooting Kell. The gunfighter had done as much to him; only he had been unable to run or fight. Chico, on the other hand, gave him pause. The man was not inherently evil, not like Kell or the others. Did his part in Santiago's death balance his effort to spare Martin's life? Did he even take an active part in what happened on the Mission road? These thoughts conflicted with Martin, distracted him until Belden's voice brought his focus back to the task at hand.

"Keep sharp. If they hit us, it'll be in that juniper thicket two miles up. Best cover available before we reach the Terraza range."

Martin nodded that he heard, and Belden pulled forward again to ride just behind and to the left of the prisoners. Martin remained vigilant, though his mind continued to wander over what would come next. When he saw the rider coming up the road, his heart jumped, until he recognized Fernando's palomino.

Fernando drew up and waited for them on the crest of the hill at the edge of the juniper forest. Momentary relief set in as Martin surmised that if the ambushers waited for them, they would not have passed up the chance to kill Fernando. Then on the heels of relief came frustration at his uncle's disregard for his warning.

"Only two?" Fernando asked as they neared.

Belden nodded. "Ride with Martin. He'll tell you what happened."

"Like it's a secret," Kell chuckled. "We pulled one over on you ranger, and you'll barely even know it."

Belden started to draw his gun to strike Kell again, but a shot rang out, and he stopped short.

Kell and Chico bolted for the brush. Martin drew and shot Kell in the back as he kicked Haze forward, trying to get between Fernando and the gunmen, but he had ridden too far back, and the second shot came almost on the heels of the first. Gunfire broke out from both sides of the road, and Fernando's palomino screamed in pain.

"*Tío!*" Martin cried as he fired blindly into the brush and spotted one of the Morales brothers behind a juniper. He charged the position, and as the man rose for a better shot, he killed him where he stood. Then he turned back to the other side of the road, but Rife was fleeing on Chico's heels as the other brother knelt behind a sun-bleached log with his long gun.

A bullet burned Martin's left arm as Haze leaped over Belden's prone body, jarring his aim. His bullet missed and splintered the top of the log. The man worked the lever and fired another round. Haze reared, and Martin dove from the saddle, landing hard on the loose sand. He scrambled for cover behind a tree thirty feet from the man's position. As he switched guns, he snatched a glance toward the fallen palomino, hoping for a sign Fernando lived.

Dust whirled from behind the fallen horse as Fernando struggled to free his left leg from beneath the dead animal.

"Stay down, Fernando!" Martin ordered as the top of the man's head peeked from behind the horse's shoulder.

A laugh cut the sudden stillness, wet and weak as a shot made Martin jump. The dust cloud behind the palomino rose in a final puff, like a soul rising to heaven, then fell still as Fernando's hat rolled free.

Rage, hot as a smith's forge, shot through Martin. It rose in a scream to his lips and descended into his legs, driving him up and out from cover. He dropped into a roll as he flanked the log and fired two quick shots into the chest and head of the second

Morales brother. Before the carcass hit the ground, Martin scrambled to his feet and vaulted the downed tree headed for where Kell had fallen.

Kell made no effort to fight. He lay on his back, blood covering his chest and trickling from the corner of his mouth. He flashed a smile that displayed blood-stained stubs of rotten teeth and chuckled.

"Should have listened to him," Kell wheezed as Martin's pace slowed and he approached on leaden step at a time, fighting to keep his rage in check. "Alvarado makes good on his word."

Martin's whole body trembled as he stood over Kell. "And I make good on mine," Martin returned through clenched teeth.

Again Kell laughed. "I'm dying, you son-of-a-bitch. What can you do to me now? No threat of death can reach me."

Martin's vision cleared. He saw Kell's horse and the lariat hanging from the saddle.

Without a word, he holstered his revolver and kicked the rifle out of Kell's reach. Then he took down the lariat.

Kell's eyes widened, and Martin remembered the many times the man had said he would prefer any other way of dying than hanging.

"Wh… What are you doing?" Kell stuttered.

Martin shook out a small loop and could not deny the sense of satisfaction the look of blossoming horror on Kell's face brought him.

"You always said hanging was the worst way to die…especially without a gallows." As he spoke, Martin was only distantly aware of his voice and his actions, as though everything was part of a dream beyond his control. "Lying there, you'll bleed out in a few minutes, but I have no intention of you dying so easily." He tossed the braided rope over a branch several feet over his head.

"Oh, God, no! Don't!" Kell's words were choked off as Martin slipped the loop over his head and took up the slack. Kell gasped and struggled, trying to loosen the noose with weak hands as Martin wrapped the bitter end around the trunk of another tree and worked the rope, pulling down and taking up slack until Kell's feet left the ground.

The dying man writhed and kicked, twisting grotesque circles as he dangled between earth and sky. Martin watched his struggles grow weaker until at last, the body stiffened and swayed lifelessly. As the dead man rotated in a slow arch, Martin looked at the face, the throat bloodied by the clawing hands, the eyes bulged in terror, the same eyes that an hour before mocked him. They were still now, no longer laughing or defiant, no longer alive with that devilish spirit.

"You know, you ain't that much different from me."

Remembering the words sobered Martin and cooled the violent lust that heated his blood. Kell had been right, and he had known it. Kell's proof was his death.

A cold, writhing sickness took Martin as he glared up at Kell's corpse. He remembered the watch and swallowed the rising bile. He stepped forward to retrieve the watch from the man's hip pocket. It was blood-smeared, but otherwise unmarked. Martin slipped it into his vest pocket and turned back toward the road.

Kell's bullet had left no room for hope. He had shot Fernando through the head, killing him instantly. Martin stood beside the body, fists clenched, fighting to keep a fresh rise of rage and grief in check, but it would not be held back, and the cry that burst from the depths of his being was unrecognizable as human. With Fernando, his heritage died. His cousins and his aunt had no reason to claim him as kin, and in protecting them, he would incur the wrath of both God and man.

Heart of Darkness

The Terraza ranch buzzed with restless activity as Martin neared the gate, but as he entered the yard, all fell silent. Men, women, and children stood watching him as he led the bay mare toward the main house burdened with Fernando's lifeless body. Martin rode with his gaze downcast, and when he looked up, he saw Filipe, Lucia, and Maricruz standing on the front porch. His throat tightened, cutting off all words he might have said. His gaze met Filipe's, but there was no warmth in his cousin's face, only virulent anger.

"How dare you come back here?" Filipe demanded when Martin drew rein.

Lucia, weeping into a handkerchief, timidly approached her husband's body. She buried her face in the blood-stained back of Fernando's coat. Martin felt her grief keenly, and his cousin's anger seemed distant.

"I've brought your father back," Martin said flatly.

"You killed him! Yet you have the arrogance to bring him here?" Filipe's fists were balled at his sides. "Murderer!"

Angry shouts rose from the people gathered in the courtyard. Only this morning, these people had been his friends. Martin refused to look at them and fixed his attention on Filipe.

"Who told you I killed him?" Martin asked in the same flat tone once the crowd quieted.

"Paco. He told us everything."

Rage again rose in Martin, but this time grief and exhaustion kept it in check. He had not thought of Paco since before the ambush.

"Paco." He nodded. "You would take the word of a coward who fled and left both your father and grandfather to face their killers alone?"

"Why should I take your word? Until two months ago, you were a stranger to us, and you have always been an enemy. I've known Paco since we were boys!"

Murmurs of assent barely drowned out the sound of Lucia's sobs. When last he looked into these faces, they wished him to go with God and prayed for St. Michael's protection over him. Now, they cried for his blood to be spilled. Still, he loathed the thought of killing any of them to save his own life. Emotions warred within him as he looked deep into the face of the man he would always know as a cousin.

"I am no enemy to you," Martin said gently. "But I am a threat and always will be."

The crowd fell silent. Martin glanced around at their faces. He did not see Paco among them. He was grateful for that. Had Paco been there, he would have beaten the little coward to death. Instead, he found Jinx's weathered countenance and saw sadness and fear in the sun-bleached eyes.

"Santiago wanted this war to end," he continued, turning back to Filipe. "I will end it, whether you see me as a friend or not." He dropped the mare's reins. "Bury your father, Filipe, and keep his name well."

With a slight pressure on the reins, Martin turned Haze toward the gate, deliberately turning his back to Filipe, placing himself at his cousin's mercy. The crowd parted, letting him go with mixed sentiments of farewell and condemnation. Filipe watched him, speechless, fists still clenched, but he made no move to stop Martin.

With no food, no bedroll, and no strength left to think, Martin turned up the road, not caring or knowing which way he went. He could return to Alvarado's ranch tonight and end it all, but Haze had as little strength left as he. Both had been grazed by bullets, and while Martin knew he could go on, he wanted to spare his horse, the agony of being run to death. With nowhere else to go, he turned toward the old mission and hoped the priest would grant him and his horse a night's rest.

From atop a knoll above the old mission, Jinx watched and waited. He had ridden many miles to be sure of his destination and then to cover his trail should anyone follow him. Now, as he sat cross-legged in the shadow of a juniper tree, he wondered how well he would be received.

He saw the look on Martin's face two nights ago and failed to recall seeing such a look of betrayal before in his long fifty years. He now waited for nightfall, hoping to catch Martin at ease with the two padres.

The sun touched the western horizon, and the shadows lengthened, then faded and vanished. Unkinking his long legs, Jinx rose, stretched, and limped to his horse. Rather than ride, he walked the mile downhill. A man on a horse would be a threat. A man leading a horse was an easy target.

The young padre met him at the heavy oak door.

"Has trouble befallen you, friend?" he called out as Jinx came near.

Jinx shook his head. "Not yet, padre." He squinted into the shadows beyond the doorway. "The man I'm looking for may cause me some, though."

The young padre's eyes narrowed at him in attempted recollection.

"Do you come as a friend or enemy?" he asked.

"A friend. Will you tell Martin that?"

The young padre hesitated. A sound came from the shadows, and he cocked his head in the direction of the door. Jinx felt his skin crawl as he recognized Martin's voice

"You are a friend of Martin's?" the padre asked.

Jinx frowned. "I sure don't feel like one just now." He turned toward his saddle. "I just thought I'd bring his things to him. He'll be needing them before long." He started untying the bedroll when Martin's voice came from the shadows.

"Let him in, father."

Jinx looked past the padre, his skin still crawling. Though he heard something different in the voice, he came to know as quietly friendly. Weariness made the words sound forced, effortful. He continued untying the bedroll and took the extra saddlebags from in front of his saddle.

The young padre held out his hand toward the door. When Jinx stepped through, he was not prepared for the man he saw.

All the youth and gentleness was gone from Martin's face. He looked pale, and his cheeks hollow. The torchlight above him cast deep shadows into his eyes and cheeks, giving him the look of Death.

"Hello, Jinx," he said roughly.

"Hello yourself," Jinx returned, trying to affect his old familiarity with the young man. "Reckon it's pointless to ask how you've been."

Martin held his gaze a moment before his attention shifted to the padre as he walked between them into the sanctuary. Then he stared down at the floor, though Jinx had the distinct feeling Martin watched his every move.

"You took an awful risk bringing those few things," he said finally.

Jinx glanced down at the saddlebags and chuckled. "When a man lives in a saddle, these few things mean a lot."

For a moment, Martin studied him. The nod was slow and grim.

"Thank you," he said sincerely.

Jinx stepped forward and set the gear against the wall. As he straightened, he noticed the torn sleeve.

"You get that the other day?" he asked.

"It's nothing," Martin replied.

Jinx shrugged. "Well, I guess I came for more than just returning your gear."

Martin tensed noticeably. When he spoke, any friendliness it held before vanished. "You come to collect a reward?"

"No. I came to warn you." Jinx folded his arms across his chest in a gesture of peace. "Filipe has sent for another ranger. After what Paco told him, those rangers will be hard-pressed to see you hang."

"What did Paco tell them?"

"That you killed Belden and Fernando both, personally, that he saw it, and that the men who killed Santiago said you told them how and when to do it." Jinx bit his lip. "He said you were in cahoots with Alvarado all along since Alvarado claims you are his heir. Unfortunately, that's all anyone knows now."

For a long, grim moment, Jinx held Martin's gaze. The younger man was measuring him, gauging his friendship and trustworthiness. For all Martin must have known now, he had no friends in this world.

"Do you believe it?" Martin finally asked.

Slowly, Jinx shook his head. He sighed.

"I know Santiago set a lot of store by you," he said. "I don't know the whole story, but I know his affection was not gained easily. And I know what I've witnessed in my time. What I found yesterday morning on the trail to Alvarados would have been proof alone."

Martin's jaw flexed, but he remained silent. The warning in his eyes was clear, but Jinx had no more patience for careful words.

"My suspicion," Jinx said neutrally, "is that son-of-a-bitch had it coming, and I doubt that anyone on his side would have done that to him."

Casually, Martin glanced toward the sanctuary. Jinx realized he stood on the threshold of a house of God and removed his hat with a muttered apology to the Almighty and an uneducated attempt at signing himself. He stepped closer and whispered to Martin.

"I don't know what you're planning to do," he said. "But if it has anything to do with getting Fernando's and Santiago's killers, I want in."

Martin lowered his head, and the shadows in his face deepened.

"You don't want any part of what I'm going to do," he said grimly.

"I want to help you," Jinx countered in a near whine.

Martin looked up sharply, his eyes catching the torchlight in sharp pinpoints that seemed to blaze in anger. Then, as quickly as it came, the expression ebbed, the fire faded, and Martin's gaze turned away.

"I'm wanted for three murders I did not commit," he whispered. "I reckon I'll give those rangers a real reason to hunt me. You don't want any part of that. *I* don't want you to have any part of that."

A sharp sickness settled into Jinx's gut as he sensed the malevolence in this young man he had helped give new life to. He remembered the boyish innocence that day at the corral when Haze chose him from the other cow   hands. Sometime in the last two days, that innocence had fled, and in its place laid a black serpent waiting to be set free. Despite his old man's cynicism, Jinx felt awkward and afraid.

"You're sure about that?" he questioned, toying with his hat.

Martin gazed into the sanctuary beyond the pews to the plain altar in front-lit by dancing candlelight.

"My soul was lost long ago," he said quietly. "I don't hope for redemption, but I'll do all I can for what family I have."

Jinx felt a surge of hope. "Family?"

Martin shook his head. "It's not important." He regarded Jinx with the first friendly expression since the old cowhand's arrival. "Take care of them for me," he said and extended his hand. "And thank you…my friend."

Taking the hand in a firm grip, Jinx nodded, too conflicted to speak. Then he pulled on his hat and turned toward the door. Past the threshold, he paused and spoke over his shoulder.

"*Viaje con Dios*, Martin."

Martin watched Jinx go and felt his sadness deepen with the fading drum of hooves on the hard-pan until the soft scrape of sandals on the stone floor distracted his thoughts.

"Perhaps you should have accepted his help, my son."

He acknowledged the old priest's words with a brief glance as he picked up his bedroll and saddlebags and headed toward the back door. The old priest followed.

Outside in the little shed, Haze looked out over the rail that confined him in a stall. His ears pricked in Martin's direction, and he turned, ready to be set free. Martin dropped the gear near the snubbing post and took the hackamore from where it lay across his saddle and slipped it over Haze's head.

"Are you going to kill Alvarado?" the old priest asked.

Martin led Haze from the narrow stall and tied the rope to the snubbing post before reaching for the saddle blanket to brush down Haze's back.

"I'll not preach to you about vengeance," the old priest continued as Martin worked. "I suspect you know that belief well enough; otherwise, you would not feel the guilt so heavy on your shoulders."

The declaration caught Martin off-guard like a splash of cold water in his face. His hands froze as he felt the burden of which the priest spoke. He hung his head, wishing the priest would say no more, but the old man continued after a moment.

"I know of the family which you spoke," he said. When Martin questioned him with a glance, he stepped closer and spoke in nearly a whisper. "I joined your mother and father in marriage not long after I came to this mission. I also baptized you."

This was unexpected for Martin. The image of his parents standing before the altar of this humble church came vividly to mind and blocked out all other thought. He studied the priest, taking in the worn brown cassock and sandals. He saw the man's age and knew his words could be true, but his trust was limited.

"How do you know it was my mother and father? Not those of some long-dead child?" He returned to brushing the dirt and hay from Haze's back.

"Because I see their faces in yours, and God was gracious when he gave me a memory for faces."

Martin's hands froze again as his heart waged war with his head. He wanted to believe what he heard, but he feared becoming a pawn to someone's game again.

"I remember them distinctly," the old priest said. "Because they loved each other so much. Your father was a gruff man when he first came here, hard, even mean, but when he was with your mother, a gentler man, you never knew. Your mother glowed with pride the day they wed, and every day after that, I saw them together. She cared for your half-brothers with such devotion, one would think they were her own, and when you were born, that did not change. She possessed love enough for all three. And your brothers, they watched over you like the seraphim guarding the tabernacle. They loved to make you laugh, and you laughed much, even in the church, when most other children cried."

From the priest's words rose a memory, a flash of two identical faces hovering over him, smiling, speaking words he had been incapable of understanding, but their playfulness was unmistakable. For the moment that he remembered, he felt whole, happy, and no longer alone.

"Can you keep a secret, Father?"

The old priest smiled wryly. "I keep the secrets of all in my parish, including Santiago's."

Martin met the old priest's gaze, and he nodded.

"I reckon I don't have to tell you after all," he muttered as he lifted the saddle to Haze's back.

"Perhaps your saying it will make it easier to believe," the old priest said. "Perhaps it will help make your path clear to you."

"I know my path, father," Martin replied.

"Is it the path you're choosing, or is it choosing you?"

Martin took a deep breath and held it as his hands tightened the cinch. When he came here two nights ago, the old priest had kept silent and granted him shelter while his horse rested. He said nothing of the darkness Martin felt eating at his heart and soul, until now. Weary with thinking and fighting what he must do and what he wanted to do, Martin wanted nothing more now than to shut his ears against the old priest's words.

"If you do this thing, if you kill Alvarado, you will destroy all the love your family had for you, and the rest of your days will be spent wandering creation, friendless and homeless until a bullet or a rope ends your life."

"That's true, father, but if I don't, how many more will be killed? Fifty? One hundred men and women?" Martin glared at the old priest. "I know vengeance is a sin, but now, I don't care what it looks like. The fact remains that as long as Alvarado lives, he will continue killing the Terrazas one by one, and I can't let that happen."

"I know." The old priest seemed crushed by Martin's words. He remained silent as Martin loaded his gear onto the saddle, checked his rifle, and filled his canteen. As Martin untied the *mecate*, he said his final words on the matter. "I pray to God to forgive you this choice."

Martin listened as the old priest turned and walked away, unable to face someone who truly could pass judgment on his immortal soul. When the door to the rectory closed, Martin led Haze from under the awning and mounted up. From the gate, he turned east and traveled overland. By the time he reached Alvarado's ranch, it would be past midnight. Without a moon, traveling fast was impossible, but no one could follow him.

His left arm was still sore, but Haze's wound seemed little more than a scratch, and the big stallion's strength had returned within a day. If he chose his escape well, any pursuit would fall behind long before Martin reached the northern border. He had thought long enough about how he would do this, but his mind still wavered on who would die first. By the time the ghostly shadows of the ranch emerged into view, he had decided.

Dismounting, he led Haze into the arroyo below the ranch and slipped up to the wall. Around the west wall, he remembered a spot where the hillside had collapsed many years before. As he stood on the berm, he listened for signs of movement within. Soft footfalls paced the fire step. He did not know who would be on guard. Part of him hoped it would be Rife or Chico.

He waited, and as the guard passed above him, Martin leaped, grasped the poles supporting the roof, and climbed over, landing lightly as a cat behind the guard. In a split second, he chose. Without recognizing the guard, he grabbed him around the neck and squeezed. The man struggled and, within moments, sagged to the walkway.

Pulling the body closer to the wall and tying the man's hands and feet, Martin searched the yard and listened for any sign that the short commotion had alerted others. Then he looked into the man's face. It was Diego, one of the stable boys, barely old enough to be called a man. He was out cold.

Martin turned him on his stomach with his face toward the wall and pulled on the boy's poncho. Then he straightened and paced toward the stairs.

Across from him, the other guard raised his rifle and waved. Martin gestured back as Diego would then descended to the yard headed for the outhouse. Once within the shadows, he slipped around to the bunkhouse and climbed in through a back window.

His heart pounded with the fever of battle, and he stood for a moment in the darkness of the room, listening to the sounds of sleeping men. One coughed and rolled in his blankets. Martin's heart stopped until the man's breathing deepened, and he once again slept soundly. Now he moved with silent, stalking grace.

He found Rife's bunk first but wrapped in blankets; he could not be sure the man lying there was Rife. He eyed the gun belt hanging from the post, reached out and fingered the tooled leather and grips. Both butts faced the same direction, confirming it was Rife's, but still, he waited for another sign.

It seemed an eternity before Rife moaned in his sleep and shifted to his back. Starlight from the window fell across his face, and Martin knew it was him.

Drawing his knife, Martin eased himself onto the bed over top of Rife. Like a constrictor, he pinned Rife to his bunk, his left hand covering the mouth in the same instant he pierced Rife's chest with the blade.

Rife's eyes shot open and stared wide into the shadow covered face that hovered over him, but Martin dragged the blade across and along the ribs, slicing open the heart beneath and prying downward to release the blood, letting it spill and soak into the blankets. Rife died quickly and silently.

Again, Martin waited and listened, but Rife's execution had gone unnoticed by his sleeping comrades. He rose, wiped his knife on the blankets, and moved to Chico's bunk.

It was empty. A cacophony of thoughts burst in his mind. Killing Chico was something he regretted having to do. He owed the man for keeping Kell from shooting him, but he also felt obligated to exact justice. He decided the time was against searching out Chico and slipped back out the window.

Glancing up at the sky, he estimated three hours before sunrise. That meant a three-hour head start once he ended Alvarado's life.

The other guard on the fire step did not look down as Martin made his way from shadow to shadow to the kitchen door of the main house. Inky blackness greeted him within, and he groped his way through the faded smells of bread, spice, and ash to the main hall. There, like a beacon, he found a light burning in Alvarado's room. He hesitated a moment, then lifted the latch and stepped inside.

The old man looked up from his book, his expression eternally stern.

"*I told you I did not want to be disturbed,*" he said in Spanish.

Forcing his nerves to steady, Martin kept his head down and turned to face Alvarado.

"*One of the men is dead, señor,*" he replied, affecting Diego's voice as best he could remember it. "*Killed in his bed.*"

Alvarado slammed his book shut and pushed up from his chair. "By whom?" he demanded.

"*We don't know, señor,*" Martin replied, reaching for the knife at the small of his back. "*Perhaps one of Terraza's men.*"

Alvarado scoffed. "*Man? There's not a man among them.*" He turned his back to Martin, facing his wardrobe. "*Which was killed?*"

"*Rife, señor.*" Martin waited for the man to look down from the mirror. Then in two short strides, he closed the distance between them and pressed the knife to Alvarado's back.

"Tell me, señor," he whispered. "What possessed you to claim me as your grandson?"

There was no fear in Alvarado's face as he lifted his gaze to the reflection and looked squarely into Martin's eyes. He smiled.

"So you've come, finally," he said as though addressing an old friend. "I've waited for a long time."

Martin frowned. "Answer me, old man. Why did you claim me as your kin?"

Alvarado chuckled. "Two years ago, a gypsy caravan traveled through here. The old woman read my fortune. She told me death would come from the seed of my enemy *con ojos oros*. When you appeared on my doorstep that night, I knew you for

Maitea's son. If I could turn you against your own, perhaps I could save my own life. When I couldn't, I tried to break your spirit."

"By killing Santiago?"

"*Si*." Alvarado hung his head. "I'm an old man. I've known you would come for a while, *La Muerte*. I am ready for you."

Martin drew a deep breath and sighed, sensing the irony. "You know what your one mistake was, Alvarado?"

The old man merely shifted his gaze.

"I hadn't considered killing you before Santiago's death. When Fernando was killed, that was the final cast. You've brought this on your own head."

"And what comes from this, *Muerto*, will be on yours. My family will never stop hunting you."

As Martin met his reflected gaze, he felt rage, cold and calculated, turn his veins to ice. What would become of this killing? Alvarado was the last of his lineage. His ranch would fall into ruin; its workers scatter to the wind. Who then would avenge this murder? No one, except Martin's own conscience.

A knock sounded on the door, and a woman's voice called softly.

Alvarado filled his lungs to shout, but Martin clamped a hand over his mouth and brought the knife around and cut deep into the old man's throat.

The knock sounded again, more urgently. Martin lowered the dying man to the bed as blood spurted from the jugular, splattering his sleeve and darkening the blue coverlet with every beat of the dying heart. Before Martin could reach the window, the door opened, and Lolita stepped through with a thin robe pulled tightly around her. Her eyes widened in fear at the sight of him. When she saw Alvarado lying across the bed, heart stilled, and eyes fixed and glazed in death; relief relaxed her features.

"Go," she whispered calmly. "I'll not tell them."

"They'll think you did it," Martin replied.

"I'll tell them I found him like this. That I don't know who killed him." Her words came in a hurried rush. She skirted the bed and put her hands on his arms. "If they catch you, they will kill you. Now go!"

He glanced at the dead man, and a thought occurred to him. "Where's Chico?"

"Gone. He came back for his things two days ago and left. Said he wanted no part of this anymore."

"And left you at the mercy of these *pendejos*?"

"It's what he had to do," she snapped back. "I've lived this way since before womanhood, and it will never change."

Martin's stomach twisted at the realization of what she meant. Any man could have his pleasure with her, and she was powerless to stop them. It was no different from slavery, and he hated himself for not understanding sooner or doing something about it.

"Come with me," he begged. "You deserve better than what's here for you."

"Like what? Starvation?" Anger flared in her turbulent eyes, but her voice remained soft, even gentle. "I have a roof over my head, clothes on my back, and food in my belly. As long as I have that, I have enough."

"No one should live like this, Lolita," Martin growled back. "No woman should have to trade her virtue to fulfill her needs."

Her eyes narrowed at him. "And you would risk getting caught to save me? *Baboso*, go before I kill you myself." She shoved him toward the window. "Go!"

He hesitated, trying to think of another way to convince her. She looked around and found Alvarado's revolver resting on the bedside table. She picked it up and leveled it with Martin's heart. Her hand did not waver, but tears sparkled in her eyes.

"Go, or I'll spare you the slow death they'll give you."

Her hand was steady, but her voice wasn't. Without a word, Martin stripped the poncho and turned to the window. He looked out first to be sure the coast was clear then swung a leg over the sill. He looked back at Lolita one last time.

"Where did Chico go?"

"*Norte*. Now go!"

He tried to think of something to say in farewell, but Lolita cocked the hammer, and he thought better of it. He lowered himself to the ground.

Blinded from the lamplight, he crouched beside the wall and waited for his eyes to adjust. When he once again could see the fire step, he gauged the distance to the ladder and decided the front gate would be an easier way of escape.

Keeping low, he moved toward the front of the house and slipped into the shadow of the old oak tree. The man on the fire step had turned and paced toward the front gate. His heart pounded as he realized he was plainly visible to anyone who happened to look out from the bunkhouse. Then, the guard paused, gazing down at the outhouse, puzzlement barely visible in the starlight. Martin had wasted too much time, and before long, Diego would be discovered.

Martin forced himself to calm and wait for the right moment. If he spooked and ran too soon, the guard would certainly see him.

The man paused above the latrine and called to Diego. Above the thudding of Martin's heart, he heard the muffled cry from Diego on the far side of the house.

The guard looked up and started walking around the wall. For a few brief moments, he would face away from Martin.

As quietly and as quickly as possible, Martin ran for the front gate and started lifting the heavy bar. Then, a thought occurred to him, and he let the bar back down. The gate would be left open, leading them directly to his trail.

Praying the guard wouldn't look his way, he climbed the gate, using the strapping and bar for holds. He heard the first shout from the guard as he vaulted over the top and dropped to the ground on the other side. The second shout covered the sound of his landing. Waiting was over, and he slipped into the mesquite and circled back to his horse.

Escape from Texas

The days that followed stretched together. He rested little and then only for Haze's benefit. More than once, he was thankful for the stallion's enduring strength and did all he could to preserve it.

For the first day, he watched the south for the ever-present dust cloud signaling the position of his pursuers and tried to think of how to outsmart them. He hoped to strike the Brazos River and find it shallow enough to follow within its waters far enough south; they would fail to find his tracks. Perhaps he could follow it as far as Austin, gather supplies, and lose his tracks among the other travelers, but that was hoping that someone had not thought to wire the capitol with his description.

It was the second day by the time he reached the water and felt relief to see it ran low for the season. Haze took to the water willingly, and both welcomed the cool moisture. Martin kept Haze close to the bank, where the water sloshed at the stallion's knees. For a half-hour Martin rode before dismounting and leading Haze on. The current was with them and made the going easy, but he wanted to spare the horse the extra burden of his weight. Nearly an hour and a half after entering the water, they climbed up the bank and pressed east.

Three days followed in which Martin slept little and constantly watched for signs of pursuit. The dust cloud no longer followed, offering him some relief, but what sleep he gained was filled with dreams of Alvarado's men catching and hanging him. In the midst of it, he thought of how stupid it was to chase Chico. He had little hope of finding the man while on the run. Still, the desire to do so lingered with him.

Nearly a week later, he came within sight of a settlement and paused in the cover of a sprawling live oak tree to consider the wisdom of riding in. The jerked beef Jinx provided had run out two days before, and he could not risk hunting or loose time snaring. As he crouched and studied the settlement, he glanced over at his horse.

Haze looked worn and dozed with his head down. Martin began to worry that he pushed the animal too hard and that if he were discovered, he would run Haze to his death, but he needed food, ammunition, and, if possible, a place to hide. Part of him wanted to know how avidly the law wanted him, or if only Alvarado's men pursued him.

Stretching his hand toward the western horizon, he determined two hours remained before sundown. Three would bring the full dark he needed to disguise Haze's mottled brown coat. Folks might write him off as another drifter, but if any reports described the brown stallion, questions would arise.

Martin cursed. He didn't like the situation but saw no other option. He settled down against the tree trunk and waited.

As he watched the sun drift toward setting, his mind wandered. He thought of his cousins and aunt in their grief. Could things have been different if they knew who he was? Martin shook his head dismissively. Once it was known he had murdered Alvarado, his reputation would only taint the Terraza name. Shame washed over him as he once again thought of his mother. Only after he had committed murder, did he think of her and how she would have wept for his immortal soul. She had been a peaceful woman despite her fiery temper, kind and gentle. She would have been shamed by what he had done, but Martin accepted that as a burden he must bear for he had seen no other way to end the fight forever.

From his breast pocket, he drew out the old portrait and studied the faces of his parents. His mother, expression holding a subtle smile, sat in a high-backed cushioned chair, a veil cascading down over her hair from a crown-like comb, her head held high and regal. Beside her, his father stared sternly, back straight and proud, his left arm draped across the back of the chair with a protective air. He seemed a giant compared to her, broad-shouldered, and light-haired. His features betrayed Nordic heritage.

Martin knew he more closely resembled his mother in his slight build and Spanish features, but somehow, he had inherited his father's fighting spirit and a subtle resemblance in his build. Would his father recognize him when they met? Did he dare confess his identity? The answers brought cold loneliness to his heart. If he was wanted for murder in Texas, he could not tell them who he was without running the risk of being caught or putting his family in danger. Lifting his gaze to the north, he thought of the miles that lay between him and Oregon. He thought of the cold nights, dry days, and the dangers he would face every time he entered a settlement like the one below and realized he likely would never meet his family. His throat tightened with grief, and he again shook his head. Too many nights without sleep, he thought. His tired mind was losing immunity to emotion.

Tucking the tintype away in its place, he removed his hat and slouched deeper against the tree. He must have dozed; for a while later, he opened his eyes and found the sky black save for a thin glow in the west. The settlement still stirred with life. He mounted up and rode in at a sedate walk avoiding the brighter lit parts of the street.

Hope slipped away as he passed one dark store after another. Then, he spotted a general store with the light still glowing, and his hope rebounded.

Glancing back the way he had come and on up the street to be sure no one noticed him, he turned Haze up an adjacent alley and left him ground hitched. Without appearing cautious, he stepped up to the porch and tried the door. It swung open easily, but the ring of the bell startled him.

The proprietor glanced up from a ledger he had laid out on the counter.

"We're closed, mister. You'll have to come back in the morning."

"Sorry," Martin said. "I was just hoping to pick up some hardtack and dried beef."

"And that cannot wait 'til morning?" The man's tone betrayed a short temper, and Martin's hand drifted closer to his gun.

"I'm riding out tonight," he said casually. "I haven't got much, but I'll pay what I can for the inconvenience."

The proprietor's eyes narrowed as he studied Martin. He had a round face, button eyes, and wore a twill vest that strained around his middle. As Martin watched, understanding came over the man like a cascade starting at his brow and descending to his lips.

"*El Muerto*," he whispered, horror running as an undercurrent through his tone.

Martin raised a hand as though he could soothe the man's fear. "I mean you no harm, mister. I just need some food and grain for my horse."

"You mean to kill me for it." Panic was rapidly taking over the man, and Martin scrambled for a plan to deal with him.

"No," he replied flatly. "I'll pay you in script, and I'll take your word you won't go running to the law right away."

Understanding seemed to break through the mild panic. Then a thought appeared to occur to the proprietor, and all common sense fled him.

"What if I refuse?" he asked with a tone of challenge.

Drawing a deep breath, Martin gritted his teeth. "You don't want to know."

He knew it was a bluff, but in a brief lapse of awareness, he believed his own threat. What mattered was that the proprietor believed him. The man's gaze darted to the window over

Martin's shoulder. His skin crawled, and he moved deeper into the store.

"When does the law make rounds?" Martin asked.

"Just about this time of night," the proprietor replied. "You should leave before Marshall Rawlins gets here. He'll shoot you dead without question."

Martin had to hand it to the man, he knew how to take advantage of an opportunity, but because of the context, Martin was willing to call the bluff.

"Thanks for the advice," he said, "but I'll take my chances. Now, if you don't mind, I'd like a pound each of jerked beef and hard-tack and four pounds of grain. Think you could get that together quickly?"

Frustration flashed over the proprietor's face. His mouth hardened. "I don't negotiate with thieves and murderers."

With a sigh, Martin drew his left-hand revolver with casual irritation. "In that case, mister, I'll ask you to show me where you keep your rope."

"You're going to tie me up?"

"Yes, sir, and I'll club you over the head if need be, but I'd rather not. I'd rather you go home to your family tonight, eat at your own table and sleep in your own bed, but if you keep up this mule-headed bullshit, you'll be spending the night here or at the doc's with a split skull. It's your choice."

The man frowned in puzzlement. "You really don't want to hurt me?"

Martin shook his head once, and the proprietor nodded.

"Alright," he said, sliding off his stool. "I'll get what you ask."

Martin holstered the revolver and followed the man toward the back of the store. Dividing his attention between the windows and the proprietor taxed his senses, but anxiety kept him alert. His nerves tightened more at the proprietor's silence as he collected the items and brought them to the front counter.

"That will be two dollars, four bits," he said.

Reaching into his pocket, Martin froze at the sound of footfalls on the porch. He did not dare look up in case the passerby recognized him. Silently, he prayed the steps would continue on, but they stopped at the door, the knob clicked, and the bell rang.

"Evenin', Clare," a man's voice greeted. "Thought you closed an hour ago."

"Rawlins," the proprietor returned, meeting Martin's gaze with wry triumph. "Was just helping this gentleman with a few supplies."

"Oh?" The marshal leaned an elbow against the countertop. "Couldn't wait 'til morning?"

"No. He's in a bit of a hurry to head north."

As casually as Martin could, he counted out the payment from the coin in his pocket and collected the sack of groceries with his left hand.

The marshal rolled his head back in contemplation as he studied Martin's face. "Where you coming from, son?"

Martin fixed the proprietor with a questioning look, expecting him to answer that question as well, but the man kept silent, and Martin did not offer an answer.

The marshal's eyes narrowed. He straightened.

"You know, I noticed that dappled brown horse in the alley. He yours, son?" As he asked the question, he straightened, letting his hand rest against the revolver on his hip.

"Don't do it, Marshal," Martin said coolly despite the shock of fear piercing his heart.

"You think you can take me?" the marshal foolishly challenged.

For the first time, Martin met the man's gaze. He knew the lawman did not stand a chance against him in an even draw. His gun was ill-kept, riding high and loose on his hip. Excitement coursed through him just beneath the surface of his flushed face. He may wear a badge, but it was clear he could not live up to the purpose of his office.

"Before I kill you," Martin said casually as if it were a polite conversation between them, "mind telling me how much I'm worth to you?"

The lawman blinked. "There's a combined reward of four thousand dollars on your head, Martin."

Martin nodded and scoffed. "I guess killing you will add another five hundred…all over two and a half dollars in grain and foodstuff. Should've just let myself starve."

"You could come along quiet, make it easy on both of us."

An alarm went off in Martin's head, too late to head off the fight. The proprietor, moving slow and careful, had reached his hidden revolver and drawn it, thumbing back the hammer as he brought it into line.

On reflex, Martin swept up his right-hand revolver and shot the man without thought, then turned as the lawman's gun barked. In less than a heartbeat, two men died in the cramped little store, their life's blood running over the worn floorboards. Before realization could sink in, Martin darted for the back door. There was scrambling on the main street as he snatched the trailing rein and swung aboard Haze. A shout from one of the townsfolk warned him, and he spurred Haze into a dead run into the back alley, but he did not dare stay there for fear that he'd be trapped and cornered.

With a turn as sharp as any cutting horse, Haze darted back toward the main street, leaping a pile of trash and cutting close to a suited man who yelped in surprise.

"Shoot him!" someone shouted.

Martin held tight to the saddle as Haze wove through the crowd of people, then flattened against the stallion's neck as the horse stretched into a full run as though he knew the urgency of their situation.

The buildings blurred past and fell away. The quarter moon had yet to rise, but the road stretched like a white ribbon through the grass under a starry sky. Martin let Haze run all-out for a half mile before drawing up and sliding to the ground. He pulled a piece of jerky from the bag and tucked the rest with the hard-tack in the right saddlebag. Then, he let Haze have a portion of the grain, all the while listening and watching for pursuit. He lingered just long enough to finish half the beef strip and let Haze have a breather. Then he put the grain away and started to climb into the saddle, but as he lifted his right leg to clear the bedroll, a sharp pain knocked the breath from him. The world spun, and he clung to the saddle horn until it passed. He looked down at his side and saw a dark patch glisten on his shirt.

He growled in frustration and pressed a hand to the wound as he kneed Haze forward.

They walked for several miles while Martin tried to stop the bleeding. He wasn't sure, but he believed it was only a deep graze. At first, the pain cleared his head, then wore him down to the point he lost track of the miles. He did not remember the moon rising or giving Haze his head. He dropped into a deep sleep and woke up to the sharp scent of sage and the first rays of dawn lighting the east. Haze stood beside him, quietly grazing on the sparse grass.

For a long moment, Martin fought to remember where he was, and as the memories returned, he questioned if it had all been a dream until he tried to sit up. He looked at his horse apologetically.

"I got us in a real mess, didn't I?"

Teeth grinding on the dry vegetation, Haze glanced over his shoulder, ears perked forward.

"I'll take that as agreement," Martin groaned. He collected his hat and staggered to his feet. He took down his canteen and shook it. His heart sank to find it barely a quarter full. Lifting his shirt, he inspected the wound. It needed cleaning, but Haze needed the water to keep going. Taking a swig, Martin offered the majority to the horse then wet his neckerchief. Gritting his teeth, he cleared away the worst of the blood and found it was indeed a deep graze that had bled badly, but it showed no signs of infection though it was stiff and sore.

Still holding his side, he put up the canteen and climbed back into the saddle. Clouds had moved in sometime during the night, bringing a chilling wind. He pulled on his oilskin slicker and watched for the rain as he rode. It appeared as a veil descending from the low clouds to the west, obscuring the gently rolling hills as it drew closer.

It came around noon after he refilled his canteen, and both he and Haze had drunk their fill at a shallow, muddy stream. All morning he had watched the north but only saw an occasional puff of dust. He had not thought to head south, but now it worked out.

As the clouds broke, he turned Haze upstream and hunched his shoulders against the driving west wind. A half-mile later, he left the water in a downpour that washed out their tracks and headed north again.

The late summer rains swelled the creeks and rivers by the second day. After nearly drowning on the third crossing, Martin decided just to follow the banks of the next river he came to. Haze had grown worn and weary and walked with his proud head hung. To spare him, Martin walked with the horse heeled beside him like a dog using him for balance when weakness came over him.

It was late the fourth day when he came to the bridge. The river running beneath it, gorged on rain, washed out the banks. The tresses and planks creaked and groaned as they crossed. Haze hesitated. When Martin coaxed him forward, Haze threw up his head and tried to pull back.

"Easy, Hazy Boy," Martin soothed as he stroked the stallion's muzzle. "We have to cross this river. The sooner we get out of Texas, the better. They can't chase us forever."

Haze calmed. Whether it was Martin's encouragement or the stallion's faith in him, Martin did not care. Haze followed him calmly onto the bridge. As they neared the far side, Haze's ears perked, and above the rush of water, Martin could hear a soft cry.

"Hello?" he called out.

The cry intensified with words unintelligible above the roar. Martin followed the sound down along the bank. There, clinging to a willow root, was a little girl.

"Help! Please!"

The bank was steep and slick. Though Martin could reach her, he risked falling in with her.

Taking his lariat, he tied off the lasso end to the saddle horn.

"Stand, Haze."

The stallion's ears perked toward him as he descended the bank.

The girl wept loudly. Her lips and little hands clinging to the root were blue with cold.

"I'm coming!" Martin shouted. "Hold on!"

He spoke too soon as the bank gave out under him, and he slid into the water upstream of her. She screamed as he collided with the root and knocked her loose, but he dove forward, and his hand shot out to grasp her sleeve in a precarious grip. In desperation, she lunged toward him and gripped the sleeve of his oilskin with both hands. He pulled her closer, wrapping his arm around her body.

"Pull, Haze!"

Steadily, one step at a time, Haze backed away, pulling them to safety. Roots and rocks dug into his ribs and back as Haze dragged them onto solid ground. At Martin's command, Haze stopped and stood.

For a long moment, Martin lay down in the matted grass and let the rainfall on his face while he caught his breath. The girl pressed her face to his shoulder and hiccupped with sobs.

"It's alright now," Martin cheered the girl as he sat up. He untangled his stiffened fingers from the lariat and brushed the dark hair back from the girl's face. "Are you hurt anywhere?"

She shook her head and sniffed. "I was just trying to get out of the rain. I tried to crawl under the bridge and fell in. Papa's going to be so angry."

"He would have been unhappier if you had drowned in that river. Come on. Let's get you home."

Still crying, but determined, she scrambled up the slope to where Haze stood looking curiously at her. Martin followed and gathered the lasso as he went.

"What's your name?" he asked as he untied his bedroll to wrap her in it.

"M…Mary," she stammered through chattering teeth.

"Alright, Mary, we can't make a fire, but we'll wrap you up nice against the rain." He unfolded the blanket and draped it around her shoulders, then the tarpaulin shell to help keep out the rain. As he did, Martin glanced toward the bridge and saw the bank had collapsed up against the footings. Before long, it would no longer hold the weight of a horse.

"Where's your home, Mary?"

She pointed to the far side of the bridge. "That way. About a mile past the fork."

He felt his shoulders sag. He could not leave the girl here alone, but if he took her home, he risked getting trapped on the south side of the river with a posse on his trail.

"How far from here?" he asked.

"A mile and a half, maybe."

He heaved a quiet sigh and rose from the mud. "Let's get you home. No point in staying out here any longer."

Martin put away the lariat and lifted the girl into the saddle. "Hold tight now. If we fall in, you hang on to Haze here. He could swim through a hurricane." He smiled, hoping to cheer the girl a little and was rewarded by the girl gripping the saddle horn with both hands.

He chose to lead Haze across the bridge, ears keen to the creak of wood as it moaned beneath their feet. He prayed it would hold, and in a mixed blessing, it did, until they reached the far bank. As Martin climbed into the saddle behind the girl, he heard the hiss and splash of the bank sloughing out from beneath the footings followed by the groaning and popping of lumber as the bridge twisted and broke and scattered lumber into the floodwaters.

The girl shivered. "Pa's going to be angry," she said through chattering teeth.

"Ain't much he can do about it." He unbuttoned the slicker and wrapped it around her, hoping his body heat would help keep the girl warm, but the chill was working into his own bones. "Which way?"

The girl only pointed, and Martin turned Haze down the road. Gradually, the girl stopped shivering. She curled up against Martin and fell asleep. As they rode, he could feel a fresh trickle of water down his collar. He reached up to adjust his hat and realized it was gone, probably lost when he fell in the water, a small loss compared to the revolvers, but his jaw tightened in frustration. He made note to take off his guns next time he attempted such a rescue. Had he not been tied to Haze, he would have been dragged down by the extra weight. The hat had been a gift from Filipe. Things being as they were, it was probably just as well.

An hour after leaving the river, they rode into the yard of a little homestead. The house and barn were well kept. The animals were penned up against the rain, and as they neared the house, Martin saw the boards were painted a bright white.

The door flew open, and a tall man in a slicker and hat hurried out to meet them. Behind him, a woman stood framed against the light in the doorway. She called the girl's name.

The girl woke at the sound of her mother's voice. Mary looked up, and when she saw the man, she stretched her arms out to him. "Da!"

Martin lowered Mary to her father's embrace.

"My God! Where have you been?"

"I fell in the river," Mary explained. "He saved me."

The man eyed Martin. A fresh chill ran up Martin's spine as he nodded in greeting. Rather than risk trouble, he decided it was best to leave soon.

"Thank you, stranger," the man said genuinely though his expression remained guarded.

"It's no trouble."

"He fell in too, Da," Mary added. "His horse pulled us out. Can they stay with us for the night? Please?"

Despite his daughter's pleas, the man seemed no more welcoming.

"That's alright, Mary," Martin said to soothe the girl. "I still have a long way to go. You folks take care now." He started to turn Haze back down the road as the man returned to the house carrying Mary.

"Please don't go," the woman called from the porch.

Martin hesitated as the scent of wood smoke from the chimney reached him. His stomach twisted with hunger and a shiver of cold ran through him. He glanced back as the desire for warmth and human contact called to him.

The woman spoke softly to the man as he set Mary on the top step beside her. The man shook his head, but the woman spoke again, and the man obligingly walked back out into the rain.

"Why don't you come inside and warm up, stranger," the man said. Though his tone was friendly, his gaze held a silent warning.

"I don't want to be any trouble," Martin replied.

The man shook his head. "Looks like you and your horse could use a rest, and no one should be out in this storm. I was just fixing to go after Mary when you rode in."

Martin nodded that he understood then turned his gaze back to the road, torn between fears and wanting. Until then, he had not realized how weary he was. He looked at Haze, who felt a little less solid on his feet than he used to. Haze needed rest more than he did, but something in the man's manner scared Martin.

"Please," the man continued. "A warm fire and a hot meal are the least we can do, as my wife said."

Again his stomach twisted, and Martin realized he had not eaten anything since two days before, and that had been little enough. He relented, but as he stepped down, the man took the reins and offered his hand.

"Bill Knolls," he said. "My wife is Anna, and you've met Mary, our daughter."

Martin took the extended hand, but his mind failed to create a name for himself.

Bill noticed this and seemingly took it in stride. "I'll take care of your horse for you." His way was firm, and Martin decided not to fight him. Instead, he took his rifle and the soaked bedroll.

"If you can spare some grain for him, I'd be grateful."

Bill smiled. "I'm sure I can."

Martin returned the smile with a tired nod and walked up to the house. The door stood ajar, but when he stuck his head inside, the front room was empty.

"Be out in a minute," the woman's voice called from the back room. "Just make yourself at home."

Feeling awkward, Martin retreated outside to shake what water he could from the slicker, then hung it and on a peg beside the door. From where he stood, he could hear Mary telling her mother what happened in great detail. Had he been better rested, Martin might have smiled at the excitement in the girl's voice, but he only glanced around the room, taking in the gun rack beside the china hutch, the little table, the rug between it and the open fireplace, and the two chairs flanking it. Beside the hearth, a wooden horse stood in a miniature corral gazing stoically upon the swirling, braided pattern of the rug.

Pulling a barely dry rag from his saddlebags, he sat on the stone hearth and began wiping down his guns. The entire belt was soaked as was the ammunition, but before he could recover his saddlebags and the dry cartridges inside it, Anna bustled out from the back room. She had blonde hair and a bright, kind face that invited Martin to trust her, but he kept his gaze averted.

"Mary insisted on going to school today," she said as she busied herself in the kitchen. "I tried to keep her home, but she refused to listen. I feel terrible."

"You did what you could, ma'am." Martin tried to reassure her as he caught the sound of Bill's footsteps on the porch. He put away his left-hand revolver and drew a deep, quiet breath in an attempt to convince himself these people could be trusted.

Anna turned an innocent smile on him and filled a cup with coffee. "Thank God for you. Mary told me you were nearly caught in the flood, trying to save her."

Martin said nothing as the door opened, and Bill stepped in, slicker in hand. He hung the coat and hat beside Martin's worn slicker, and as Bill turned toward the fire, the flash of a silver badge stopped Martin's heart. Resting a little heavier against the hearthstone, Martin kept his gaze on Bill. The knife in its leather sheath dug into his back. It did not reassure him, but it took the edge off his sense of vulnerability.

"That horse of yours has put down some miles," Bill mentioned in an attempt to start a conversation. "Where were you heading?"

"Wherever I could get," Martin replied in an attempt at friendliness.

Bill scoffed. "Not many places you can get in this rain. I'm surprised that bridge to Wichita Falls hasn't fallen in."

"It did, just after your daughter and I crossed it."

Bill cursed quietly. "Guess I won't be going to town for a while."

Martin turned his gaze to the flames and hoped the heat would hide the sudden chill running through his veins.

"Where's Mary?" Bill asked his wife.

"In bed," Anna replied as she brought an iron pot and hung it over the fireplace. "I'll bring her some food. You're welcome to sleep here by the fire, stranger."

It took Martin a moment to realize she was talking to him. "Oh. Thank you, ma'am."

She smiled and returned to the sideboard to mix biscuit dough.

Bill sank into the rocking chair facing Martin, sighed, and dug a pipe from his pocket. Out of the corner of his eye, Martin saw his attention catch and linger on the revolvers. He feigned ignorance of the man's curiosity, picked up a splint, and played with it while Bill packed his pipe.

"What's your line of work?" Bill asked, again attempting conversation.

"Cattle," Martin responded after a moment.

"Drover?"

Martin nodded. "When I can," he lied. "Between jobs at the moment."

Bill nodded. "Seems that's the way to make money since they started driving north and east. They pay pretty well?"

"Well enough for my needs," Martin replied.

Again Bill nodded and openly eyed the guns, but he said nothing as he put the pipe between his teeth. Martin stuck the splint against a burning log and held it while Bill puffed the tobacco into flame.

Martin studied Bill as he lit the pipe. He was not much out of his twenties, a deputy sheriff, according to his badge, but his expression and manner were wise. Martin relaxed a fraction when he realized this man was smart enough to not try something in front of his wife or daughter. That also meant he was smart enough to gain an edge before tipping his hand, and in his current state of exhaustion, Martin stood no chance against him in a battle of wits.

If Bill was aware of Martin's scrutiny, he gave no sign and thanked Martin genially as he sat back in his chair.

Anna nestled the biscuits in a Dutch oven and settled it into the coals. As she straightened, she noticed the bloodstain on Martin's side.

"You're hurt!"

Martin held up a hand to halt her well-intended advance. "It's alright, ma'am. I just tangled with a branch a few days ago." The lie came easily, but like a doctor feeling a pulse, Bill watched him while quietly puffing on the pipe.

"Even a little cut can turn septic," Anna warned. "You're sure you wouldn't like to clean it."

"Maybe later." He offered her a smile. "I'd really rather just sit here and dry out, ma'am."

"I have some antiseptic. I'll get it."

As she stepped between them headed for the back bedroom, Bill caught Martin's gaze and held it. The deputy was smart. He knew the truth, and in his gaze was a quiet warning. Anna left the door open, and both men could hear her speaking to Mary. In a gesture of good faith, Martin folded his hands in plain sight and kept them there. Bill pursed his lips and nodded once.

"Here you are." Anna handed him a bottle and a scrap of cloth. She went to the water bucket and ladled water into the basin she pulled from the cabinet then set it on the hearth beside him with a cloth. Then she knelt beside him and started lifting his shirt.

"Please, ma'am." He caught her hand and held it firmly but gently. He did not want her to see the wound, lest she could tell the difference between a bullet graze and the lash of a branch.

"No need to be modest," Anna countered gently. "I've tended enough of Bill's wounds in his life."

Bill scoffed and puffed his pipe. Reluctantly, Martin relaxed his grip. She showed no sign of unease at Martin's resistance to her care and no shock at the sight of the wound.

"It's a little red," she commented as her fingertips traced the swelling. "But, it's healing." She dipped the cloth and pressed it over the wound. Martin tensed but made no sound.

"You said you tangled with a branch," Bill asked. Martin nodded.

"Was trying to find a place to hole up for the night," he lied. "My horse ran me into a tree."

Bill hummed acknowledgment as though he did not fully believe him. Martin wondered how good a judge of horses Bill was.

Anna finished with the water and soaked the cloth with antiseptic.

"This will sting," she warned.

Martin nodded that he understood, but he wasn't prepared for the explosion of fire in his side. His breath caught, and stars erupted in front of his eyes as he fought to not pass out. By the time the burning eased, he could barely keep his eyes open.

"Hold this," Anna instructed, putting his right hand on the cloth. Then she straightened to check the stew. "We'll wrap it. Keep the infection out."

"That carbolic probably just burned out whatever infection he might have had," Bill teased his wife. "She's a great believer in it."

Martin scoffed and nodded agreement then realized there was no trace of a joke in Bill's expression. Bill betrayed no fear or even real concern. Anna sensed it, for she fixed her husband with a gently imploring gaze.

"Take off the badge, Bill. This man is our guest."

Bill looked up at her, then over at Martin, weighing his choices. With Anna standing so close, Martin doubted Bill would try to shoot him. He could easily reach out and pull the woman to him as a shield. Perhaps Bill thought the same thing, for he reached up with his left hand, unpinned the badge, and laid it beside him on the table.

Anna nodded approval. "Good." Then she went back to the bedroom and returned with a rolled bandage.

"Lift your shirt," she instructed. Martin obeyed, and she wrapped the bandage just above the line of his belt. "There. Feel better."

Martin smiled gratefully. "Yes, ma'am. Thank you."

"Thank you for saving our daughter."

Her words and the touch of her hand on his arm were the first signs of friendship he had experienced since the day Fernando died. Even at the mission, the padres held him at a distance, whether out of respect or pious devotion. Like the fire, Anna's gesture was more welcome than Martin could express.

Anna must have understood this. After gazing into his eyes for a moment, she straightened and started serving the stew. Even Bill's expression had softened some.

He waited for Anna to place the stew and coffee on the table. She had set the place nearest the fire in consideration for how cold he was, but sitting there required putting his back to Bill for the duration of his meal. Deciding to take the chance and show faith he did not feel, Martin sat and began to eat. Anna disappeared into the bedroom to feed the girl, taking with her the calm Martin felt until then. He ate slowly despite the ravenous hunger but managed to finish the stew and two biscuits. Then, he sat in uneasy silence, trying to think about what to do next.

"Would you like more?" Anna asked when she came back with a tray balanced against her hip.

Martin shook his head. "Thank you, but no."

"You look like you've been a while without a hot meal."

He feigned a shy smile. "Believe my stomach's shrunk from it, ma'am. But thank you. It was very good."

She glanced at her husband but gave no acknowledgment to his sulking mood.

"I believe I'll clean up and turn in," Anna said as she cleared the table. "Help yourself to more coffee. Bill, will you give me a hand?"

Bill's gaze locked with Martin's, more question than warning this time. The man did not want his wife to worry, and Martin did not blame him, but standing at the washtub would put his back squarely to Martin. Deliberately, Martin cradled his coffee in both hands and nodded toward the woman, a silent promise he would not harm either of them.

Bill seemed to believe him though his fingers tapped his holster deliberately as he rose slowly and turned to the washtub.

Martin filled his cup again from the pot beside the fire and watched the windows. A chill ran up his spine. His whole body felt heavy with exhaustion and craved the warmth of the hearth.

"Reckon I'll sit close to the fire," he said, giving Bill ample warning of his intentions. Then he rose and moved to sit on the hearth again. He knew it was unwise to sleep in such company, but it crept upon him and pounced soon after he sat down. He woke a few minutes later to a light tap on his arm. Fortunately, he came to quickly enough to realize Mary stood next to him. He half laughed, half sighed with relief.

"You startled me, little one."

Without pretense, the girl wrapped her arms around his neck in a strong hug. After overcoming this second surprise, he hugged her back, keenly aware of the moisture in his clothes soaking into the girl's thin cotton nightdress.

"Thank you," she said in his ear and kissed his cheek.

He patted her back and swallowed the lump forming in his throat. "You're welcome." In that moment, he did not care if he died tonight. This family was complete, whole, and loving. Only that mattered to him. Gently, he drew the girl back. "Careful, you'll get all wet again."

"Don't you have any other clothes?"

Martin coughed and glanced up to see Bill and Anna watching them. With a weak smile, he shook his head.

"I'll be alright, darling. Now you go on to bed."

But the girl remained. "Will you be here in the morning?"

"Maybe," he told her. "If I'm not, you be a good girl and mind your ma and pa. Y' hear?"

Mary nodded that she would and trotted away. She stopped at the door and waved. "Good night, mister."

Martin waved back, and the girl disappeared into the back room. He settled back and picked up his coffee as the sound of clanking dishes resumed. Glancing up, he caught Bill watching him, but the deputy's expression had lost its edge, and Bill turned away, hiding his face.

A log settled in the fireplace sending embers up the chimney. Martin watched the flames dance across its surface. He wondered briefly if his brothers had children if they were boys or girls. By his reckoning, his brothers would be near thirty. Likely, they were settled with families, probably on their own homesteads.

The clank of a dish on the floor made him jump. His right hand dropped to the revolver as his gaze shot to Bill, but the deputy, stone-faced, bent and picked up the plate. Martin's heart continued pounding long after the plate was washed and put up. Consciously, he relaxed his muscles, but tension lingered. He tilted his head back and tried to remember what he was thinking before the noise, but his mind refused to grasp it.

Finished with the dishes, Anna took the basin to the door and tossed the water onto the saturated ground. Bill put up the last plate and hung up the towel.

"Will you be staying up a while, dear?" Anna asked Bill, who nodded.

"I'll be up a little while yet." He hooked his thumbs in his belt and gazed down at Martin. Martin caught a frown of displeasure on Anna's face.

"Bill, you'll see to our guest's comfort?" Anna took Bill's arm. Martin averted his eyes, giving them what privacy he could without leaving the hearth.

"I will, Anna." Bill bent and kissed her cheek. "I'll be in before long."

"Don't be too long." She passed the rocking chair and paused. "I'll never be able to thank you enough, stranger."

A flood of thoughts froze his tongue. How could he express the value of her courtesy? Instead, he smiled his quiet, little smile, bowed his head briefly, and said, "Have a good night, ma'am."

"And you have the same." Her smile seemed so warm, so gentle; Martin was suddenly reminded of his mother and how much he missed such kindness. His heart began to ache at the sound of her skirts rustling against the doorframe. Then the latch clicked into place, and he was alone with Bill. In Anna's absence, a chill settled over the room again. Martin felt more than saw Bill's hand inching close to his gun.

"Don't," Martin whispered loud enough for the man to hear without his voice carrying through the closed door. "Don't make me kill you here, where your family will have to know and remember."

"Strange sentiment coming from a murderer," Bill whispered back.

Martin smirked and nodded. "I suppose it is." He lifted his gaze to the man. "Only I have some sense of family. Being an orphan, I know the pain of loss."

"Did you think of that when you killed that ranger and your employer? Terraza had a family as you must have known."

A fresh pain knifed his heart. Martin lowered his gaze. "Care to hear my side of things?"

Bill scoffed dismissively. "You'll just claim you're innocent…that someone else killed those men."

"No. I killed my share, but that's not what I'm referring to."

Bill frowned in confusion. His right hand lingered against the leather of his holster. As Martin sat with his arms crossed, he was at a disadvantage, but he had cards to play in this game of poker. Tired as he was, he would see the hand through.

"You've got a good thing here, Bill," Martin continued. "Before a couple of weeks ago, it was something I'd thought I'd lost forever. Then I found hope of having it again, a family to love and care for, and to rely on when I needed them. Then things happened, I had to make a choice, and that choice cost me that dream." Again he looked up into Bill's eyes, part pleading and part warning. "Take my advice, Bill; don't take the chance of losing what you have here."

Bill's expression softened as he considered this. He glanced toward the bedroom door, and the rigidity left his spine. He swallowed.

"I can't just let you walk out of here," he said.

"Yes, you can," Martin responded. "I'll not spend the night, and when Anna and Mary wake in the morning, they'll wonder if it really happened. In a few days, they'll forget I was ever here."

The deputy seemed unconvinced. His right hand twitched, and Martin relaxed his arms, readying himself to fight.

"Don't risk it," Martin pleaded. "You may kill me, but I'll kill you too. Which do you think Anna would rather have? The reward money? Or the husband she loves? Warm, alive, and loving like you are toward her and your little girl?"

"You're just trying to talk yourself out of this," Bill countered.

"Am I?" Martin let the challenge hang before going on. "That store clerk had the same choice…so did the marshal. They chose to take me, and they both died, and I walked away with a single scratch, nothing more. You're one man. Think you'll be luckier than those two combined?"

In the dancing firelight, the color drained from Bill's face. His shoulders relaxed as he seemed to decide.

"Alright," he said finally. "I owe you for saving my daughter, but I'll not let you stay in my house."

Martin nodded. Moving deliberately, he rose from the hearth, his clothes still damp, but that was a small price to pay for leaving this family as he had found it and better than it would have been without him. He pulled on his slicker and collected his rifle and saddlebags.

"Martin."

He stopped at the sound of his name and waited for Bill to speak.

"Thank you for talking me out of it."

Weary from long miles and worn by these last few moments, Martin could only offer a smile and a nod before stepping out the door and hurrying to the barn.

The rain had eased. He saddled up and headed north again, pausing to look back at the homestead where the firelight still glowed in the front windows. What happened there paled compared to his sins of days before, but this small victory buoyed his spirits, and he rode on, thankful for his good horse, the smell of wet earth and sage, and even for the chill that lingered well after dawn.

The Red River roared like a hungry cougar bringing down game. Martin stopped at the edge of the water and climbed down from the saddle to stretch. His sides ached from the nagging cough that started the day before. He knelt as Haze cropped grass and considered which direction to follow. Thought had become an effort almost beyond him with every additional day, adding its share of fatigue. Many times in the war, he and those he fought beside had marched and fought on will-power alone, but rest had always been in sight. Now, he pushed on, unsure if rest would come without death. In an effort to focus, he closed his eyes and bowed his head, willing the tension in his body to ease.

The morning was cool and still. A light breeze swept through the prairie of North Texas. Fall was coming, and for a moment, he laughed at himself for heading north into a cold, white winter, but he could not stay in Texas. New Mexico and Arizona held only vast loneliness and reaching them required several more weeks in a land that wanted his execution. North was the only direction left open to him, whatever he found.

Through the stillness, Martin heard a distant shot. He opened his eyes and listened. Another shot came from upstream. He climbed into the saddle and turned Haze east along the willows at a quick lope.

In a small hollow, a man lay dead. Two others hunkered, one behind a wagon, the other behind a log. Martin stumbled into the open it too suddenly in the close confines of the brush. The man behind the wagon fired at him. Martin veered Haze to the left, drew, and fired back on reflex. A second-round from the other man whistled past his head so close his ear tingled. Haze whirled as the man in black and white prisoner's stripes, stood up for a better shot. Martin killed him with two rounds to the chest.

The prisoner wilted like a dropped rope, and Martin turned back to the wagon where the man behind it now lay still. He circled around and drew up staring down at a Texas Ranger badge pinned to blood-stained gray vest. Martin felt sick at his string of poor luck, and knew things held no promise of improving. He slid off his horse and crouched beside the man, taking the revolver from his limp fingers.

Struggling to breathe, the man looked up at him. Blood foamed at his mouth, and the wound in his chest sucked and hissed.

"I didn't know," Martin muttered in apology.

"You're not…one of the gang?"

Martin shook his head.

The ranger laughed, and the laugh grew into a racking cough that ended in a wheeze. Martin went to his horse for a canteen. He knelt beside the ranger and offered water. The ranger pushed it away.

"Don't waste it," he said. "Did you get him?"

Martin nodded. "He's over yonder."

"Least that's done." The ranger's eyes wandered to the distance. "Which way you headed?"

"North."

The ranger grunted understanding. "Goin' by Amarillo?"

"Maybe."

Right shoulder shattered, the ranger dug a watch from his hip pocket with his left hand. He handed it to Martin and unpinned his badge.

"Take that," he said of the watch, "to the teacher, Miss Leighton. Tell her, I love her." He gulped air before going on. "Take my badge, and Carl's…" He nodded toward the dead man a few feet away. "…to the ranger captain up there. Tell him what happened."

Martin stared down at the badge smeared with blood, the sickness thickening. He looked back to the ranger. His mouth now gaped with effort for breath that would not come. He reached out with his remaining good hand and, gripping Martin's arm, pulled himself up. Martin held him there, the bloody fingers digging deep through the cloth until the ranger's eyes lost focus and his muscles relaxed. Martin eased him back against the wagon wheel, but the hand remained clamped on his arm, frozen in a vice-like death grip. The back of his throat tingled. He tried to pry the fingers loose, but they refused to bend. The dead ranger's eyes still stared at him, and Martin had the sudden irrational image of the dead man dragging him down into Hell.

Steeling himself against the nightmarish image, Martin drew his knife. He sliced wrist, spilling blood not yet clotted. The fingers relaxed, and Martin worked his sleeve free. The hand dropped with a light thud to the sandy ground, and Martin scrambled away to a willow thicket. There the sickness overcame him. On hands and knees, he heaved his stomach empty. When the convulsions stopped, he remained there, trembling. Ironically, he felt thankful he consumed only water that morning, having no food to eat. Martin sat back on his heels and filled his lungs with cool morning air before a fit of coughing seized him. When it ended, he sat hunched and winded. His side and head ached worse now, and he deserved it.

Glancing over his shoulder at the scene, he wished it had only been a dream. Texas once meant hope for him, now it only meant sleepless nights and dreams with the faces of dead men constantly reminding him of the trail he fell on and would follow him to his own grave.

On shaking legs, he walked down to the river and rinsed his mouth. Then with dutiful weariness, he searched the wagon for a shovel. Finding none, he took a plate from beside the fire.

It took a day and a half to dig two graves in the muddy earth. The rangers he buried first, covering them with what stones he could find. Deciding the dead men would not need what they left behind. He searched their pockets before he covered them, finding ten dollars and a letter between the two corpses. It was then Martin decided to leave the prisoner where he fell despite the ongoing noise of scavengers gorging themselves on his flesh. The prisoner was a member of the Jackson gang raiding along the border of the Indian Nations, and Martin did not care to further abuse his skinned and bloodied hands by digging a third grave.

As the ranger asked, Martin took the watch and the two badges and rode north, keeping to low ground where possible. He camped without fire despite the constant chill and worsening cough. With what lay behind him in that hollow, he had reason to worry. Jackson's gang roamed this country, and if they found the prisoner's body, the trail Martin left would not be hard to follow. Once or twice, it occurred to him he was being a fool. What did it matter that the ranger's sweetheart knew he was dead or not? But the thought of leaving it undone left a worse sense of dread in the pit of his stomach than the threat of being caught. He realized this, but could not understand it. Despite the lingering anxiety, he slept more often than he cared to. He blamed it on the growing illness.

The little town of Amarillo looked as thin as Martin felt when he rode down the main street six days after the rangers' deaths. He paused near the general store and gazed down the street at what looked to be a church on a short ride outside of town. Cast in deep shadow by the setting sun, it looked no different from any other building.

"Help you, stranger?"

Martin glanced over into the eyes of a man with a sheriff's badge and nearly laughed at his luck for finding lawmen without trying. He managed to speak without mirth in his tone. "I'm looking for Miss Leighton. Would she be over to the school?"

The lawman shook his head. "T'day's Saturday. No school held today."

"Where might I find her?"

"Why are you asking?" The man settled his left hand on his hip; his right rested palm-inward against the holster on his hip. His finger tapped the leather lightly in absent thought, apparently an unconscious habit, but Martin wearily took it as a warning.

"It's my concern, sheriff," he said calmly. "I don't intend trouble."

The lawman studied him as though weighing the truth of his words. Martin gave him the time in still silence. He had no intention of letting the sunset with him in this town, but rushing a lawman could get him pushed out sooner or settled in the jail at the far end of town. Finally, the lawman nodded toward the silhouetted building.

"Down at the end of the street," the sheriff said. "You'll find a little wagon trail leads out behind that church to a rooming house, not quite a mile out of town. Ask for her there."

"Thank you." Martin nodded to him and walked Haze to the end of town. All the while, he was aware of the stares from the people on the boardwalks and the street. They were the typical stares such settlers gave drifters, or so he tried to convince himself. Still, a small measure of relief settled his nerve once he was out of sight down the little wagon trail.

The shack could barely be considered a rooming house, one story with a lean-to added on the west side for a small extra room. Martin worried he took the wrong turn or heard the sheriff's directions wrong. He stopped at the gate, unsure whether to proceed or turn back when a woman stepped out on the porch. She ran her empty hands down her apron, and Martin realized it was near the evening meal.

"Come on in," she called. "The gate's not locked."

Martin nodded and leaned down to unlatch the gate. He rode through and closed the gate without dismounting. The little farmyard was neatly kept with chickens and a handful of goats loitering near the haystack. Haze pricked his ears at the goats and snorted a warning. Martin slapped the stallion's neck with a sharp, "No," and Haze continued forward, but his left ear pivoted toward the little herd. Martin decided it was not worth the fight. He turned his attention to the woman on the porch.

She was thin-faced with a harsh expression. Her hair was tied back in a tight bun. Martin wondered if her expression came from the hairstyle.

"Have we met before?" the woman asked, cocking her head as Martin neared the porch.

"No, ma'am."

She set her hands on her hips. "If you've come for food, I haven't anything for drifters."

Her tone cut deep, but Martin forced himself not to react.

"Thanks, ma'am, but I've come on another matter." A shiver ran up Martin's back. Despite it, his skin felt hot. "I'm looking for Miss Leighton. Might you be her?"

"No, I'm Missus Reardon. I own this place. Alice Leighton is my tenant."

"May I speak with her?" He barely finished before he noticed her standing in the doorway. She stepped forward. Young, pale, and dark-haired, Martin saw why the ranger had taken to her.

"What is it?" She read the grim lines in Martin's face, and they brought her fear.

Martin dismounted and climbed the steps to stand before her. He started to reach for his hat and remembered he had none.

"Miss Leighton..." His throat tightened. He looked down at the porch boards as he reached inside his vest pocket. "I've come to bring you this," he said finally, holding out the watch.

She took it and stared at the plain gold case. When she opened the lid, her beautiful lips parted, and her cheeks blanched.

"It's Dillon's." Her hand went to her mouth as tears welled in her eyes. "How did you get this?"

"Your man was killed in a shootout," Martin explained, remembering cutting himself free of the dead man's grip. "I was with him when he died. He asked me to bring you this and tell you...he loved you."

Her eyes flared. "Is that all?"

"Yes, ma'am."

She glared at him, then turned away sharply and disappeared inside, slamming the door behind her.

Martin didn't move. Words of apology burned inside him, but their sheer inadequacy kept him silent.

"Is that all you came for?"

He glanced at Missus Reardon. Her face, ashen by nature, had taken on a deeper frown.

"Yes, ma'am." He descended the steps, depriving her of the opportunity to order him off her property. When he reached Haze, he turned back. "Could you tell me where I might find the captain of rangers?"

"Captain Neil lives at the jail. He dislikes his own cooking. So, if you don't find him there, he'll be at one of the cafés."

"Much obliged, ma'am." Martin climbed back into the saddle.

Missus Reardon stood on the porch, arms crossed, watching him leave.

Martin exited the gate and turned Haze back down the trail to Amarillo, glad to be done with the place and Missus Reardon. He had hoped that with telling Miss Leighton, some of the weight would lift from his shoulders. Instead, it rested harder. Telling her had been easy. Seeing her grief hurt him as much as the ranger's death.

Two hours of daylight remained when he walked his horse back through town to the jail. With no one there, he led the brown down to the livery for water, then returned and waited for the lawman in a chair left beside the door where he fell asleep. He awoke to find two men with badges staring down at him.

"You're looking to get charged with loitering, son," the white-haired one said with more mirth than malice.

Martin ran his hands over his face. The sun was gone. He'd have to wait nearly an hour for the moon or ride slow if he rode again at all. He looked back up at the lawmen and recognized the sheriff.

"We tolerate little from saddle tramps in this town," the sheriff said. Silent warning exuded from his posture and tone.

Ignoring the comment, Martin looked to the other wearing the ranger's star.

"Would you be Captain Neil?"

The man nodded.

"If I could speak to you for a few minutes, I'll be on my way."

"Certainly. Come inside." He unlocked the door and stepped into the darkness, where he struck a match and lit a lamp on the desk. The sheriff followed, but Martin held back at the doorway.

Neil checked the pot on the cold stove. He glanced back at Martin and waved him inside. "Come on in. We don't bite unless you're a lawbreaker. Sorry, I don't have any good coffee to offer."

"That's alright." Martin took a step across the threshold, eyeing the walls. How long since he stood within a building, let alone one of stone? Too long, and the quarters felt too close.

"Could I get you some water?" Neil asked.

"No. Thank you."

The captain turned a mildly puzzled look on him. "In a hurry?"

Martin stupidly shot the man a look, and his blood chilled. "Not particularly," he replied in his best attempt at a casual tone.

"Well, if you don't mind, I would like a cup of coffee while we parlay. Have a seat."

Reaching up for his hat, Martin self-consciously ran his fingers through his now shaggy hair. He sat down in the chair at the front of the desk facing the door. Inwardly he cursed himself for tipping his hand. He had to slow down and let them have some control. If he kept calm, casual, he would walk away from this and go on with his life.

Leaving his hat on the rack beside the door, Neil went out back with the coffee pot and returned with it filled with water. He added grounds to the percolator and stoked the fire in the little stove.

The sheriff took a seat behind the other desk in the corner and picked up a stack of papers.

"Missing your hat?" the sheriff asked.

"Lost it in a storm a few days back."

"Bad luck, losing your hat," Neil commented as he shut the stove door and adjusted the pot over the hole. "A man usually finds another pretty quick in this country."

"I haven't the money," Martin lied.

Neil grunted that he understood, then held up a finger and disappeared through a side door into what looked like a bunkroom. Martin listened to the scrapes and clatters of a trunk being dragged across the floor and opened while fixing his gaze on the window beside the sheriff's desk, aware of the sheriff's scrutiny. A minute later, Neil returned with a black, flat-brimmed, flat-crowned hat with a tooled leather band.

"Try that," he said. "Came off some drifter that got shot a few months back. Looks like he just bought it."

Martin raised an eyebrow at Neil. If losing a hat was bad luck, how much worse was wearing the hat of a man who died shortly after purchasing it? But he was a beggar and tried it on. It fit a little snug but would stretch in time.

"Now," Neil said, easing his weight onto the edge of his desk and crossing his arms. "What did you want to talk about?"

Martin pulled off the hat and set it on his knee, keenly aware of the captain's position between him and the door.

"It's about a couple of your men," Martin said. "They were killed in a shootout with a prisoner six days ago."

"Where?"

"On the banks of the Red, about a hundred miles southeast of here."

"And how do you know about it?"

Moving slowly and deliberately, Martin reached inside his vest and pulled the badges out of his shirt pocket. He laid them on the desk in front of Neil. Then he drew the paper from his jacket pocket.

"I stopped for water one morning. I heard the shots and followed them to where I found your two men. One was dead. The prisoner was killed, and your other man, McGannon, was wounded but still alive. He lived long enough to tell me where to bring those."

"And that was all?" Neil's gaze was piercing. He barely glanced at the badges.

"There was a watch he wanted to be returned to Miss Leighton."

Neil's jaw worked as he looked over to the sheriff who had listened without pretense.

"You believe what he's saying, Johnny?"

The sheriff nodded once. "So far."

Neil turned his measuring gaze back to Martin. His right hand perched on a stack of papers. "So you just go around doing errands for dead strangers, is that it?"

Again, Martin's unease deepened, but he made no effort to speak. Absently, his hand rested on the brim of the new hat, his right trigger finger stroking the band.

"I knew Dillon McGannon, and I doubt he waxed poetic about his Alice Leighton. He wasn't that type. In fact, he wrote her a letter to propose. Never was a man for words or ways." Neil sipped his coffee. "So, there must be some other motive for you coming here."

"I was headed this way."

"Really?" Neil's sarcasm was plain. "Where from?"

"South."

Neil chuckled briefly, straightened, and paced around the desk to stand by the chair on the far side from Martin. "I heard about a man from the Hill Country, headed north and running from a noose for killing a ranger. You kind of look like that man's description. Apparently, he is one too quick to use his gun."

Martin felt the blood drain from his face. His throat tightened, and his breath stilled. The image of the dead man pulling him down to Hell returned as the stone walls seemed to close in on him. Bowing his head, he tried to find comfort in knowing he could now sleep.

"Didn't you hear, Neil?" the sheriff asked without looking up from his work.

"Hear what?"

"That *El Muerto* fellow drowned outside of Wichita Falls. Never found his body, but a deputy down there saw him go in trying to save a little girl."

"You don't say." Neil considered Martin again. With hope renewed, Martin met the captain's gaze and never looked away. His path to the door was now clear, but he didn't look at it and didn't consider it. He kept his silence.

Neil scoffed. "Got a poker face like a professional gambler." He looked down at the badges, and his mouth hardened into a grim line. "I didn't hold much love for either those boys, but McGannon left Alice Leighton with a child on the way and no ring. For that reason, I'd like to see the man that killed him dead. I don't suppose you'd mind telling me what happened that morning from the beginning."

"I already told you."

"Why don't you tell me more? Like how the prisoner came to have a gun."

"I have no idea what happened before my arrival."

"And you came riding in at the end of the fight?"

"That's right."

"And you made sure the other two were dead?"

"I checked them, yes."

"Where were they shot?"

"Hays in the heart and the prisoner in the head. McGannon took two bullets to the chest and died slow."

"And you buried them?"

Martin nodded. "I buried the rangers. I had no shovel and left the prisoner to the buzzards. After I found the letter of execution, I figured it would be fitting."

Neil studied him again and smiled. "Guess I'd've done the same thing." He went back to the stove and lifted the pot. "You want some coffee now?"

"If it's all the same to you, I'd rather get some rest."

Curiosity lifted Neil's brows. "It's early yet."

"I'm used to sleeping with the sun."

Neil's eyes narrowed. "Alright, but see that you don't leave town. I want to talk to you in the morning."

Martin nodded that he understood and rose from the chair.

"Of course, if you don't stay in town, I might be inclined to think you killed those rangers trying to save your friend Jackson."

Martin glanced down at the dead man's hat.

"You didn't give a name either," Neil said casually, but it was like the warning rattle of a snake.

"Chigger," Martin replied, falling back on a nick-name the men of his regiment had called him after his first fight.

Neil considered the name, repeating it twice as though testing the sound. "Heard of a man in the war that went by that name. They said he could slip behind enemy lines and kill Yankees while they slept. You heard of that?"

"A time or two," Martin replied, keeping his tone light despite his skin beginning to crawl at the lawman's recollection.

Neil's expression became haunted as a memory surfaced for him. He shook it off. "We've all done things we'll regret," he said. "Best, it's all left behind us."

Martin nodded in agreement and pulled on the hat.

"Good night, gentlemen."

Stepping into the darkness brought no ease to Martin's mind. From the end of the street, four men rode side-by-side. They stopped a shop-keeper closing up his store. As Martin untied the stallion, he noticed the shop-keeper gesturing in his direction. He mounted up and turned the brown toward the church.

"Hey, you! You, with the Mex nag!"

Haze stopped almost without Martin's command. Martin stared straight toward the church as the lights from the town reflected off the white headstones of the cemetery.

"We know you killed Jackson, left him to the buzzards."

With a heavy sigh of acceptance, Martin turned his horse sideways to the four riders.

"How do you know?"

"You're the only one to ride away from that camp. Couldn't've faced Jackson in a fair fight if you did that." The one that spoke sat to the right of the middle. The moon glowed at the edge of the horizon and cast a ghostly light over the town. Martin was aware of people beyond the windows and doors, a world away from where he sat. Even Neil and the sheriff stayed inside. Quietly, Martin smiled and shook his head.

"You know, gentlemen, with the way my luck's gone, I was beginning to worry death would never catch up to me." His lips hardened, and the fear stepped back, yielding to the fighting spirit. "I guess it's up to you to tell the devil I'll be along in a minute."

There were four, and Martin was no fool. With the town watching, he opened the ball and shot the speaker before his hand was half-way to his gun. The man to his left went down next, and Martin charged between the last two shooting the one to the right as his gun came to level. The one on the left struggled, his gun hung up in the holster. Without hesitation, Martin put a bullet in his brain.

Haze twitched and pranced as Martin turned him back to the line of bodies sprawled motionless across the hard-packed dirt street. The speaker laid face up, blood pouring from a wound in his throat. He choked and gagged, eyes bulging. Martin stared down at him, knowing this would one day be his fate.

"Rest in peace...if you can," he said without malice as the body stilled, and the head fell to the side.

Holstering his revolver, Martin looked up to find Neil, the sheriff, and the town in general staring in disbelief and horror, but these dead at his feet brought little unrest. He walked Haze up the street, pausing beside the jail.

"You're welcome, Captain." He touched spur to Haze, and the stallion leaped into a dead run. Once out of town, he found the North Star and followed it.

By moonlight, he rode until dawn twilight. Then he found water tucked in a thicket of willows. He was tired, but he had made yet another choice he would pay badly for, and other than to rest Haze, he would have to ride straight through to the border. With little available cover, he hid in a willow thicket and unsaddled Haze and dried him letting him graze. Though logically, he knew any posse was likely hours behind, Martin felt pressured to move on. He forced himself to rest for Haze's sake. Once Haze ceased grazing and napped, Martin saddled up again and rode out at a steady pace.

The miles fell away, and he kept glancing at his back trail. No column of dust followed him, but the nagging sense of pursuit lingered. He didn't know when he passed out of Texas into the Nations, but the land ahead gave him little hope for water. That night, the waning moon gave too little light, forcing Martin to stop. He didn't sleep. With hunger and thirst nagging him, he leaned against a rock wrapped in a blanket and dozed. He woke repeatedly in the night to Haze's nervous knickers. Coyotes howled in the distance but never came close enough to threaten horse or man. Martin moved closer to the stallion, and Haze lowered his head to be scratched.

"Only you and me, Hazy Boy," he said as he ruffled the stallion's forelock.

Comforted by the contact with his companion, Haze slept, but Martin remained awake agitated by his dulling senses. When the first rays of sun came, he saddled up again, keeping a northern heading. The days and nights blended together, and he lost track of time. There was little chance they could pass through the Nations without attracting attention, but there was also little chance Texas law would follow them through the territory.

Then one late evening, he came upon a homestead. Like so many others, it was clean and well-kept. Unlike others, paintings marked the adobe walls. Martin knew little about Indians. What he did know was that with the white-man's ways, these settlers could just as easily know from where he came and why his horse was worn down from hard riding, but he had been two days without freshwater, and without that, Haze could not go on. The well at the center of the yard offered that much. Getting to it was risky.

As the first lamp was lit, the front door opened, and a man stepped out and lit a pipe. He sat down against the wall and smoked quietly with his dog beside him. Through the window, Martin could see and hear a woman's voice as she readied her children for bed. Then she joined the man on the porch. Martin watched and waited until the man and woman also turned in for the night. He waited an hour longer to be sure they slept. Then through the inky blackness, he led Haze to the well and drew water for him.

Inside, the dog barked. The windows had been left open, and Martin in his exhaustion had failed to judge the wind. He turned to mount and froze as a hammer clicked to full cock.

A voice spoke to him from the shadows of the barn. He shook his head that he didn't understand.

"What do you want, stranger?" the voice asked in clear English.

"Just water for my horse, that's all."

"You too proud to ask water from a Cherokee?"

"No, sir," Martin tried to ease the nerves that threatened to shake him, but he'd been too long without food.

"On the run?"

Hesitating, Martin nodded.

"What for?"

Keeping his hands in plain sight on the saddle, Martin turned his head, trying to see the man.

"I killed four men in Amarillo," Martin explained.

"Were they white men?"

"I think so."

"Bad men? Or Lawmen?"

"Arlo Jackson's gang, what was left of it."

The man chuckled. Gravel grated under his boots as he walked into the open.

"In that case, take all the water you need. Bad Texas white men don't mean anything to me."

The man came and stood across the well from him as Martin reached out and started pulling up the bucket. It took more effort than his body remembered, but finally, the bucket reached the edge, and he poured it into the trough for Haze. Then he dropped the bucket again for himself. Halfway up, the rope slipped, and the bucket dropped back to the water below. Martin gripped the rope again and fought to bring the bucket up. When it reached the edge, he almost lost it again, but the man caught the rope.

"Thanks." Martin uncorked his canteen and pushed it into the bucket. It gave out a long, satisfying gurgle as it filled.

"How long you been riding?"

Martin shrugged. "The moon was four days past full when I left Amarillo. I don't know how many days."

"When last did you eat or sleep?"

Martin lifted the canteen to his lips and drank deep of the cool water. It sent a chill through his body. The night was cool, and the man wore a coat, but the thin slicker offered Martin little warmth. The chill overcame him, and he couldn't hide it.

The man looked over Haze and seemed not to notice Martin.

"Your horse needs rest. He's been ridden too long. If you want to keep on, I'll trade for him."

"Nothing can replace him." Martin finished filling the canteen and hung it on his saddle.

"I don't have room in the house, but there is space in the barn for you to rest, and my woman has some food. It would be cold, but it would be food."

Martin said nothing as he readied to ride. He turned to gather his reins and the man stopped him.

"Do it for your horse, friend," he said. "You won't trade. Would you instead run him to his death?"

For seemingly the first time, Martin looked at Haze. The horse stood head down. He'd thinned down some, and though the dog still barked inside, Haze didn't even raise his head in curiosity. Then he studied the man and sensed only friendliness in him. How long had he gone without a friend? Had it only been a few weeks?

Worn past the point of strength or will, Martin relented. "I can pay you for what he eats in work or coin. Whatever you think fair."

The man held up a hand. "We'll worry about that later." He called over his shoulder to the house in his Indian tongue. A light came on, and Martin saw the woman's shadow moving in the kitchen.

"Come." The man gestured for Martin to follow him to the barn. With a gentle touch, Martin woke Haze and led him after the man.

The barn was not big, but it was adequate and efficient, allowing enough room in the stalls for a big draft horse to turn easily. There was an empty stall near the door, and while Martin unsaddled and dried Haze's back, the man forked hay into the manger.

"You come on up to the house when you're ready," the man said before he left.

Martin watched him go, grateful for the kindness shown. He led Haze into the stall and left the horse to sleep or eat as he pleased. Before he made it to the door, the haystack caught his eye. They could wait a few more minutes while he made up his bed. Food would only make it that much harder to do later.

Laying out his bedroll, he dropped into the hay to test the feel and instantly fell into a deep, un-waking sleep.

Refuge

Sunlight seeped through the cracks in the siding when Martin woke. From the gold hew, he guessed it was just past dawn, but as he stepped out into the light, he suffered momentary disorientation.

A child's voice spoke from behind him, making him jump, but his hand stopped short of reaching for a gun. Calmly, he faced the boy who spoke again, but he shook his head that he did not understand.

What the boy said then sounded derogatory, and he jabbed his thumb toward the house. When Martin frowned questioningly at him, the boy grabbed his arm and pulled him forward, shouting orders to his two siblings.

A woman stood at the sideboard, working bread dough. She glanced up when they entered and spoke sharply to the boy. Martin frowned, trying to divine her meaning in the gestures and expression. She repeated herself, this time waving her hand toward the table near the fire. Still groggy, Martin moved to the chair and sank into it. He was rewarded with a curt nod. Then the woman shooed the three children back outside and turned to the fire. She bent and stirred a pot that issued scents that made his stomach rumble.

"Coffee?" she asked, the word heavily accented. It took Martin a moment to realize what she asked; when he did, he felt like an excited little boy.

"Yes, please!"

It was hot and fresh and soothing. Martin grasped the cup in both hands and almost huddled around it. If this was all she gave him, he could have felt no less gratitude.

Silence fell over the room, but it was friendly and threatened to draw Martin back to sleep when a man's voice called through the open window. Starting out of a doze, Martin's hand went to his gun, dropping the cup as the door swung open. When he recognized the man from the night before, he felt instant shame as the man, the woman, and the children stared questioningly at him.

"Please forgive me," he pleaded, picking up the cup. He started to untie his neckerchief to clean up the spilled coffee, but the woman crouched beside him and stilled his hands with a gentle touch.

He was afraid to look into her eyes, afraid of what he would find there, but she spoke gently to him, and there was no holding back the emotion he felt. To hide it, he rested his elbows on the table, covered his face with his hands, and fought to control his breathing while the spell passed.

He was distantly aware of them moving about the cabin, speaking to each other as though nothing had happened. When he was ready to join them, the food was ready.

"Here," the man offered him the chair with its back to the fireplace. "You'll be warm, and you can see out all windows." He gestured to encompass the three windows and door.

"Thank you," Martin said, but doubted the words fully expressed what he felt.

"I understand these things," the man said as he slid into the chair at Martin's left. "Have no fear. You're safe here, friend."

A new uneasiness sparked in Martin's brain. "You call me friend very easily."

"Indeed. It's the way the missionaries have taught us."

"What missionaries?"

The man thought for a moment. "I believe the whites call them Quakers."

Understanding struck Martin. He had known a Quaker woman who had tended the sick and wounded in a Yankee camp and remembered her ways.

"Please forgive me."

The man waved his hand. "Ah. You haven't had much reason to trust. You've been a long time running. After all, you slept for nearly two days."

Martin choked off a curse and started out of his chair. The man put a hand on his arm.

"Sit down, friend. Relax. Once you have eaten, you can run off again, but I think it would be foolish to miss my woman's cooking."

The woman spoke to him, and he chuckled. "She doesn't like me bragging about it."

Martin looked up at the woman as she served him. "You understand English?" he asked.

She nodded.

"She doesn't speak it, but she understands it well. So do the children."

The oldest boy, with his stern look, spoke to his father, who rebuked him.

"Uzumati dislikes everything about the whites," the man explained. "Please forgive his rudeness."

Martin regarded the boy who openly glared at him. "Reckon you got reason," he said. "You don't seem like the type to hate without a reason."

The man nodded. "He does. His mother died at the hands of bad white men who came here as you have. He was very small, but he remembers."

Understanding cut deep. There were no words fitting for a response.

"Ah, I forgot. I am called Silas. My woman is called Ahyokah, and my sons, Uzumati, Honovi, and Hakan."

Martin nodded to each as they were introduced.

"Shall we call you 'Stranger'?"

He considered giving them the name he had given the lawmen in Amarillo, and then decided against it.

"It's fitting," he said.

"Good." Silas turned to his family, and Martin sat quietly while they prayed.

The food proved to be better than Silas's boast. Martin ate two plates full before stopping himself, afraid he'd become sick from eating too much. The children helped clean up, and though he did not understand their words, Martin believed he understood them. Most of all, he believed he understood the oldest boy, and wished somehow to extend to him some sympathy, but he did not know how.

"Your horse could use much rest," Silas said after filling his coffee cup.

"I know."

"You could use rest, too."

Martin smiled. "Yes."

"And I could use another man to help prepare for winter," Silas continued. "Uzumati is still a boy. He works hard, and will fill a man's roll in a year or two, but..." Silas shrugged. "Rest your horse, Stranger. Get your own strength back. Perhaps, hiding here a while will let your trail die."

His reasons were valid, and Martin had failed to consider the last one. But as he watched the woman and children do their chores, he worried.

"It's not worth the risk to them," he said quietly.

Silas scoffed. "You're the first white man we've seen in nearly two years. No law comes into the Nations, and you could almost pass for one of us if you kept yourself shaved."

Martin ran his hands over the scruff of beard that had taken over his face.

"Hide here, friend. Put your guns away and become peaceful again."

"What makes you think I was before?"

Silas appreciated his candor and smiled, but his expression sobered. "It's the guilt I see in your eyes. I don't know what you did, or why. I don't want to know. Every man deserves a chance to gain God's love. You believe that much, don't you?"

"Never thought much of it," Martin replied. "Been a long time since I thought I was worthy of it."

"You are worthy, friend. I sense that about you."

Ahyokah stepped around the table and put an arm around her husband's shoulders. The boys were climbing to the loft. The oldest held back warily studying Martin.

Raising his hands in a peaceful gesture, Martin hoped to at least ease the boy's fears, but it did nothing to win the boy's favor. He turned and climbed the ladder, slapping each rung as he went. Martin shook his head and stared into the fire.

Silas pushed up from the table. "We'll sit out on the porch a while. You're welcome to join us."

"Thank you, but I believe I'll return to the barn," he said with a shy smile. "I guess I'm not done sleeping."

Silas chuckled and took his pipe down from the mantel. "You can decide in the morning if you'll stay or not."

"Yes, sir, and…thank you."

Silas smiled and nodded in return, then followed Martin out to the porch but said no more as Martin crossed the yard back to the barn.

It took a while for him to fall asleep. He had to admit the offer was tempting, but he feared what staying here too long would do to endanger the family. Perhaps he could stay a few weeks, let Haze rest and regain the flesh he'd lost. If trouble followed him, he could move on before the threat involved this family. He would stay, he finally decided, for a little while. When he finally dropped off to sleep, he felt a vague sense of humanness return to that dark void inside him.

The work proved rewarding. In the weeks that followed, fear settled and fell away with each passing day that failed to bring unwanted visitors. A neighbor stopped on his way to town and spoke with Silas. Martin kept his distance out of worry that word of his presence would spread. He made friends with the two youngest boys, and they began teaching him words, proudly showing him their favorite places to play and things to do. Even the oldest boy took part in this, his strict corrections doing little to unease Martin. With time, his manner seemed less harsh, and grew more patient and proud to teach his ways to a stranger.

Then one day a rider and wagon appeared on the horizon. They were a mile out when Silas recognized them as old friends and welcomed them warmly. The rider, a grizzled man in fringed and beaded buckskins, hurried ahead and greeted Silas and his family with a whoop. His horse to a stop and the big man slid from the saddle to embrace Silas in a playful bear hug.

"Silas! You old cougar! How have you been?"

"Very well. Life has been good to us."

Martin hung back as before and watched as the big man, with his age whitened blond hair and laugh lined face, greeted Ahyokah with a gentler hug and each boy with a man's handshake. His attention shifted to the wagon as it rattled into the yard with a scruffy gray dog trotting along beside the front wheel. A woman, young and lithe, guided the horses with a firm hand from the seat. She cast a suspicious glance at Martin as she pulled up beside the trough.

"Lena, come see how much these young 'uns have grown."

She hopped down with the grace of an antelope, and her expression instantly turned friendly as she faced the family. She spoke to them in their Cherokee and quickly engaged their attention, but her companion regarded Martin for the first time.

"And who's this?"

"We call him 'Stranger'," Silas explained. "He has been helping me ready for winter."

The big man offered his hand. "Jack Miller."

Martin took the rough, big hand and returned its strong grip easily. "Mister Miller."

"Ah!" Miller waved his hand. "No need to be so formal. Few enough people in this country without formal society butting in." He turned his attention to Silas. "Lena and I were on our way west. Wondered if you wanted to come with us."

Silas shook his head. "Sorry, Jack. My place is here."

"Even for a few weeks? I need a skinner."

"I gave that up; you know that."

Miller sighed. "Well, I figured it wouldn't hurt to ask. You were one of the best skinners I ever had working for me."

Silas looked at Martin. "I can't join you, but Stranger here might."

Martin shook his head. "I don't know if I'd be of any use."

But Miller's interest was piqued. "You know anything about skinning, son?"

"I've skinned a few deer, but nothing really to speak of."

"He's handy," Silas put in. "He'll learn quick. He's picked up enough words of Cherokee to understand us in just a few weeks."

Miller's eyebrows went up. "Well, if you can spare him…"

"Silas…" Martin started to protest, but the man cut him off with an upraised hand.

"Your work here is done," he said wisely. "Here's a chance for you to move on without riding alone."

Not until then did Martin realize he had become too comfortable here. He knew from the beginning he could not stay forever, but that knowledge had faded in a very short time.

"If you're sure," he said, trying to let the idea settle.

"I am sure, and Jack here is a good man to work for."

Martin forced himself to relent. He looked to Jack Miller. "When will you leave?"

"In the morning, if it ain't too much trouble for us to stay here one night."

"No trouble."

As their conversation wandered to other topics, Martin became aware of the two women looking at him. Ahyokah smiled deviously. The young woman, Lena, looked less than pleased, and suddenly, Martin felt like a prize bull being considered for stud. Both women smiled at the color that rose to his cheeks. Awkwardly, he excused himself and climbed into the wagon, ignoring the warning growl of the dog. A stern word from Lena silenced her, and Martin moved the wagon to the barn. Then he busied himself unhitching the team.

Lena silently joined him, and they worked without a single spoken word between them. Once the horses were watered and turned out into the pasture, Lena returned to the house. Martin resolutely ignored her and returned to his chores. That was how he stumbled across Uzumati hiding in the loft.

The boy turned his face away, but not before Martin saw the tears. Puzzled, he glanced back down the ladder, considering what other work he could do, but all was done except for feeding the stock. So he took up the pitchfork and went to work.

"You know," Martin said lightly. "Hay dust has a bad way of making my eyes water."

The boy looked up with swollen, curious eyes.

"Yeah," Martin went on. "Every time I go and hide in a loft, my eyes just start pouring."

"Not hay," the boy retorted in the first English Martin had heard him speak.

Martin stopped his work and considered the boy, waiting to see if he would offer more.

"Why do people have to leave?" Uzumati asked finally.

"I don't know, son," Martin replied. He leaned the pitchfork against a rafter and sank down beside the boy. "I've asked myself that question many times. I still don't have an answer."

"Then stay. Papa needs you. He just don't know."

"Your papa's got you, and that's a whole lot more than I could ever be for him."

"But I can't work as hard as you."

"You will someday, and then you'll wonder if the work will ever stop."

Uzumati grunted disdainfully. "I already wonder."

Martin chuckled. "Yeah, I guess so."

They were silent then, and Martin considered leaving before the boy asked him another question, but he waited too long.

"Will you ever come back?"

Martin thought about it a long moment. Too many possibilities lay ahead of him, most bleak and unpromising, but Uzumati wanted and needed hope, so he simply said, "I don't know."

"You should. Then you could teach me how to shoot."

Martin's expression darkened, and the boy seemed to shrink from him. Realizing it, Martin ran a hand over his face and regained his composure.

"Let me tell you something," he said confidentially. "You remember when I came here, how worn out me and my horse were?"

The boy nodded.

"I still ain't real comfortable around people, and I'll have to live with that fear of people, because I chose to kill. You understand?"

The boy shook his head, and Martin considered another way of putting it.

"Your papa will teach you a way of living where you'll always have a place, a home. You'll know who you are and who to trust. The way I live, I have none of that. No home, no family, no one to trust. Do you understand now, Little Bear?"

"Yes."

"Good, 'cause I can't think of any other way to explain it." With a grunt, he hauled himself to his feet and offered the boy a hand up. "Now, how about we go over to the house and get some supper? My stomach says it's about ready."

The boy returned to his old serious self, and did not speak another word to him. When morning came, he was nowhere to be found, and Martin did not take it personally. Knowing someone would never return was hard enough to face without watching them leave.

He said good-bye to the family that had so warmly welcomed him when he so badly needed refuge. He had not known them before, and would never see them again, yet he owed them a debt too great to ever pay.

As he followed the wagon west, he paused on a low rise to look back at the rising sun and south, toward Texas. How many miles lay between him and Santiago's grave? How many more to his own? The thought chilled him, but he did not shiver. Silently, he bid farewell to the place with a tip of his hat and turned to catch up to the wagon.

Jack Miller chuckled when Martin pulled up beside him.

"Saying your own good-byes, eh?"

Martin glanced south again, as though at a door slowly closing.

"Say," Miller said a while later. "You got a different name we can call you by? Stranger's just...too telling. A man goes by that, you know he's running from something."

Martin considered it. Then from a distant part of his memory, he recalled part of Santiago's story.

"Call me Shiloh," he said, deciding the name was twice fitting.

Miller nodded, pleased. "A place of unity and peace in the Good Book. A good name to start a new life with."

"That's what my great-great-grandfather thought." He glanced south one last time, then it no longer held his interest to him, as though the door had shut and locked behind him. "I'll never go back," he said to himself, and with that decision, he tucked the name of Martin Santiago Hidalgo Mercer away in the back of his mind and tried to think of himself only as "Shiloh", a man with no past and no future.

"We ain't going back either," Miller offered. "No huntin' left worth having in the east."

The old man's words were definite, and Martin took his word. He looked west and wondered how many days they were from the mountains. He decided it did not matter. For now, he was among friends, and he held fast to his thin hope for the future.

Lena's Gift: Spring 1870

Blood, thick and sticky, covered his arms from hands to elbows. The scent panged his senses with its coppery sweetness masking the fresh scent of the spring wind.

Martin straightened, stretched his aching back, and mopped his face on his sleeve. He stared down at the doe, the last of four he had gutted since early that afternoon, the last they needed to make the trek north to meet with the wagon train.

"Weather won't hold," Miller commented from the back of his bay gelding a few feet away.

Glancing at the sky, Martin nodded. "Reckon so." He reached inside the carcass with both hands to cut the windpipe.

Miller slid from the bay's back and stood watching as Martin dragged the doe's steaming innards clear of the deflated rib cage. They would skin it when they returned to the dugout then dry the meat for trade and travel.

"Reckon we'll leave in three days for Grand Island," Miller stated after a minute.

"How many days travel up there?" Martin asked.

"About a week." Miller loosened his cinch and let the bay graze. He untied the packhorse and led it beside the doe. "You know coming in with furs is the dangerous part of the job."

Stooping beside the doe, Martin cleaned the knife blade in the grass. Then he cut a handful of brown blades to clean his hands and arms. It had taken nearly two weeks before the gutting and butchering ceased reminding him of slitting Alvarado's throat. With time, the memory had lost some of its edge, but it still returned, unbidden, now and then and brought with it that same sinking feeling. It was not the death or the gore that unnerved him; knowing he killed without feeling or care for the life he took made his blood run cold and his stomach turn empty.

Gritting his teeth, he scrubbed harder with the balled up hunk of grass.

"You make this look easy, son." Miller chuckled, staring down at the doe. "Remember the first time you skinned a buffaler? Thought you was about to cut yourself."

"I did," Martin said coldly, still cleaning the blood from his hands. "Sliced the inside of my wrist. Didn't know it until I washed up."

"Ah, yes. Lena nearly had a fit." Miller stood silently for a long while after that, his weather-beaten face betraying deep thought. "You know she's taken a liking to you."

Martin rose from his crouch and wiped his face on his sleeve, scratching an itch on his nose. He knew Lena's feelings but did not know how to deal with them. On days when the men stayed close to the Miller's dugout, Lena would always find something to do near him though she rarely talked without purpose. At first, her silence seemed awkward, but as time went on, the quiet became companionable, yet she always seemed reserved and guarded as though afraid to come too close. Martin forgave her, believing that he could never be fully trusted ever again.

"She'd never leave you, Jack," Martin said. "Besides, you two got along without me before. You will again."

"But having you around has changed that girl. I have never seen her wear skirts before you came to live with us. Now, that's all she wears around the homestead or whenever she don't have to ride horseback."

Martin gritted his teeth and slipped the knife into its sheath at the small of his back. Miller was right. Lena had changed since that first week Martin lived with them on their little homestead after he fled Texas. He worried she had grown too attached to him, making their inevitable parting harder on her.

Gripping the doe's forelegs, Martin helped Miller load the carcass across the pack horse's back. As they lashed the doe in place, Miller eyed Martin.

"Shiloh, I know you have business in Oregon," he said finally. "Please, at least don't leave without giving Lena something to hold on to. If she won't go with you, at least go easy on her."

Martin took a deep breath and held it a long while. "Jack, Lena's a fine woman, but I'm just not ready for the responsibility of a family."

"How long you been with us?" Miller asked.

"About two years."

Miller frowned in thought. "What you did was that bad, eh?"

Martin cast him a questioning look.

"What you did in Texas," Miller continued. "It was bad enough it wouldn't have settled after a year?" Still frowning, he nodded to himself, then shook his head. "Reckon I wouldn't want my little girl tied to a man still looking over his shoulder."

Stepping around the packhorse, Miller went to his bay and tightened the cinch. Martin watched him for a minute, wrestling feelings of insult and sadness, before going to where Haze stood grazing and mounted up. Miller's wisdom was sound, but that made his words no less painful.

He rode over to the packhorse and leaned down for the lead rope. Martin let the silence hang between them on the ride back. His mood reflected the gathering clouds as it often did after thinking too long about his situation.

Lena stood in the yard, stoking the fire in the squat smokehouse, her rust-colored dress catching Martin's attention as he and Miller rode into sight of the homestead. She looked up and saw them, but returned to her work without any gesture of greeting. This was her way, and Martin had grown used to it.

Light faded from the overcast sky. By lantern light, they butchered the deer and salted most of it. The rest they hung in the smokehouse to dry for the trail.

Martin and Miller found stew and ash cakes on the table when they finished their work. The meal was quiet. For the first time in months, Martin felt tension in the air, especially in the way Lena avoided eye contact. Despite the unease, Miller talked steadily about the old days trapping in the north country along the Missouri River. This narrative rarely failed to grace the supper table, and Martin listened, knowing it was an old man's reminiscing. In some ways, he wondered if Miller suffered from senility, for he often repeated stories in a single telling without appearing conscious of the fact. Most nights, Martin patiently waited for an opportunity to retire for the night, but something bothered him this night.

With his stomach upset by unease, Martin tried to force himself to finish his meal but failed. He fed the rest to the gray dog and washed his plate. Miller fell silent when he did this, and he and Lena finished their meal without a word. Martin bade them good-night and retired to his bunk in the outer shed that doubled as storage.

As he lay staring into the darkness, he thought of what Miller said about Lena that afternoon. He puzzled over what the old man meant by leaving her with something. There was nothing he could give her as a gift, at least nothing significant. Despite having spent the whole winter with her, he knew little about her other than her fondness for the vibrant colors of a fall sunset.

After a while, Martin gave up on the puzzle, believing the answer would come in time. The dreams filling his sleep came as distorted memories of Lolita. Guilt for not helping her filled him as once again, he stood in Alvarado's bedroom. Only this time, he heard the rustle of cloth behind him as Alvarado reached for a hidden revolver in the last throes of death. In reflex, Martin found the grip of his gun and whirled to face a shadow in the darkness as his waking mind scrambled to make sense of reality.

Silhouetted in the moonlight flooding in from the cracks in the door, Martin saw the sleek, curving lines of a woman's form and whispered Lolita's name.

"No." It was Lena's deeper, rougher voice.

Martin sighed as his mind grasped that he was in a safe place. He lowered the revolver and swung his legs over the edge of his little cot. There he sat with his head down, trying to slow his racing heart. He was vaguely aware of Lena's approach. As she crouched before him and placed her hands on his knees, he caught the sweetness of her woman's scent.

"Your dreams are bad?" she asked, her words accented.

"Not always," he said, drawing a deep breath and letting her take the revolver and set it aside. Then Lena took his hands in hers, her touch gentle.

"That is not how I've seen," she said in a near whisper. "I have watched you sleep many times. You often wake suddenly with fear in your eyes."

Shock brought a frown to his face. He looked at her and saw the moon glow on her bare shoulder. His heart stopped.

Lena moved closer, pressing her body against his knees, and he became painfully aware of her warmth, unabated by clothing, sending fire through him.

"I did not mean to wake you this night, not as I did. I wished to comfort you."

As she spoke, Lena drew his hands to her. He felt the silken softness of her bare skin, and the rush of heat surged through him, followed by hunger and longing. Martin wanted what she offered, tenderness, closeness, physical contact that up until that moment he had not been aware of desiring. For several long beats of his heart, he sat there, tracing his fingers over her body as she came closer. Light and gentle as a dove, she eased onto the cot, straddling his lap and kissing him. He could feel the lusty anticipation in her and knew she felt his, but before she could reach down and undo the first button of his shirt, he wrapped her in a fierce embrace, staying her efforts.

"I can't..." he whispered against her breast. "I can't do this."

"I am not ashamed," she told him, waiting to continue, but when he continued to hold her, she put her arms around him, stroking his hair.

Seemingly forever, they sat like this. Martin remained on the brink of letting it go on, but the one thought of what it could mean for the both of them cooled his blood. He had grown up without a father, seen his mother struggle to provide the basic necessities of living. He refused to do that to a child, or to Lena. Yet, he still wanted her, clung to her with his cheek resting against the soft, warm curve of her breast while the conflict within him brought tears to his eyes.

"I'm sorry, Lena," he said, looking up into her face. "But we can't do this...not now."

Neither could he see her face in the darkness, nor could he feel a rise of tension in her as she stared down at him, his expression plain to her in the moonlight. Still gentle, she brushed the tracks of tears from his cheeks.

"You are a good man," she said softly. "Father said you would not leave a woman to raise a child alone. I thought I could convince you to stay."

Martin swallowed and asked himself how much his family meant if he could live without truly knowing who he was. Never again could he use his real name or live as the person he discovered in those few short days before Fernando's death no matter what he found in Oregon. To his father and brothers, Martin Mercer was only a memory rarely brought to life by recollection. It would not matter to them what he did here and now.

But it did matter to him. His heart still wanted to cry out, claiming the name Mercer as his own with honor and pride. Though he loved Lena, his love for her did not extend beyond friendship. If he bedded her and left her with a child, he would lose that pride in himself. For a moment, he gazed up into the shadow of her face. She offered him a gift he could not accept. He hated himself for what it might mean to her.

Shaking his head, he again whispered a sad apology.

He expected her to push him away, to strike him or take up her robe and storm out of the shack, but after a moment, she drew him close and held him in a long, comforting embrace. Then she kissed his forehead and slid off his lap before sweeping up her robe and leaving without a sound.

Threshold of the Past

After years away from large settlements and towns, Martin felt uneasiness grow in every fiber with every farm they passed. The day before reaching Grand Island where homesteads dotted the landscape every dozen miles, anxiety kept him restless. First sight of the big town made his heart nearly leap from his chest. His eyes continually scanned the faces he passed even as he tried to keep his vigilance unnoticed. Most of the men stared at Lena, seated in the wagon with her father. Martin guessed that the presence of one with Indian blood was now rare in this civilized town. He welcomed the distraction. Still, he worried someone would recognize him. How far could stories travel over time? Had folks here cared enough to listen to news from across the plains from a world that had little to do with theirs? Had the law in Texas sketched his likeness on posters sent this far north?

All he could do was wonder and wait.

As they drove in among the warehouses, Miller startled him with a loud whoop. Throwing the wagon break, he vaulted from the seat to greet another man clad in buckskins with a rough bear hug.

"Jean Ramsey! You old wildcat!" he declared through laughter. "Ain't seen you since the cholera!"

The man called Jean grinned. "Takes more than dysentery to kill me." His attention lifted to Lena, who took up the dropped reins. Jean's expression sobered. "This your girl?"

"Sure is! She's grown a bit since last you saw her."

"That she has," Jean assented. He lifted his hat and bowed. "Pleasure to see you again, Lena."

Lena nodded and spoke in Cheyenne. Martin had yet to grasp the language and sat in his saddle beside the wagon with his head down as the two exchanged a few words.

"That's our partner, Shiloh," Miller said a moment later. Martin nodded and caught a look of worry on Jean's face. He whispered something to Miller, and Martin felt his nerves go taught. Miller nodded then turned back to Martin.

"Keep your head down and follow me," Miller told him as he flicked he reins against the mules' rumps. He nodded to Jean. "I'll meet up with you at the Stern Wheeler around sundown."

Jean nodded that he heard and watched them roll away.

Bile rose in Martin's throat. Tension ran down his limbs as his senses became acute to the cacophony of sound around him. He followed the wagon down the row of warehouses and in through the open doors of one filled to the rafters with bales of hides.

"What did he say?" Martin asked as Miller set the brake and looped the reins around it.

"He recognized you from posters," Miller said with a touch of worry in his voice. "It's been six months since he saw one, but he said it's probably still hanging under a few others. He'll hold his tongue, but he said you should keep out of sight and slip out of town tonight."

"Maybe I should ride out now," Martin stated.

"You don't have the supplies for a long ride." Lena met his gaze with an impassive expression. "Besides, with the cover of darkness, it's less likely anyone will be able to follow you."

"I doubt anyone else took the time to look at you closely enough," Miller added. "Old Jean has a memory for faces better than most."

"Even so, I might have just got you in trouble."

"Nothing worse than what I've been in before," Miller grunted as he threw his leg over the side of the wagon and climbed down. "Let's get this wagon unloaded. You can hide out here until dark. The guy that owns this place is a good friend of mine. He'll keep quiet."

Despite Miller's reassurances, Martin remained jumpy the rest of the afternoon. Even after taking refuge among the bundles of hides, their raw animal stench seeping into his clothes and skin, he remained edgy at every sound of the warehousemen as they worked. Lena took Haze for rest and feed at the livery and agreed to return with him ready for travel at sundown. So Martin tried to settle down and rest. It might be his last chance to sleep for a long time.

Miller stepped through the doors of the Stern Wheeler Saloon almost an hour before twilight. Jean Ramsey sat alone in the corner with a bottle of rum and two glasses on the table in front of him. True to his custom, the glasses sat empty, the bottle unopened. No matter how long he had to wait, Ramsey never drank before his company arrived.

As though the years between meetings did not exist, Miller approached the table and sat down without a single word spoken. Ramsey pulled the cork from the bottle's mouth, filled the glasses, and held his up for a toast.

"*Au passé,*" Ramsey said. They clinked glasses and drank. Then they sat in silence for a long moment afterward, each remembering his own story of the past.

Ramsey broke the silence first. "Is that partner of yours in a safe place?"

Miller nodded. "Thank you for the warning. Lena and I weren't sure if word traveled on him."

"It did. Best thing for him will be to keep away from all settlements, but even that will buy him little time."

Miller's jaw hardened. He reached for the bottle and filled the glasses again. "Shiloh has not spoken a word about what happened. I didn't ask."

Ramsey nodded once. "I remember when a man could disappear into the wilderness and live out his life in peace among the tribes." He drew a deep breath and sighed with a rueful shake of his head. "Those days are gone. The Army shut down the Bozeman, part of the agreement with the Sioux." He shook his head again, and his expression morphed into a disdainful sneer. "Hell, you and I should be fighting alongside the tribes. The land is as much our home as theirs anymore, and these farmers with their civilization ain't doing it any good."

Watching the change in his friend as he drank, Miller felt a stab of empathetic sorrow. "Times are changing, Jean. No stopping that."

"That's what the chiefs have said. Some have already relinquished their hope of freedom. Others will die free, even if that means fighting until there is nothing left." Ramsey fixed Miller with a respectful look. "Civilization never completely left you, Jack. I understand why you have accepted what's happening."

"I don't like it any more than you, Jean." Miller stared down into his glass. "I just know all the tribes of the Upper Missouri and their white friends together can't stop what's coming. Already people are moving west faster than they were five years ago thanks to that damned railroad. In ten years wagon trails may only be a memory."

"No." Jean shook his head. "They'll still travel by wagon." He sighed. "What I don't understand is why you're helping them. Scouting for the settlers moving west."

Miller shrugged. "It's the only way a man like me can make a living. It's the last bit of the past I can hold on to. You know I never could stand dandies playing trapper."

"*Oui.*" Ramsey chuckled. "I remember what happened with that emperor."

"Maximillian was a prince, and I couldn't stand him either."

Ramsey chuckled. "I doubt he's ever spoken of it. Too embarrassing for his royal blood to admit someone like you bested him in a joke."

They laughed, each remembering their own part of the story. Again, amiable silence fell between them and lingered a long while. Before Miller realized it, the sun had set, and he felt a grim sadness for the young Shiloh. Miller lived his share of time on the run from warring Indians and other trappers who took offense at his sense of humor, but most of his fights had been fun as a young man often found the edge of death a way to feel alive. What remained of Shiloh's life would not be spent among friends.

"When are you leaving town again?"

"Once the furs are sold."

"Will you and Lena take the train?"

Miller frowned. "Haven't decided yet. Can't say I'm fond of going faster than a horse can run."

"Was that Shiloh going with you?"

Miller nodded.

"Is he of any use?"

Miller nodded. "He's a good student. Took to the knife naturally enough and can shoot well."

Ramsey scoffed. "No doubt he's good with a knife, from what they say."

"What have you heard?"

Glancing over the room, Ramsey leaned closer and spoke low. "They say he slipped into a rancho and killed two men in their sleep then escaped before the guards knew what happened. He never opened a gate."

"With a knife?"

Ramsey nodded.

"Makes sense. First time he skinned an animal for me, he turned pale as a sheet."

Again, Ramsey nodded. "They call him 'Death' in Spanish. Unfortunately, there's a good chance anyone could recognize him. Texas wants him on suspicion of killing a ranger."

Miller's eyes widened. "They won't give up on him with that charge."

Ramsey nodded in agreement.

Miller tossed back a mouthful of rum, hoping it would soothe the rising sense of regret, and refilled it from the bottle. "He's heading out tonight. Hopefully he can get away clean and find someplace where no one knows him."

Ramsey nodded that he shared the sentiment. From a pouch on his belt, he dug out a pipe and tobacco. As he packed the bowl, Miller remembered something and leaned close to ask Ramsey a question.

"Have you heard anything about folks wanting revenge against him?"

Ramsey frowned as he tucked the tobacco pouch away and fished a match from the pocket of his linen shirt.

"I recall hearing something about two bounties on his head, one by the State of Texas and one from a private person. Two thousand dollars in all." Ramsey struck the match and lit his pipe.

Miller stared down at his glass, then guzzled it. Two thousand dollars would go a long way for him and Lena. He could retire comfortably to a new homestead far from civilization; maybe wait for grand-children if Lena would find the right man. Then the thought of what he would have to do to a man whose trust came slowly. He considered Shiloh, his quiet, humble manner of speaking. His actions spoke more than his sparse words, and though darkness always resided deep within him it never showed in how he treated man or beast.

"It seems," Ramsey went on after a short silence, "that this *El Muerto* killed an enemy of his employer, but he also killed his employer. The man I heard it from thought he may have been hired by the one side to kill the other, and the other side hired him to kill the first." Ramsey paused with a shrug. "It makes as much sense as drunken tales ever do." He studied Miller a moment through a haze of smoke. "You've been a good judge of character, Jack, long as I've known you. What do you think of him?"

"I think he's a young man in a lot of trouble," Miller said with a sigh. "Haven't decided yet whether to help him escape it or make him face what he's done. We never liked courts, I know, but we believed in justice."

"Best to get his side of things."

Miller nodded. "That's what I plan to do. If I get a chance."

Silence fell between them, and Ramsey scratched his cheek with the stem of his pipe in contemplation. "He could have easily killed you."

Miller knew that, and it contributed to the sourness in his stomach. He refilled his glass and glanced toward the front window, where a rider walked his horse by headed west out of town. Though Shiloh had never given him a reason to fear him, the threat of being turned in to the law could change a man. Maybe it would be wiser to turn him in, then hit the trail and leave the whole thing for the law to sort out.

Martin watched the sun descend the western sky through the open chinks in the warehouse wall. Restless and restricted from moving around, he chewed the inside of his lip until it bled. Every time the warehouse workers came close to his hiding place, his heart pounded so hard he felt it in his throat. When darkness came at last, and the warehouse was closed up for the night, he ventured out and waited for Lena.

She brought Haze, saddled and loaded with supplies. He placed a hand on the full saddlebags and cast a questioning look at Lena. Her cheeks flushed with deep crimson.

"In case you leave forever," she said. "You'll be well prepared."

His jaw hardened at her tone of disappointment. "I'm sorry."

Lena shook her head. "You belong to no one, not even me." She smiled wryly, her eyes bright in the faded twilight. "Your heart is not mine. I know that now, and I am not angry." She reached up and touched his cheek. "Promise me that if we meet again, you'll not treat me as a stranger."

He felt her loneliness. It so closely resembled his own, a need to belong among others. As the daughter of a white man and a Cheyenne woman, Lena had no people to truly call her own. She was an outcast by both, and for the first time, he felt true sorrow for leaving her.

"I promise we will always be friends," he said, taking her hand. He tried to remember the words of farewell in the language she used so often with her father, but they escaped him, and even if he could remember, no words were enough. He released her hand and turned away.

Haze moved forward as Martin climbed into the saddle, and Martin did not look back even after he knew she was out of sight behind the warehouse.

The strangeness of town closed in on him as he turned Haze down a side street. He rode through the squares of light cast from windows as he passed but kept his face in shadow. Few people moved about in the darkness, and their presence made him wary. As he rode, more and more people crossed his path. By the time he reached the tracks, a crowd staggered along singing "Annie Laurie" with thick Irish accents.

The thought of his brothers came to him. From Jinx's description of them, Martin believed they grew into men who enjoyed spirits with vigor now and then. He wondered what it would be like with them. Would they accept him readily enough to share a drink with him? Or would they enjoy cards and the company of a lady? He smiled wistfully at the dream as it played out in his imagination. Then the question arose in his mind; what did his brothers look like?

He reached inside his coat and drew out the daguerreotype and held it so the faint lamplight would play off the picture. He studied his father's face and build, not for the first time, but this time to deduce his brother's features and bearing.

They would be tall, he decided, blonde like their father and perhaps as broad. Cormac and Damien, he mouthed their names as he put the picture away. Damien was the quiet, thinking one. Cormac was the rough, bull-headed one. Together, they were capable of taking on a mob as boys. How much tougher were they as men? The answer he grasped with a sense of comfort was that they were men he would be proud to stand with.

"Martin!"

His head came up sharply at the sound of his name, and his eyes locked on a lone figure standing in the street ahead of him. At first, he remained frozen, hoping the figure had called out to a companion, but the way this man stood facing him, feet wide, knees bent and hands ready, spoke clearly of his intent to fight.

"*El Muerto!*"

Martin reined Haze in. The Irishmen fell silent and looked toward the lone figure. The perfectly spoken Spanish identified him as a Mexican or Tejano, and Martin felt cold resignation spread through him. For a short while, he had tasted reassurance that he might escape Alvarado's revenge, but Alvarado's ghost had found him, and he would die here, never knowing his brothers' faces or the sounds of their voices.

Alvarado's Revenge

"What do you want?" Martin asked.

"Don't you recognize me?"

Martin squinted at the shadowed face, but even after moving so that the saloon light no longer blinded him, he could not make out the man's features.

"I'm sorry. I don't."

The man chuckled, a tight, almost painful sound. "I once joked with you that if you fought Kell again, I would make money selling tickets. Too bad I didn't get to see you kill him. That would have been worth the money I lost."

Recognition sent pain through Martin's chest. "Chico?"

The man nodded. "*Si.* It is I, the man who was once your friend."

"You never should have taken part in Santiago's killing. We would have remained friends."

Chico barked a sharp, humorless laugh. "Is that what you think?"

Martin frowned, trying to divine Chico's meaning. "You were a hired gun. You had no blood ties to Alvarado."

"No?" Then Chico's voice lost all pretense of levity. "Didn't you ever wonder how I could defy Armand's wrath and protect Lolita?"

The memory of the day he rode with Belden to Alvarado's ranch came easily to Martin. He remembered Lolita, bruised and battered, appearing to cling to Chico and believing it was because Chico had defended her against Armand. Now, as he recalled the image, he could not remember a single mark on Chico's face.

"Alvarado married once, late in life," Chico explained. "She died giving birth to me, making me my father's only legitimate heir."

"How do you know? Alvarado lied when he said I was his grandson, and that *I* was his only legitimate heir."

"*Abuelo* knew who you were the night you came to the *hacienda*. He thought if he could sway you to our side, break you, he could have a quiet little end to the feud with a little bit of irony known only to him. He was glad when he found out that we left you in the desert. Never did we think you would live."

"But you defended me. Tried to convince Kell not to shoot me."

"I thought of you as my friend!" Chico's voice choked on these words. "I would have gone on believing you were my friend if you had not murdered Alvarado. Now...I must see that you pay...that you die as he did, drowning in your own blood."

Perhaps it was an act of desperation or a lingering sense of owing Chico for trying to spare his life, but Martin raised a hand to gesture truce, and in that instant, Chico drew. Martin failed to anticipate his speed. Chico's gun came up and spat flame before Martin could reach his revolver. He felt the hot piercing pain as the bullet entered his right shoulder. The darkness spun as Haze darted sideways at Martin's reflexive cue. Unbalanced, he fell from the saddle and hit the ground so hard it knocked the wind out of him. He was aware of Chico running, closing the distance between them. He started to reach for his left-hand gun, but Chico was on him, lamplight flashing off the knife blade as he drew it from its sheath.

As the blade came at him in a wide arch, Martin rolled backward and felt the nearness of the blade's edge as he scrambled to escape, but Chico followed through in his charge. Martin drove himself forward into Chico's middle and held on in a tackle that sent them both into the dirt. They came down hard. Chico gave a bear-like growl of rage.

They scuffled, each scrambling for an advantage against the other. Chico pushed his feet against the ground and rolled, pinning Martin beneath him. Before he could bury his knife in Martin's chest, Martin wrapped his left leg around Chico's neck and pushed him backward. With Chico off him, he scrambled to his feet and stepped back to the cheers of a gathering crowd.

Chico glared up at him with a malevolence that Martin once believed impossible in him. His knife had fallen beside him. Martin felt the urge to run but stood his ground as Chico gripped the knife again and rose to his feet.

Martin flexed the fingers of his right hand and drew his own knife while Chico circled grinning with morbid obsession. As he stared into the rage-filled eyes, Martin saw Santiago's face, ashen with death, and knew the rage Chico felt. Only one of them would walk away from this fight.

Like a viper, Martin waited for Chico to move within striking distance. He lunged and cut deep into Chico's right wrist as Chico lashed his blade across Martin's arm. Martin threw up his hand to block the knife as it swung back and took the blade through his forearm. Chico shoved him down and jerked the blade free.

Martin growled as Chico rallied and dove at him. He pulled his legs up, planted his boots against the Tejano's chest, and threw Chico into the crowd. The men caught him and kept him from falling. Chico seemed to bounce off them, giving Martin little time to recover. He shifted his body and rolled into Chico's planted foot, mid-stride, and spilled Chico face-first into the dirt. Martin righted himself and drove his body at Chico. Flipping onto his back, Chico faced him, and Martin felt the pressure of Chico's blade against his ribs as he buried his own knife in the center of Chico's chest.

Shock filled Chico's face, now vivid in the light of a lantern. Rage flared in his eyes. Thrusting his hips upward, he threw

Martin over and rolled up, straddling him. Chico yanked his knife free, flipped it around, and brought it down. Martin squirmed at the last second and took the blade in his left shoulder. Teeth bared, Martin twisted his own knife, trying to free it.

Coldly, Chico reached up to grip Martin's scalp. He pulled and slammed Martin's head against the ground. He reached across to bring his knife to Martin's throat, but Martin grabbed the blade with his free hand.

"Give up! You son of a whore!" Chico roared. "Give up and die!" He jerked the knife, and the blade slipped from Martin's hand, leaving a burning line across his palm. The force of Chico's rising arm shifted the blade in his chest. Martin pulled it free, and before Chico could recover, Martin's fist shot out as though in a punch, driving the blade across the side of Chico's neck. Blood spurted from the severed jugular in sparkling black droplets that descended on Martin in a warm, sweet, raw-scented shower.

Chico released Martin's head and put his hand to the gaping wound that barely missed the windpipe. Now the look of shock came and stayed as all color steadily drained from his face. In that long moment, filled only with the sound of his pounding heart, Martin watched the life leave Chico's eyes as his body wilted and fell to the hard-packed dirt of the street beside him.

Chest heaving, Martin reached over and took the knife from Chico's lifeless hand. The fight was over, and Martin felt no satisfaction. Shaking with chills and weakness, Martin pushed himself up and lurched to his feet.

The fight had taken his bearings. The lanterns from outside the saloons now surrounded him and he couldn't see Haze through the crowd which now closed in on him. He stumbled and fell to his knees. Despite the growing pain of his wounds, he tried to rise and fell again. Through the sea of voices, he heard a familiar name, but his overwhelmed mind failed to recognize it. A cool hand touched his cheek gently, and a woman's face filled his vision. Fear filled her eyes, but she spoke gently telling him to lay still.

Panic filled Martin. He pulled away and became aware of the blood on his hands, black as ink in the dim light. Something hit his side, then his shoulder. Then a blow to the side of his head drove him into darkness.

The Marker

It glowed in the noon sun, a wide, rough-cut plank with a name burned into it. Miller stared down at it grimly as he finished setting it into the loose earth above the grave.

"That's all you can do," Jean said over his shoulder.

Miller hung his head. "I just hope it's enough."

"A grave usually means the end of a life," Jean went on, gazing up at the open sky. "His at least."

Miller nodded agreement, then stood with a grunt as his knees crackled painfully. He picked up his shovel.

Jean stood with his hands resting on the handle of the pickaxe as he once stood leaning with his Sharps. "What will you do now?" he asked.

Miller shrugged. "We'll move on, I guess. Given time, this will all fade from memory."

"Not for Lena."

"No. Not for Lena." Miller followed his friend's gaze out to the western horizon. "I just hope this is the last grave I dig for many years."

Jean turned a grim stare on him. "Death always rides with us. If it's not from another's hand, it will be by fate's hand or your own."

"I know. Though, it's not every day you bury Death himself."

Jean's stony visage did not crack at the jest. He stood silently a long while before he spoke.

"You ride carefully, my friend, and never turn your back on any Indian, even the tribes who were once our friends."

Again, Miller nodded that he understood. He extended his hand. Jean took it, gripping the wrist in the old way. They embraced briefly and parted without another word spoken.

Miller descended the low bluff alone, glancing back once to see his friend still watching the distance from beside the fresh grave with "*El Muerto*" burned into the wooden marker. A shiver ran up his spine at the thought of this being the last time he saw his old friend, but as Jean said, death always rode with them. The old-timers were good at not being caught by it, which he saw as both a blessing and a curse.

He rode into town in the direction of the tracks. Past there and overlooking the river, a rooming house stood with sagging slats and peeling paint. The widow there, a youngish woman, had opened her home to them willingly after they pulled Shiloh from the midst of the crowd, bloody and unconscious. The doctor held out little hope of his recovering, but Shiloh held on through the night and regained consciousness briefly in the early morning.

Miller entered the little house which offered two bedrooms on the second floor, besides the room where the widow slept with her two sons. The rooms were just large enough for a bed and bureau, but they were clean and surprisingly warm.

He found Lena and the widow in the room with Shiloh.

"How is he?" Miller asked quietly to keep his voice from waking the wounded man.

"Awake, but in much pain," the widow, Judith Banks, whispered back.

"Hmm." Miller glanced at his daughter as she bent over Shiloh.

"It's a miracle he's still alive," Missus Banks said.

"It would have been a mercy if he had died," Miller stated flatly.

Missus Banks frowned deeply at him. "Surely you don't mean that, sir," she declared in vivid shock.

Miller made no reply. He did mean it both for him and Lena and for Shiloh. His left arm and hand was nearly useless. If infection didn't get him in a slow death, he would most likely be crippled the rest of his life.

Missus Banks gave a soft sigh and turned toward the door. Miller let her go without a word. He knew she would be in the kitchen. Moving closer to the bed, Miller put his hand on Lena's shoulder. She pressed her cheek to his buckskin jacket and cried softly. Her tears startled him. Only twice, in his memory, had she cried.

"It's alright," Miller told her. "Everything's going to be alright. You're very tired. That's why this is coming over you."

Lena sniffed. "I don't like seeing him suffer like this."

Miller nodded that he understood. The doctor refused to give Shiloh pain killer out of worry that sedatives would worsen Shiloh's condition.

Lena sat up, wiping away her tears. "He won't be ready to travel by the time the train leaves. Bouncing around in the back of that wagon will kill him, and we can't leave him here."

Miller drew a deep breath and thought. "Perhaps we should."

Lena stared up at him. "We can't do that, papa. We can't abandon him here among strangers!"

"At least you won't see him suffer anymore."

She closed her eyes tight and fought back a new rise in tears, and Miller realized his humor had once again come at a bad time. He gritted his teeth and silently scolded himself. Reaching down, he patted her hand.

"I'm sorry, dear girl, but we couldn't keep riding with him for our sake or for his. Jean showed me the poster. Shiloh has killed seven men in cold blood."

Lena's face paled as she stared down at Shiloh. If he heard their conversation, he gave no sign. Miller leaned down and spoke softly in Lena's ear, just in case Shiloh only pretended to sleep.

"We have to leave him, girl," he said firmly. "He'll bring trouble. Even if he doesn't hurt us, others will come for him, and there's no telling what they might do to get him."

Lena didn't move or speak. She continued to stare blankly at Shiloh's bruised and cut face. He had never given Miller cause to worry or fear him, but that had been far from civilization. Things changed when people got too close to folks.

Miller sighed and sat on the edge of the bed. He hated having to hurt his daughter like this, but in the long run, she would be better off for it.

"We'll board the train tomorrow," he told her. "He'll never even know we left."

"He'll know," Lena stated. She reached up and brushed a lock of hair back from Shiloh's flushed face. "He always knows, and he remembers."

A chill ran up Miller's spine. Maybe he was taking too much of a chance by abandoning this outlaw to whatever fate may come while he had no chance of protecting himself. Miller studied the lines of Shiloh's face. He seemed angry with pain lining his eyes and mouth. Imagining him as a killer was not hard in that moment. The more he thought about it, the better he liked the idea of leaving him. If Shiloh decided to hunt them after this, Miller could hold his own in the mountains among the Nez Perce.

He pushed up from the bed. For a moment, he stared down at Lena. She hated his plan, but he refused to consider the alternative.

"I'll find a buyer for the wagon and mules. Be at the station by morning..." He gritted his teeth against the shame he felt at what he had to say next. "...or I'll leave without you."

Lena half turned toward him, but he pulled the door open and stepped into the hall before she could protest.

Alone

Every fiber ached as he slowly roused from sleep. He fought and managed to return to a dreamless doze, but a sharp pain in his shoulder brought him to full wakefulness a short while later. He did not know where he was. For a long while, he lay staring up at the slat ceiling lit by twilight through the thin curtain and tried to remember.

Bits and pieces came back to him. He felt the tight restriction of being trapped, cornered, but did not know why. A glance around the room told him nothing except that he was alone without clothes or guns. The absence of his guns worried him more than his missing trousers.

After two attempts to get up, he surrendered to the relative comfort of the husk mattress and soon fell asleep again. When he woke, the sun shined bright and clear through the curtains. A strange woman, plain and skinny, with a long face laid his shirt and trousers on the short bureau beside the window. He remembered his traveling companions.

"Lena?" The sides of his dry throat raked together causing him to cough. He almost recovered by the time she offered him water. He drank all of it and asked for more. The water was cool and cramped his stomach, but it was welcome. Once he drained the second glass, he settled back on the bed and gathered his thoughts.

He studied the woman, trying to remember if he knew her, but he had no recollection. This woman could not be considered beautiful. Her eyes were spaced too far apart, and her upper lip was too large to match the lower, and her expression had a calculating nature to it.

"I'm sorry, ma'am, but I don't recall you," he said politely.

"I know. You've been unconscious since the night they brought you here."

"My companions?"

"Two old men and a half-breed girl?"

Martin nodded. "That's them."

She looked down at her hands, her lips tight in a not-quite believable expression of pity.

"They left you behind."

Martin's heart sank. His gaze shifted from her to the wall then up to the window. A gut-wrenching sense of loneliness set in.

"They left a little money to pay for your care and your outfit. They said they could not afford to wait for you to be well enough to travel."

Slowly, sullenly, Martin nodded that he understood. Though he felt abandoned, he wondered how much the fight had to bear on Miller and Lena's choice to leave him behind.

"Did they say anything else?" After he said it, he realized it did not matter. They were gone, and he was on his own again. Nothing would change that.

The woman shook her head. "The girl stayed until early yesterday morning. She seemed reluctant to leave."

He believed that. Leaving him probably tore Lena's heart out, but given the choice between a half-dead drifter and her father, he doubted she could have done any differently. Silently, he said good-bye to them and closed his eyes, trying to think what he would do next. A long time passed before he realized the woman remained at his bedside.

"What do I call you?" Martin asked without opening his eyes.

"I am Missus Judith Banks," she said crisply. "You may call me Missus Banks."

"Yes, ma'am."

Still, she remained beside him. He opened his eyes and found her watching him expectantly.

"What is it, ma'am?"

"I was hoping you would give me your name," Missus Banks said flatly. "Your companions did not offer such information when I let them bring you here."

Martin squinted up at the woman. He wondered how Missus Banks could miss his name entirely, even if Miller or Lena never introduced him.

"It's Shiloh, ma'am."

"That's all of it?" Missus Banks asked after a short pause.

"Yes, ma'am. That's all you'll know me by."

Her expression hardened. "What are you running from?"

Martin's jaw hardened against her question. Neither could he lie, nor could he answer truthfully. Either choice could be fatal, and silence offered no guarantee of safety.

After it became clear she would receive no answer, Missus Banks straightened from her chair and paced to the small, high window. She stared through its dirty panes a moment before she spoke.

"I am a good, Christian woman," she declared. "I cannot have a strange man with an unknown background in my house. I never assumed your companions would leave you here with no prospects if you recovered."

Neither had Martin believed Miller would abandon him like this, but he guessed she was about to throw him out anyway. He decided to save his breath.

"As soon as is practical," Missus Banks said sternly, "I want you out of my house. The sooner, the better. I'll not tolerate a possible troublemaker under my roof." She turned on him, bending forward as though to bite him like a rabid dog.

Anger, frustration, and betrayal filled Martin, and he fought to hide it in the face of her obvious indignation. Though it was not clear what the source of her aggression was, she wanted him gone despite his current condition. He made no effort to hide his anger from her.

They stared at each other for several moments before Missus Banks turned toward the door.

"I will feed you today. Tomorrow, you'll eat at the table with everyone else or not at all."

She closed the door behind her. Martin guessed he would be confined to eating what she prepared whether or not his stomach was ready for hard food. With a heavy sigh, he closed his eyes and tried to turn his mind to other things, but the situation consumed him. What would he do now? If he recovered, how would he make it to Oregon? How would he get started soon enough to find his family before winter?

His mind, still fogged by his long sleep, struggled to unravel the mass of trouble that had fallen upon him. Soon he gave up solving the problems and tried to wash it from his mind. He gave up on that too after a short while and fell into a restless sleep.

He woke hungry, and found a small bowl of cold soup beside the bed. Despite the lingering weakness, he managed to drink it down without bothering with the spoon. It tasted thin; more water than broth and failed to satiate his hunger. It was all he got that afternoon.

The next morning, he managed to dress and put on his boots before making his way one slow, shaky step at a time down the hall. He rested often, leaning against the wall. He could hear the soft clink of dishes in the dining room, but no conversation carried down the hall. By the time he reached the doorway, most of the food was gone, consumed by the two men, two children and Missus Banks.

The two men sat with their backs to him. They were dressed in neat, twill suits, the outfits of townsmen. When Missus Banks looked up from her plate, they turned.

Neither man looked familiar, or even threatening, but Martin felt a shock of fear under their scrutiny as he faced them with no weapons. He had not left the guns in his room. He had no recollection of what had happened to them after the fight. Even with them, he stood little chance if these men chose violence.

"Glad you could join us, Mister Shiloh," Missus Banks said in obligatory greeting. "There is not much left, but you are welcome to it."

Her words registered distantly. The two men had Martin's full attention. The one on the right only glanced up at him and turned back to his plate. The one on the left took a longer look at him, long enough to concern him. When finally the man bowed his head back to his meal, Martin stepped around to the far side of the table and eased into a chair.

The biscuits were hard, the eggs dry, and the bacon undercooked, but it was food. Unfortunately, the food he got down sat heavily in his stomach. Neither man spoke to him and left once their plates were empty. If they recognized him, they gave no sure sign. Despite that, Martin could not shake the nakedness he felt.

As he watched them leave, Martin remembered his conversation with Missus Banks. His sense of betrayal turned to anger.

"You children finish up and get on your chores before school," Missus Banks ordered. Within minutes the boys excused themselves, and Missus Banks began clearing the table. When she came near his place, he spoke firmly, but quietly, lest his tone alarm any prying ears.

"Where are my revolvers?" he asked.

"Do you not know?" she replied with an odd tone of affection that belied the condemnation in her eyes. She reached for his plate, half the food still left. He caught her wrist with his good hand and gripped it tighter than he thought he had the strength to. She released the plate and stood staring down at him. Her mouth gaped in shock.

"Where are my revolvers?"

Her wide-set eyes narrowed, but she spoke with genuine song-bird sweetness. "I don't know where your filthy guns are."

Martin drew a deep breath and let it out slowly, releasing the tension in his muscles which threatened to overflow onto her. He shoved her hand away and returned to his food.

Missus Banks finished clearing the table and disappeared into the kitchen. By the time Martin finished his breakfast, she had not returned.

Though the food was terrible, it satisfied Martin's hunger. Fortified by it, he rose and limped back up to his room. He stretched out on the bed, but despite his longing for it, sleep spurned him. His mind kept mulling over where his guns might be. Finally, he sat up and searched for his gear in the room. He found the saddle bag and bedroll tucked between the dresser and the wall. He unrolled the blanket and found nothing. His saddle bags yielded everything they should but the revolvers. Exhausted by the effort, he fell back on the bed, cursing the lump by his hip. For a long while, he lay there staring at the ceiling until he slept out of pure exhaustion. By the time he woke it was late afternoon. He shifted his position on the bed to relieve the pain caused by the only hard spot in the straw tick.

A frown creased his forehead as he thought it strange that a single spot could be so hard. Stiffly, he swung his feet over the edge and slid his hand under the thin mattress. Relief cooled his agitation as his hand closed over the tooled leather of the cartridge belt. He pulled it out and habitually checked the revolvers. Then he peeled back the tick and found his rifle near the wall.

"Thank you, Lena," he whispered, knowing she would have thought to safeguard his most important possessions.

Having these back, he felt a little less vulnerable and a little more ready to leave though his limbs still felt as solid as wet grass. With Missus Banks to deal with, he figured he would rather take his chances alone on the trail. His only concern with that was access to food.

Strapping on the revolvers, he searched the saddlebags and bedroll again for his share of the hide money. Martin doubted Miller would have taken the money with him. The old mountain man was honest enough not to. Then he remembered Missus Banks stating Miller had left money for his care. Martin doubted the cost of his care exceeded fifty dollars. The problem was figuring out where she kept it. That would take time and strength he doubted he had unless he held her at gunpoint.

Even with her heartlessness, he disliked the idea of robbery, especially when it would put the law back on his trail. He decided he would ask her for it. If she surrendered it, he would take it, but he would stop short of pulling a gun on her.

It was an hour before supper when he walked down to the kitchen. He paused outside the door, silently laid his saddlebags and bedroll on the dining room table, and reached out to push the swinging door open. He found her by the stove working the dough as though it were a living thing struggling to escape. Rather than address her, Martin let the kitchen door swing back, its ill-fitted frame clattering loudly. Missus Banks screeched and jumped, spinning to face him with her right hand pressed to her breast, eyes wide as though the Devil himself had reached out and touched her. He knew the sight of him in dark range clothes and holding the black rifle at his side was enough to scare the life out of her.

"How dare you scare me like that?" she cried, betraying a strong recovery.

"Imagine discovering that every cent you earned over the last two years had gone missing."

Her hand dropped to the counter behind her. "I don't know what you are talking about."

"Keep your hand at your side."

Her homely face blanched in a look of utter horror. Martin was angry and a little scared of her. He wondered what showed on his face.

"Where's my money?" he asked, almost lazily.

"Ah…" Missus Banks searched for words. "I…I think your partner, the old man took it."

"Don't lie to me," Martin told her flatly.

"I'm not lying. He paid me twenty dollars to look after you until you were well enough to move on."

Her palpable fear brimmed into tears. Martin refused to believe them. He knew she was lying. He also knew she would kill him if she got the chance.

"How long have I been here?"

She looked down at her hands and counted off on her fingers. Martin waited patiently, listening for sounds of the two men returning from work.

"Five days," Missus Banks replied.

"Keep ten dollars and hand over the rest."

She attempted to neither protest nor comply. Martin glared at her.

"W…would you please turn around?" she asked awkwardly. "I need privacy to retrieve the money."

"Why don't you turn *your* back?" he countered, refusing to give her an edge.

Her cheeks flushed with anger. "You worthless..." she growled but did not finish. Turning her back on him, she dug a pouch from inside her bodice, counted out ten coins before slapping the pouch into his outstretched hand. Her washed-out blue eyes glared at him. Now Martin knew why she had taken him in. She wanted to make a raw profit off of his misfortune.

"Where did they stable my horse?"

Missus Banks nodded toward the back door. "My barn."

Martin's eyes narrowed. "You didn't sell him, did you?"

She scoffed loudly. "How could I when he bites everyone who enters that corral?"

A tired, knowing smile lifted the corners of Martin's mouth as he backed toward the kitchen door. "He has good sense."

Even as he said it, he remembered Jinx and longed for the old cowboy's company. Fighting to shrug the sudden wash of melancholia, he stepped backward through the kitchen door just as Missus Banks reached for a plate on the sideboard.

"Get out of my house, you worthless trash!" she screeched. Martin had every intention to leave before she threw the dish, shaky and weak or not. He did not like leaving in daylight, but perhaps in a town this big, he could move about freely, especially with a week of stubble hiding his face.

He moved slowly down the hall, careful not to cause himself pain but watching over his shoulder all the way to the barn.

Haze whinnied at the sight of him as though eager to leave as well. Whip marks showed on his flanks, and Martin felt the sudden urge to find the whip and take it to Missus Banks for her efforts, but doing so would only land him in jail.

It took a long time to saddle up, and by the time he was done, Martin worried about climbing aboard. Finally, he relented to stepping up on a box and climbing into the saddle from there. For a moment, he considered the folly of his intention, but he shook his head, dismissing any thought of staying. Missus Banks had made herself clear, and he wanted nothing more to do with her. Staying in her house certainly set him on a path to a gallows somewhere. So, he cued Haze into a slow walk and pointed him out of town.

He dropped south and followed the broad, braided riverbed of the Platte, stopping often to drink. The sun reached the horizon before he realized hunger pained him as much as the wound in his side. Pausing at the river's edge to let Haze drink, he reached into his saddlebags and dug out the dried venison Lena left for him. Relieved to find it still good, he chewed a strip and rode on into the coming darkness.

How many homes and farms he passed along the way he did not know, but as the moon rose, fresh fatigue crept into his limbs. He stopped Haze in a shallow draw to ease the agitation of his wounds. Touching the bandage covering his side, he found it moist with fresh blood. He needed to rest and to tend his wounds, but he felt agitated and uneasy despite his increased faltering. Shaking his head as though to free it of the rising fog, he glanced back along his trail and focused his whole mind on what he had to do. He considered turning back to a cottonwood grove he passed a half-mile back but shook it off as a waste of time that would take him too close to civilization. He decided to push on and stop in the next thicket he entered.

Martin rode heavy in the saddle and nearly slid from it more than once before fatigue overtook him. Thick prairie grass on a low rise broke his fall and he rolled down it to settle in a cup of land still warm from the sun.

When he woke, the moon remained high in the sky behind Haze's looming silhouette. Despite the sweat soaking through his wool shirt, a chill coursed through his body. Martin thought of his bedroll lashed behind the saddle, but that was as far as his mind got before dropping back into nothingness.

The Doctor

The engineer squinted out from beneath a stiff-billed cap as the setting sun blinded him. He adjusted the throttle, hoping that a slower speed might prevent the train from derailing should a stray cow wander onto the tracks.

Dragging thousands of pounds in supplies, livestock, and passengers, the engine chugged along the tracks which split the prairie with a silver line. The engineer, Townsend, let his eyes wander to the north ahead, resting them from the glare. That was when he saw the brown horse, fully saddled and bridled, watching the train approach from the bottom of the grade alongside the tracks. He frowned at the horse. No animal fully tacked would be alone, but the engineer saw no sign of a rider. The short grass afforded no cover for anything larger than a jackrabbit.

Reaching up, Townsend pulled a thick cord, and the dissonant wail of the train's whistle pierced the air. Nothing moved except for the horse which eased closer to the tracks. Knowing better than to kill the horse and leave his rider stranded, the engineer backed off the throttle and threw the engine into reverse.

Thankful he saw the horse in time, he worked the throttle, slowing the train without the jerking of a sudden stop which could injure passengers or worse, derail a car or two. The engine puffed and chugged against the hissing grind of the drive wheels spinning backward on the rails, but the horse just stared at the oncoming hulk of iron and steel with dumb curiosity.

Tommy, the fireman, leaned out behind the engineer.

"Stopping for a horse?" he asked around his usual stutter.

"His rider. Thinking there might be trouble. Look out that side. See if there's anyone else out there."

Tommy stuck his head out the other side of the cab and scanned the open prairie.

"Nothin'!" he reported as he crossed back to the engineer's side and stepped out onto the landing.

The horse shied away as the engine rolled past him at a walking pace. That's when Townsend saw the body lying in the ditch below. When the train finally came to a stop, the two men climbed down from the engine.

The horse watched them approach, ears pricked and standing proud. He snorted as the two came nearer and stomped the ground in warning.

On the ground beside the horse, the heap of human flesh moved, rising feebly before falling back to earth.

"What do we do?" Tommy asked, nervousness exacerbating his stutter. "We g...get much nearer, and that animal will d...do his best to k...k...kill us!"

"Any way you can distract that horse?" Townsend asked.

Tommy frowned in thought for a moment. Suddenly, he snapped his fingers excitedly, "Apples!"

Townsend nodded, and Tommy darted back to the engine.

The man on the ground lay unmoving now, and the engineer wondered if they had the time to wait. He glanced up as a handful of passengers climbed down from the train following the conductor who pumped his arms like plump drive shafts as he stormed toward the engine and the horse.

"Townsend! What the hell...?" The scrawny, black-clad conductor halted in his tracks when the horse whirled to face him. He threw up his hands in a reflexive gesture of surrender.

"Do we have a doctor on board?" Townsend called to him.

"Yes!" the conductor squeaked. "A young fellow!"

"Go get him! The rest of you fan out and stay back! We have to draw that horse away."

But the stallion had more sense than most humans and stood his ground. When the man moved again, the engineer knew from the groan he was injured and not simply drunk.

"Stranger!" Townsend called. "We're trying to help you, but your horse won't let us!"

The man on the ground lifted his head a little and seemed to listen. Then he settled back into the grass, his face hidden behind the brim of his hat.

Tommie touched Townsend's shoulder and showed him two apples before he advanced toward the horse. A third was tucked under his left arm. He moved slowly toward the stallion with the first apple outstretched.

The stallion sniffed the wind. His brown eyes showed no fear as he watched the group of men slowly close in. His attitude dared them even as his attention focused on the treat in Tommy's hand.

"That's it," Tommy said to the stallion, his stutter fading. "Got a fine apple here for you. You'll like it."

Townsend saw the man on the ground move a split second before he understood what the action meant.

"Hold it."

The voice was rough, deadly, and just audible over the engine's pressure relief valve hissing rhythmically. Tommy stopped two paces from the horse and looked down at the man who pointed a revolver at him. His face blanched and his tongue tied in fear.

"We're here to help, mister," Townsend explained.

A weak, grim scoff showed how much the stranger believed him. With apparent effort, he pushed himself up to his knees and looked around at the others. His gaze fixed on Townsend, and his teeth flashed in a vicious grin.

"No, you aren't." He coughed. No doubt, his throat was dry. He had the look of a man who was very ill, and the hand that held the blue steel revolver shook badly. Townsend waved the passengers back as the conductor re-emerged from the rear passenger car with a lanky man, dressed like a dude, following close behind.

Tommy swallowed hard and stuttered, "Please, d...d..don't k...k..."

The hardness in the stranger's face faltered as Tommy struggled with the word, but he did not put the gun away.

Townsend frowned and seriously considered what they were doing. He had thought of a hold-up scheme, but nothing about the man himself, whether he was running from the law or some other trouble, but without help in the middle of the prairie, he would not live long.

The conductor stopped several feet from the man. The passenger with him was a young, toe-headed man carrying a black leather bag. Purposefully and intentionally, the man moved around the group to stand near Tommy. He raised his free hand in a peaceful gesture.

"Sir, my name is Phineas Hall. I am a doctor."

The injured man glowered at him and cocked the revolver.

Doctor Hall let his hand fall to his side. "I will tend you, one way or another. From the way you are bleeding, sir, you will pass out in only a few minutes. Then you will have no say in how I do my work. I, myself, would prefer to address a conscious patient."

The injured man's gaze brushed over the doctor. He swayed badly, but for a moment, seemed determined to hold out. In the end, he barely possessed the strength to hold the revolver up, let alone keep it steady. Relief washed through Townsend when the man lowered the weapon and let down the hammer.

"It's alright, Haze," the injured man said to his horse.

The stallion's left ear pivoted toward him. Then the horse took a step forward, reaching for the apple Tommy offered. The fireman smiled broadly, betraying his youth when the horse took the treat.

Townsend moved closer, but before he moved three strides, the man wilted sideways into the grass. Dropping to his knees, Doctor Hall put his ear to the man's chest.

"He dead?" the conductor asked.

Hall shook his head as he unbuttoned the man's shirt, exposing bandages spotted and patched with dried and fresh blood. Townsend gritted his teeth at the sight of it.

"Say, I'll bet that's the fellow who survived that knife fight in Grand Island last week," one of the passengers declared. "I wondered where he disappeared to. That was one hell of a fight!"

Hall lifted the bandage from the injured man's side, exposing a purpled wound that issued a rivulet of blood. The young doctor looked grim as he turned and spoke to the conductor.

"I will pay this man's fare to the nearest safe haven. He is in dire need of care in a sanitary place where he can rest."

"That won't be necessary," Townsend told him. "If that is the man called 'Shiloh', I'd be honored to have assisted a fighting man like him."

"I'm not sure we have room for the horse," the conductor stated, not liking the idea.

"He'll be alright in the stock car," Townsend offered before the boot-licking conductor could protest further. "Think you can get him up the ramp, Tommy?"

The boy nodded enthusiastically as he fed the stallion another apple.

"Good!" Townsend declared. "You men give us a hand. We've lost enough time already."

A handful of passengers shuffled and condensed to make room in the last car as a porter converted the end bench into a bed. As they laid the injured man down, Phineas Hall felt keenly aware of the prying eyes of the other passengers, especially the children whose mothers were too curious themselves to shield the youngsters' eyes. As he took inventory of his patient's injuries he could only frown in concern.

"Is he going to live, doc?" a gentleman asked from across the aisle.

"I do not know," Phineas replied. "Would someone please get me a basin of hot water?"

"What was that man doing out here?" a woman wondered out loud.

"From what I heard, probably fleeing the friends of the man he killed," explained the passenger who first proposed the theory outside. He leaned over Phineas's shoulder to study the wound the doctor was cleaning in the man's forearm. "No doubt this man is Shiloh. Fought a man to the death with knives and guns and fists...a true testament to man's endurance and fighting spirit!"

"A true testament to stupidity, if I may say so," Phineas stated dismissively as the train jolted into motion. He felt uneasy with so much attention focused so near him.

"The other man tried to kill him, doc! He had to fight or let himself be killed."

Shaking his head ruefully, Phineas applied carbolic acid to a folded cloth and pressed it to the wound which slashed down to the bone. The flesh around the stitching appeared enflamed, warning signs of infection. Phineas recognized the knots in the bandages and knew they were the original wrappings when the wounds were fresh. His gut twisted in rage.

The conductor pushed through the wall of bodies crowding the aisle. "North Platte is the next best stop."

"I see." Phineas turned down the edge of the bandage covering Shiloh's side. "Would it be possible for me to remain with him and continue my journey at a later time?"

The conductor frowned in dissent. "I'm sure there is a doctor in North Platte. I doubt it will be necessary for you to stay with him."

"Perhaps," Phineas said as he dribbled the carbolic over the exposed wound. He made the mistake once of leaving this man to his fate and held no desire to do it again. "I will make that decision when the time comes, but this man should not be moved unless necessary. He is very ill, and I have no doubt these wounds are painful."

"Wounds generally are," the conductor commented haughtily. He turned away and disappeared through the crowd.

"I wouldn't delay your travel for him, doc," another bystander offered. "He is one they call a 'coyote' out here. Do him a good turn, and he'll bite you the first chance he gets. Be warned. I would not trust him if I was you."

There was a guarded look in the doctor's eyes, but the bystander said nothing more as he turned and sat down in the seat in front of the berth where Phineas sat with the stranger called Shiloh. He drew a bit of cotton from his bag, doused it with the carbolic, and treated the more minor cuts and gashes with it. Finding a routine returning, the others also disbursed as the swaying motion of the car over-rode the curiosity sparked by the break in the monotony.

Phineas stared down at the rough, scarred face of his patient. After a brief interaction with a colleague in Grand Island, Phineas maintained little faith in western doctors who were as likely to be faith healers as men of science. After hearing the stories which drew him out West, Phineas felt compelled to stay with this man for his own well-being. Phineas was a gentleman, used to a civilized way of life with occasional bouts of excitement over a poker table. The violence he evidence of marked in this man's flesh concerned him. He had no choice but to continue west, and this man seemed to be the answer to his prayers for Divine protection. He would not leave this man again if he had a choice.

Retrieving a blanket from the overhead rack, Phineas spread it over his patient and settled into the seat beside him, content to wait and watch over the lip of one of his books of poetry as the miles fell behind them and the sun slid below the horizon.

A Partner

As he surfaced out of sleep, images and thoughts flooded Shiloh's mind, unbidden and unwanted like the lingering bits of a dream. Fears both irrational and real flooded his consciousness until he felt on the verge of tears. Finally, his mind latched onto his name, fighting to summon it from the depths of his brain. He rubbed his eyes as though to work the memory loose, and gradually bits of thoughts came together.

"Martin Santiago Terraza Mercer," he whispered to himself then glanced around to make sure he was alone. This slip of awareness shook him to the core, and he pushed his name into the back of his memory. He had to forget it and remember that he was Shiloh, one name with no past.

Again he ran a hand over his face, annoyed by the beard. It was full and thick and hid the hollowness of his cheeks. His trousers were loose enough he would have to cut a new hole in his belt. His arms and legs were shaky as he sat up in bed.

The room was sparse with a single bed, a short dresser in the corner, and a chair sitting beside the door with a blanket draped over it as though dropped from someone's shoulders. He remembered the doctor and a moment later recalled his name and wondered if Hall had left that blanket there. Beside the bed, a window stood open admitting a fresh, cool breeze carrying the soft scent of rain.

He heard footsteps beyond the door but didn't register the approach in time to locate his revolver. The door opened and the doctor appeared balancing two plates of food on one arm.

"I am afraid it does not smell appetizing," Hall said with a touch of humor in his green eyes. "But it is better than I can cook. So it will have to do."

Shiloh welcomed the distraction and found the food an improvement over Missus Banks's. The stew teamed with hearty chunks of beef, potatoes, and carrots and emitted a plume of fragrant steam that instantly awakened Shiloh's appetite. He accepted the plate from Hall and immediately scooped up a gravy slathered chunk and shoved it into his mouth.

"I brought biscuits as well," Hall said, digging a cloth-wrapped bundle from the pocket of his coat. "You're welcome to both."

Accepting them with a grateful nod, Shiloh set them on the bed beside him and continued devouring the stew, barely aware of Hall as he removed his hat and coat. He filled a glass of water from the wash pitcher and held it out to Shiloh who accepted it and drank half the contents before his stomach cramped. Without a word, Hall took the glass from him, topped it off, and set it on the windowsill within easy reach.

Then Hall sank into the chair and watched him with keen interest. Silence hung between them while both men ate. By the time Shiloh picked up the first biscuit, Hall had yet to touch his food.

"You're not eating, Doc," Shiloh said, hiding his concern.

Hall glanced over at his plate, frowned, and picked it up. From the wrinkle in his nose, it was obvious he didn't care for the food. He picked through it, critically analyzing each chunk.

"Where's my horse?" Shiloh asked after a short silence.

"The store owner downstairs put him up in one of the livery's in town," Hall replied. He was again frowning at Shiloh as though wanting to say something but unsure of how to do so.

"Out with it, Doc," Shiloh commanded as he speared a fat chunk of potato. "I don't like people staring holes through me."

Phineas felt a shock run through his chest. Even half-conscious, Shiloh's black eyes seemed to cut into a man. Now, with the full force of consciousness behind them, Phineas doubted the wisdom of what he was about to do. He decided caution was the wisest action to take.

"Forgive my naivety," Phineas said by way of apology. "I have not been long in the West, and I am still learning the ways of men out here."

The hardness of those black eyes softened as Shiloh either took pity on Phineas or lost the strength to maintain his guard. Either way, Shiloh returned his attention to his food.

"I understand you were in a fight in Grand Island and may be running from some trouble," Phineas continued. "I, myself can't afford to return east for similar reasons. I believe both of us could benefit from another's company."

Shiloh was young, only two or three years older than Phineas, but his eyes held the same steely glint Phineas remembered seeing in his grandfather's gaze. His mother called it a visible mark left on the soul by war. However, this man's eyes seemed harder than his grandfather's, who had seen the horrors of the Mexican War. In fact, they looked almost feral as he stared silently at Phineas.

"Mister Shiloh, I…" Phineas felt awkward as he searched for the right words and avoided making eye contact. "I realize you possibly would not appreciate having an inexperienced Easterner following you around. But, I promise it will benefit us both."

Those eyes lost none of their edge, but Phineas could see the mind behind them working as they gazed unblinkingly into his face. He had survived some of Phineas's worst nightmares and had the grit to show it. Indeed, this was the answer to his prayers. He simply had to convince Shiloh of the advantages he stood to gain.

"You aren't just a doctor, are you?" Shiloh asked finally.

"I play cards on occasion," Phineas offered. "Sometimes the other players don't care to lose."

At this information, Shiloh's eyes narrowed and he turned his attention back to eating. Sensing he had lost Shiloh's attention, Phineas continued.

"The day I left St. Louis was my first time west of the Mississippi, and I am afraid the ways out here are much different from what I have known so far. I have much to learn and am in need of a teacher…or a bodyguard. I promise I will be as little of a hindrance as possible, and I will make it worth your while."

As though ignoring him, Shiloh broke one of the biscuits and ran it through the gravy on his plate. He popped it into his mouth and sullenly stared at the bandage around his arm as he chewed. "I don't know if I'm the right man for the job."

"Oh, I do not see you as incompetent." Phineas waved his hand dismissively. "You have survived hardship and bear the scars to prove it. That is more than could be said of the man who gave you those wounds."

Shiloh seemed to ignore the compliment as he sopped up more gravy with another chunk of biscuit. Phineas guessed he was a quiet man of few words and would come to his own conclusion in his own time. No more talk on Phineas's part would change that.

"I'll do what I can for you," Shiloh told him after a long silence. "But I can't guarantee you'll be safe with me."

"Understood," Phineas replied, hoping the word imparted his gratitude. He held back the fullness of his relief. Solemnly, Phineas cut a chunk of potato in half.

"It seems we are to be each other's keeper," Phineas said thinking of the secrets they kept for each other as well as looking out for one another.

A shock of worry flashed through Shiloh's expression. He gave Phineas a warning look to which the doctor reacted with an easy smile.

"I trust you, Shiloh," he said. "I hope you can trust me."

But that edginess didn't leave Shiloh's eyes. For several moments he stared down at his plate with a single hunk of biscuit and a bit of gravy remaining. Woodenly, he wiped the plate clean with the bit of hard bread and ate it.

"You should eat more," Phineas told him offering his own plate with the overly salty slop.

Shiloh shook his head. He set the plate on the windowsill and picked up the glass of water. In short order, he drained the glass and stretched out on the narrow bed, his face looking pale and drawn.

"Yes," Phineas agreed. "You need plenty of rest. You'll feel better later."

Shiloh gave no sign he heard. He covered his eyes with his good forearm and after a few moments, breathed the deep slow breaths of sleep.

Satisfied that they had struck a deal, Phineas forced down what he could of the stew and considered what time he should go down to the poker tables. For the time being, he had to play carefully, but before long, he could go back to his old ways and make them both rich men.

An Agreement

Two days later, restless and feeling strong enough to venture outside, Shiloh pulled on his boots and revolvers and emerged, squinting, into the afternoon sun. Though his limbs still felt shaky, his mind was keen and hungered for more than what the little room offered. The last thing he wanted was to look at or be seen by strangers, but he needed to look at more than the four walls and the narrow view from the small window.

Perhaps he should have waited for nightfall and the comparative safety of darkness, but he welcomed the warmth of the sun on his face as he stood at the bottom of the stairs for a moment and surveyed the street. He wanted to check on Haze and knew the livery lay somewhere to the south, but he had the time and felt no need to hurry.

On the far side of the main thoroughfare from him, a round-faced, heavy-set woman stepped out of a milliner's shop with what looked to be a younger copy of herself. As the woman turned back to speak to an unseen person inside, the girl caught sight of Shiloh and gave him a kind, shy smile. She wasn't exactly pretty and the rosy blush that filled her cheeks spoke of naivety, but Shiloh acknowledged her interest with a casual touch of his hat brim. The girl's smile brightened and barely faltered when her mother grasped her hand and pulled her down the street. Both snatched glances at him, one hopeful for his attention, the other despising it.

It caused Shiloh mild humor as he turned south, inadvertently following them. He walked slowly, allowing them to gain distance and disappear onto a side street. He guessed their reaction was the same to anyone wearing pants. The girl stood on the threshold of womanhood, and the mother seemed unhappy about it. Despite knowing the conflict it caused, Shiloh envied the simplicity of normal life.

A few buildings down, a handful of patrons loitered outside a saloon. None of them paid attention to him as he walked past.

They were too busy discussing something of greater interest, though he could not hear what it was.

He found Haze in the corral behind the first stable he came to looking well-fed and moving with the eagerness of pent-up energy. The horse came at his whistle, and Shiloh reached over the fence to stroke the mottled muzzle.

"That's a fine stallion."

Shiloh turned to glance over his shoulder. A tall man in a beat-up hat and mule-eared boots sauntered toward him hooking his thumbs in his faded red suspenders. He carried himself with an air of importance and authority. Shiloh guessed he was the proprietor.

"A horse like that would carry a man from one end of this country to the other without breaking a lather."

"I know," Shiloh said quietly. "I own him."

The man shifted his weight uneasily and his eyes narrowed. "You sure? An eastern dude brought him in here and hasn't paid for his feed. If it doesn't get paid up, I'll have to take that animal in payment."

For a moment, Shiloh studied the man, unsure whether he was joking or trying to swindle him out of money or the horse. The proprietor read the suspicion in Shiloh's face.

"He paid for the first day, but hasn't been back since," he explained, unhooking his thumbs from the suspenders and leaning against the corral fence within an arm's length of Shiloh. "There's four days board outstanding on that animal. Comes to two dollars."

"Two dollars and you think it's right to take a horse worth easily five times that?" Shiloh demanded.

"Business is business," the proprietor responded, but the corners of his mouth softened into a suppressed smirk.

His hands were rough from work, and Shiloh guessed he was most inclined to fight with his fists. On a good day, Shiloh might push the point. A dollar a day to board a horse was on the high side, but nothing worth getting thrown in jail for. Sliding his left hand into the front pocket of his jeans, Shiloh found it empty. He checked his other pockets, and frowned down at the hard-packed earth, questioning his memory.

"You got the money? Or did you lose it in a poker game?"

Shiloh drew a deep breath, reining in a rise in anger that gathered stars at the edge of his vision.

"You'll get paid," he said coldly turning toward the street.

"See that you get it to me before sundown."

Pausing, Shiloh turned back to the proprietor and spoke in an advisory tone. "I wouldn't try putting anyone else on that horse if I were you."

The proprietor tried to look smug, but his mouth twitched slightly, betraying cracks in his confidence.

Leaving the big man there to contemplate the meaning of what he said, Shiloh headed back toward Main Street. He wasn't so worried about Haze. Once the liveryman tried to pass the horse to another rider, the price would drop with every injury the stallion inflicted. It was the thought that Hall had stolen his money that heated his blood.

The question remained, where was Hall? He couldn't skip town until the eastbound train came in sometime in the next couple of hours. He also had left his black bag up in the room, but he could have returned for it in the last few minutes. Shiloh wondered if he'd counted on slipping out while Shiloh was gone.

Emerging onto Main across from the saloon where the loiterers smoked and drank companionably, the thought occurred to him that Hall might not be as big of a tenderfoot as he believed, and that worried him beyond the value of a few dollars. A lapse in judgment about a person could cost Shiloh his life.

Guessing that at least one of the loiterers might have seen Hall, Shiloh crossed the street to the saloon. His approach piqued their interest, and they fell silent.

"Howdy," Shiloh greeted amiably as he stepped up onto the porch into a gap in the wall of men. "I'm looking for a young fellow about my height, dressed like an eastern dude."

A rough-looking man kicked back in a chair by the far window let out a shrewd laugh. A few others snickered knowingly.

"You know who I'm talking about, mister?" Shiloh asked him.

"Sure do!" He took a long draw on his black pipe and blew the smoke into the light breeze. "Cleaned me out of about forty dollars in poker last night. Easterner, he may be. Dude? Not likely."

"You know where I might find him?" Shiloh felt his blood boiling, and he questioned the wisdom of seeking out the doctor with the anger that brewed inside him. There was honesty in a man who faced someone he sought to kill. There was also honesty, at least grit, in a man willing to stab another in the back. But stealing from an unconscious man and then running was pure cowardice and the actions of the lowest form of humanity.

"Well, he ain't here," the man answered. "Saw him walking toward the station a couple of minutes ago."

"Did he have a black bag with him?"

"I don't recall. Didn't seem in any particular hurry. Looked like he was on his way to church."

Shiloh looked west. Though the buildings obscured most of the flat landscape, he could see the shiny thread of rails leading into the distance. No plume of black smoke marked the presence of a train.

"That train ain't due for another hour, and it's always a couple late. He ain't going nowhere unless it's on horseback."

These words did little to ease the tension in Shiloh's gut. He stepped off the porch. "Much obliged, mister," he said as he headed toward the train station.

The man with the pipe chuckled. "Don't beat him too hard, son!"

Ignoring the comment, Shiloh kept walking. He couldn't think of a reasonable excuse for Hall taking his money. Granted he owed the doctor for his services, but thirty dollars was far more than what the doctor had coming.

Before he reached the station, he heard raised voices and recognized Hall's as one of the two men arguing.

"I'm not asking that you personally go in search of my luggage, but I would appreciate at least some effort on your part to locate it!" The doctor was practically shouting at the stationmaster, who, from the look of his clothes through the dirty window, took as much pride in his work as necessary to keep his job.

"It's just things, mister," the stationmaster declared. "I don't understand why you're so worked up over losing a few things."

"Don't understand?" Hall's voice nearly cracked with fury. "What if I took your life savings and threw it in the Missouri?"

"That's a long ways away," the stationmaster countered seriously. "You planning on walking?"

Shiloh stepped through the door just in time to see Hall take his hat off and throw it on the floor.

"I should..." His voice trailed off at the sight of Shiloh. He bent and swept up his hat, face still livid. "Shiloh, if you are at all capable of explaining things to idiots, would you kindly make this *gentleman* understand the value of a person's personal effects?"

"I could do a damn-sight better than you right now, Doc."

Hall's visage blanched at Shiloh's icy tone.

"Outside." Shiloh nodded toward the door. Without protest, Hall obediently exited the station. Shiloh gave a cursory nod to the stationmaster and followed Hall. Once they were out of sight past the windows, Shiloh grabbed the doctor by his twill coat and pinned him to the wall. "Where's my money?"

"Is that what you're angry about?"

Shiloh shoved him, causing the doctor to wince. "The stablemaster is threatening to sell my horse if he doesn't get paid. I had thirty dollars on me when I left Grand Island, and you're the only one who's had the chance to go through my pockets. Now, where is it?"

"Good God! Have you no faith in your fellow man?" Hall retorted angrily.

"Don't talk to me about faith!" Shiloh growled. "The only thing standing between you and my guns is a single dose of gratitude, and if you don't return my money right quick, there ain't nothing going to save you."

"Except you do not want the law knowing you're here," Hall countered.

Shiloh blinked, drew a deep breath, and held it for several beats of his heart. Hall had called his bluff.

The doctor glanced toward the station window then whispered, "I sewed it into the mattress next to your hip. There was a small hole and I figured it would be safe there."

Shiloh glared at him. "You're stalling."

"No!" Hall shook his head adamantly. Then he sighed, appearing to relent. "I borrowed it without permission."

"That's the same as stealing."

"Except I returned it!"

Hall didn't look away now as Shiloh glared into his eyes. The doctor certainly feared him enough to not keep up the lie. He released Hall but didn't step back.

"Why'd you take it in the first place?"

Sighing, Hall straightened his coat. "When they put us off the train, they failed to leave my trunk as well. It had all my money and everything I had of value. I thought it would be safer there than on my person should I encounter robbers."

"So you figured you'd help yourself to my money?"

"Not exactly."

Shiloh's frown deepened. "Start talking, Doc, or we're going to pick up where I just left off."

Again, Hall glanced around and dropped his voice to a low whisper as he leaned close and explained.

"I used it as a stake in a poker game," he explained. "Believe me when I say it was never in danger of being lost."

It took several moments before Shiloh comprehended what Hall meant. Reflexively, his fist clenched.

"You cheatin' bastard!"

"Before you strike me," Hall said, raising a hand to ward off Shiloh's threatened punch. "I more than doubled your money and split the winnings with you. It's enough to pay room, board, and train fare for both of us and your horse with plenty to spare."

"Mind explaining your generosity?" Shiloh demanded, still unwilling to trust someone who could so willingly swindle another man out of his hard-earned pay, no matter what means he used.

Hall looked sheepish. "As I'm sure you have guessed, I need protection. Whether I play fair or not, there are men who will not like losing. I chose my targets carefully for that reason these past couple of nights just so we wouldn't be exposed. I will pay you to act as my bodyguard as well as keep your secret."

Cold fear washed through Shiloh. Rather than look triumphant, Hall looked genuinely sympathetic.

"I know your story. I was the doctor who attended you in Grand Island. Lena told me the story."

Shiloh hung his head in defeat. No matter where he went, his past would find him. It would have been better had he died out on the prairie alone.

Putting his hand on Shiloh's shoulder, Hall spoke comfortingly. "I know it seems like blackmail, but you and I both have secrets we want to keep. I'd prefer we keep it as friends. For what it's worth, I promise I will keep yours no matter how or when we part. It would be mutually beneficial for us both, having another person looking out for us."

Hall had a point, but Shiloh still glowered at the doctor. In the back of his mind lingered the sense that this eastern dude hid something more.

"If you still don't believe me, go look," Hall challenged. "You'll find you were well compensated for the loan."

"Meanwhile you find a nice hiding place until the train comes in," Shiloh countered, anger returning to replace fear.

Something about that thought didn't sit well with Hall. He grimaced and shook his head.

"I can't take the eastbound train. As it is, I took a chance staying here with you."

"You don't seem scared enough to worry about being seen around the poker tables."

Hall looked hurt and exasperated by this. "What will it take to convince you I bear no ill intentions toward you?"

Drawing a deep breath, Shiloh considered the question. He couldn't just walk away and let a weasel go on stealing. More than that, he couldn't turn his back on someone in need, if Hall was such a person.

"Come on." Shiloh took Hall by the arm and led him back toward the dry goods store.

Hall didn't complain about the roughness as Shiloh escorted him to the outside steps leading to their room on the second floor. Once in the room, Shiloh drew his revolver as Hall sank to one knee beside the bed.

"No. You stand in the corner."

Again, Hall shrugged in surrender as he complied.

Shiloh held him at gunpoint while he pulled back the sheet exposing the straw tick. Probing it with his fingers, he could just make out a lump with a different consistency than the rest of the filling.

"There's a hole underneath," Hall explained. "Should be able to reach through easily."

With a warning glance in Hall's direction, Shiloh lifted the edge of the mattress and found the hole. He reached in carefully, tense for any form of trap the doctor might have set for him. His hand closed over the small pouch and withdrew it. Then he felt around the bed frame for any weapons Hall might have stashed. Finding none, he let the tick fall back into place and sat down.

He undid the knot around the pouch opening with his teeth and dumped the contents onto the quilt. At first glance, he counted nearly one hundred dollars.

"I was going to pay for your horse as soon as I got done at the station," Hall explained. "I thought you needed another day or two of rest before we could move on. Otherwise, I would have purchased tickets."

The thought occurred to Shiloh that if Hall had more than tripled his stake, how much more had he kept.

"Tell me one thing," Shiloh said quietly. "Did you play honestly?"

Hall blinked once, then nodded. "I did."

His answer eased the last of the tension in Shiloh's gut. Holstering the revolver, he gathered the collection of bills and coins back into the pouch.

"I want some things set straight between us," Shiloh said. "I won't back a cheat, and I won't retrieve what you lose. I take half, and I'm free to part company with you whenever it suits me."

"Forty percent," Hall retorted. "Forty and I will agree to the rest."

When Shiloh considered that Hall would be in the middle of things, unarmed while he tucked back in the corner, out of sight as long as trouble didn't start, forty percent seemed fair. The problem came down to when a fight broke out.

"You're paying me for what I might have to do," Shiloh countered. "And that's worth fifty."

Groaning, Hall bit his lip, openly disliking the thought. Shiloh didn't fall for it. A man like Hall who could play poker that well showed what he wanted others to see. Though Shiloh didn't know what constituted a fair split for such an arrangement as theirs, he lost nothing by walking away.

Seeing that Shiloh would not budge, Hall gave up the antics.

"Agreed, even split," he conceded and extended his hand.

Shiloh hesitated. Finally, he decided it was his own fear bred out of the past that kept that tension in the back of his mind. He accepted Hall's hand, binding them both to the agreement.

"Well, then," Hall said excitedly. "Shall we leave on the train tonight?"

"I reckon." Shiloh tied the pouch shut and tucked it back in his pocket. "No need to linger where we may not be wanted for long."

"A sound thought." Hall moved to the door. "I'll purchase the tickets and meet you over at the cafe. May as well have a decent meal before we embark on this new journey."

As Hall looked back at him, Shiloh nodded that he understood. Then Hall disappeared outside, his footfalls fading as he descended the stairs.

For several moments, Shiloh sat staring out the window. The sun hovered a hand-width above the horizon which showed as a flat line between land and sky marking the known and the unknown. Though he wanted to like Hall, too many people had betrayed his trust in his life. Some time would pass before Shiloh fully trusted the doctor. At least he could sleep easy knowing the good doctor had not taken the opportunity to kill him while he slept thereby keeping all the money and secrets to himself.

Stretching his neck to ease the tension, Shiloh stood and walked out into the sunlight. From the landing outside, he traced that horizon north and saw the split where a plume of black smoke marked the passage of the eastbound train. He waited there, watching the station until Hall appeared. He tucked something into his coat pocket and walked back down the street away from the tracks. His step was light, and his expression content. Life looked good from the doctor's perspective. For now, they were business partners, but with time, Shiloh hoped that Hall would prove trustworthy.

Descending the stairs, Shiloh headed to the livery. He'd settle Haze's bill before meeting Hall at the café, just so the stable master wouldn't have the satisfaction of making extra off the stallion.